THE FINAL SILENCE

Also by Stuart Neville

The Ghosts of Belfast
Collusion
Stolen Souls
Ratlines

THE FINAL SILENCE

Stuart Neville

Published in the United States in 2014 by
Soho Press, Inc.
853 Broadway
New York, NY 10003

Library of Congress Cataloging-in-Publication Data

Neville, Stuart, 1972-
The final silence / Stuart Neville.
pages cm

ISBN 978-1-61695-548-9
eISBN: 978-1-61695-549-6

1. Heiresses—Fiction. 2. Family secrets—Fiction.
3. Murder—Investigation—Fiction. 4. Police—Fiction.
5. Conspiracy—Fiction. 6. Northern Ireland—Fiction. I. Title.
PR6114.E943F56 2014
823'.92—dc23   2014017698

Typeset in Adobe Garamond by Palimpsest Book Production Limited,
Falkirk, Stirlingshire

Printed in the United States of America

10 9 8 7 6 5 4 3 2 1

For Ezra James Neville

THE FINAL SILENCE

1

Raymond Drew wanted to die on the towpath. Even if there was no sun, no blue sky to die beneath, he wanted it to be by the river. He didn't care if the ground was sodden with rainfall as he collapsed.

If he could manage it, he'd fall dead into the water. At least that way he could be sure. To survive and be brought to a hospital was unthinkable. They would contact his family, such as it was, and his sister Ida would go to his house.

And the things she would find there.

He should have destroyed them, but he couldn't, he was not strong enough to take that action and endure the consequences. It would be easier simply to die. At least if he was gone, he would not have to face that terrible discovery. The real Raymond Drew, the creature that had hidden beneath this human skin for more than six decades, would be revealed.

Raymond locked the front door of his house, the three-bedroom semi on Deramore Gardens he'd lived in for thirty years. Just one of many identical structures on this street, red brick, early 1900s, the kind of houses that middle-class couples and property developers were falling over themselves to buy until the financial crisis. Raymond had shared the first two years here with a wife he'd barely known, let alone loved. Dead and buried now, and he hadn't missed her for a moment.

He tucked the keys into his pocket. The grass of his lawn

looked like stubble on a drunkard's chin. He hadn't cut it in years. The man next door, Hughes his name was, gave up asking Raymond to mow it and did it himself every few weeks. The spring would soon start it growing again.

Not that it mattered to Raymond any more.

He left his car on the driveway, closed the gate behind him, and walked. The Vauxhall Corsa didn't have an MOT or tax. It hadn't been driven in months.

A few minutes took him down the shallow incline of Sunnyside Sreet, past the corner shops and Chinese takeaways, to Annadale Embankment. He avoided eye contact with students and house-wives on the way. At the bridge by the river, he waited at the pedestrian crossing for the green man to appear and tell him to go. Like a good boy. Raymond had learned to be a good boy long ago, to be quiet, respectful, obey all rules while outside his home. Not to draw attention.

Once across the dark slow-moving water to the Stranmillis side, he walked south along the river's edge, beneath the bony branches of the still winter-bare trees. Past the newly rebuilt Lyric Theatre, on further, the blocks of apartments with their waterside views. Traffic rumbled to his right, cars, vans and lorries filtering in and out of the city, heading north or east.

That sickly swelling in his chest, pulsing, robbing him of breath. He did not slow his pace, even as the sweat dripped from his eyebrows. Cold on his back, running down his spine.

Raymond had gone to the doctor two months before. A soft-spoken and serious young woman, she had talked about medica-tion, pills, things to ease the tired muscle in his breast. She talked about more tests, bloods, wires tethered to his skin, a specialist at the Royal Victoria Hospital.

It was serious, the young doctor had said. It was only a matter of time before an attack came, perhaps a big one. Appointments were made, a prescription printed on patterned paper.

Raymond did not keep the appointments, nor did he have the prescription filled. He simply wanted to know.

It had been a month since the fluttering in his chest had intensified. Then the dizzy spells, the cold sweats, the feeling of his torso being crushed by some invisible hand. He awoke throughout the night, gasping, wild horses galloping inside his ribcage.

Only a matter of time.

A cool wave washed across his brow, and his legs weakened. He gripped the railing to steady himself. Waited while the blood coursed through his body.

A pub just ahead, perched on the riverbank, tables and benches and umbrellas damp and pathetic in the grey. A drink. Just one last swallow to see it done.

Raymond entered the pub. The only other patrons were a pair of businessmen comparing charts over cups of coffee. They did not notice him. But the girl behind the bar did.

He approached. The girl smiled. Blonde hair tied back, dressed in black trousers and a shirt that clung to her form. He stared for a moment. Felt his teeth with his tongue.

"What can I get for you?" she asked.

A foreign girl, Eastern European.

Raymond had been to Eastern Europe more than once. Even before the Soviets lost their hold. He had tasted many things there. Things few men ever taste.

He went to reply, but his throat and his tongue would not obey. Sweat tingled on his cheek. Something pulsed inside his skull.

"Are you okay?" the girl asked. "Do you need help?"

"Whiskey," he said, his voice crackling in his throat.

She hesitated, a thin line between her eyebrows. "Bush, Jameson, Jack Daniel's."

"Black Bush," he said. "A double, no water."

She fetched him the drink, served it in a tumbler. The liquid glowed amber, swaying in the glass as it clinked on the bar top.

A shrill thought sounded in his mind, causing a moment of giddy panic. Had he brought any money? Raymond checked each pocket in turn, the fear building in him, until his fingers touched leather at his hip. He opened the wallet, sighed when he found a twenty-pound note, and handed it over.

"Keep . . ." His lungs betrayed him. He inhaled as much air as they would hold. "Keep the change."

A smile flashed on her face, then was swept aside by concern. "Are you sick?" she asked. "Do you need a doctor?"

Raymond shook his head, no breath to spare. He took the glass to the farthest table, pausing on the way to let another dizzy wave pass. Raising the tumbler, he smelled warm earthy peat, sweet caramel, spice. Heat in his throat, the aftertaste of aniseed.

As he sat sipping at the whiskey, a knot of pain tightened around his left arm. It travelled up through his shoulder and neck before hammering on the inside of his skull. He held the table's edge.

Not here. Not here.

Raymond downed the rest of the whiskey in one gulp, coughed, and marvelled at the constellations that flowered across his vision.

The girl approached. "Sir? I can call a doctor."

He shook his head, stood, made for the exit, carried more by his momentum than his legs.

Outside, he went to the towpath.

Here?

Too close to the pub and the houses. Half a mile downriver, past the boat club, the buildings would recede, nothing but grass and trees along the river's edge. He had walked the towpath many times, letting the quiet air enshroud him, the calm seeping in through his pores.

Another charge of pain coursed from his arm up to his brain, stronger than before.

Walk. Jesus Christ, walk.

His legs obeyed. Time bent and cracked around him. Grey turned to green. Civilisation faded into the distance, only the rough ground and the sound of the wind through leaves.

A woman and a dog. It sniffed at him as he passed, whined, smelling the death on him. His and that of the others.

A cyclist, wrapped in Lycra, a helmet on his head, skidding to avoid a collision.

"Fuck's sake, watch where you're going," the cyclist shouted as he pedalled away.

Raymond did not answer.

He stepped off the gravel path, toward the grass and weeds at the edge. His shoes sank in the wetness. Hard, needling cold swamping his feet. The river flowed past, fat from the rainfall.

"God, let it be now," Raymond said.

He laughed at the futility of his prayer. He and God had parted ways half a lifetime ago.

He dug his fingers into his pocket, the tips already going numb. His keys snagged on a thread. He pulled harder, and they came free. It took the last of his strength to toss them six feet. They splashed in the water without a sound. At least none that he could hear.

Another shock of pain, bigger than his body could hold, raging up through his left arm, his shoulder, his neck, then an explosion in his brain like the birth of a star.

"Now," he said.

The water came to meet him, swallowed him, as tender as it was cold. A million images streaked through Raymond's mind, each one as bold and brilliant as the last, faces he'd known, many he hadn't, some of them twisted in terror.

They sparked and fell like the scatterings of a firework, falling into black, down to where the fire awaited him. Down into the final silence.

2

Rea Carlisle sat on the stairs, looking at the black plastic bags, a man's life wrapped up and ready to be dumped.

She hadn't seen her uncle for twenty-eight years, and she remembered the occasion better than the man. She had been six years old, a funeral in a draughty church whose location she could not recall. People had whispered, asking what her mother was doing bringing a child that age to a funeral? The babysitter hadn't turned up, and Rea's mother had scrubbed her face with spit and tissue before bundling her into her best Sunday school dress and dragging her out to the car.

Uncle Raymond had stood quiet and still throughout, had smiled and shaken hands with people who seemed to be as strange to him as they were to Rea.

Her mother embraced him.

"Och, Raymond, I'm so sorry," she said.

His arms remained by his sides, his back stiff and straight. "Thanks for coming, Ida," he said.

When they put his wife in the ground, Uncle Raymond brought a finger to his eye. But there was no tear to wipe away. Even though Rea could recall only the most vague image of his face, she remembered clearly how silly the action of wiping away a non-existent tear seemed to her.

She asked her mother about it on the drive home in the Mini Metro.

Ida stayed quiet for a while, watching the road ahead. Then she said, "Well, he was always an odd cratur."

After that, they never talked much about him. Rea knew her mother had tried to contact Raymond, by telephone, by letter, but never a reply. He faded from their lives like mist from a window.

The phone call had come a week ago.

Rea had been sitting at her kitchen table, eating a microwaved ready meal straight from the plastic container, scrolling through the listings of a jobs website on her iPad. She lifted her mobile knowing it would be her mother's name on the display. Ida had a knack of calling at awkward moments. When Rea was eating, or in the bath, or on the toilet, or trying to get out the door, she could almost guarantee the phone would ring.

"It's Raymond," Ida said.

Rea's mind scrambled to connect the name to anyone she knew. God help her, she didn't want another one of those verbal tennis matches where her mother insisted Rea knew someone while Rea swore blind she didn't.

Och, you know him surely, Ida would say.

I don't, Rea would counter.

Och, you do.

No, I don't.

Back and forth until Rea would be ready to scream.

Before any of that could happen, Ida said, "He's dead."

Rea heard a watery sigh in the phone's earpiece.

"Who's dead?" she asked.

"Raymond," Ida said, exasperation in her voice. "Your uncle Raymond. My brother."

The white wisp of a man by the graveside came back to her. The finger at the dry eye. The features she could not form into a real face.

"Jesus," Rea said.

Ida tutted at the minor blasphemy.

"Sorry," Rea said, not meaning it. "How did he die?"

"They're not sure," Ida said. "Maybe drowned, but they don't know."

"Drowned?"

"He was found in the Lagan yesterday afternoon, all snagged up in the weeds."

Rea heard a crack in her mother's voice. A sharp, high-pitched inhalation. She pictured a tissue screwed up in Ida's fingers, ready to dab at her cheeks. Keeping it all bound up tight like a ball of string in her breast in case she made a show of herself. Ida Carlisle was the kind of woman who wept at her kitchen table, a cup of tea going cold in front of her, at least one closed door between her and anyone else.

"They found out who he was from his wallet," Ida said. "It took them a day to find out he was related to me. The police called at the house this evening."

"Was Dad there?" Rea asked.

"No, he was at a party meeting. He says he'll be home as soon as it's over."

Rea suppressed a curse. Graham Carlisle made his wife look like a well of warm emotion. God forbid he should let Ida's bereavement get in the way of his ambitions. He'd had a seat at the Stormont Assembly for five years now, and they were grooming him for Westminster. They would announce his candidacy at the next general election. To him, all else was secondary.

"I'll come over," Rea said. "Give me half an hour."

Before she could hang up, Ida said, "I didn't know him."

Rea kept silent, left the space for her mother to fill with whatever troubled her.

Ida took a quivering breath and said, "He was my brother, and I didn't know him. I haven't seen him in near thirty years. I don't know if he still lives in that wee house. I don't know if he married again. I don't know if he had any children. I could've passed him on the street, and I wouldn't have recognized him. I should've known him better."

"You tried," Rea said. "I remember you writing him letters and sending him Christmas cards. You did try."

"I should've tried harder."

Ida brought another bin liner from the living room and added it to the row in the hall. The black plastic jarred against the clean featureless white of the walls. Even the stairs on which Rea sat had been painted the same colour. Combined with the aged black and white tiles of the floor, it gave the hall the feeling of an institution, as if it led to a headmaster's office, not a home that should have sheltered a family. Only the stained glass in the front door offered any relief from the monochrome decor.

Rea's father had promised to drop by and take the bags to the dump in his big four-by-four Range Rover.

Not that there were many to carry.

Raymond Drew had gathered little of the clutter that most people do throughout their lives. His wardrobe had been filled with cheap chain store and supermarket clothes, invented brands, shirts that come in packs of two, a suit made of a material that crackled with static electricity under Rea's fingertips. Every item of apparel he owned filled one bin bag—minus the suit, which he was buried in—with another for shoes and belts.

A box rattled and clanged with a meagre selection of pots and pans, cutlery, and another held a toaster and a kettle. Yet another held a yellowed dinner set, plates of different sizes, cups, a teapot, all covered in a floral pattern.

"I bought that," Ida had said when Rea found the set in a cupboard. "A wedding present for him and Carol."

An old cathode ray television in the back living room looked like it hadn't worked in years, and a music center complete with a turntable. The tone arm didn't have a stylus. Rea looked, but couldn't find a pair of speakers to go with it.

It was as if these things, along with the scattering of clocks and ornaments, were placeholders. Items set around Raymond Drew's house to give it the appearance of a home. Like a film set, Rea thought. Props. She imagined knocking on the walls and finding they were facades made of plywood.

Most important of all, they had to search for letters, bank statements, bills, any official looking paperwork. Rea's father had called his solicitor, David Rainey, before he'd even thought to comfort his wife. Rainey had told Graham to find any and all documentation that might help determine the size of the deceased's estate. They'd need everything they could get their hands on to take to court and apply for a grant of letters of administration, the authority to deal with Raymond's affairs. Once that was done, Ida would be her brother's sole heir.

"I think that's the last of it," Ida said.

Rea counted them. Eight bags and boxes in total.

Ida read her mind. "Pathetic, isn't it?" She climbed the stairs and sat next to Rea. Her voice resonated between the hard surfaces of the stairwell and the hall. "What kind of life did he have? Here all alone. He had nothing. No one. There's not even a photograph around the place. Him or Carol. You'd think he'd have a picture of his wife, wouldn't you? But there's nothing. Just . . . this."

She waved a hand at the packed-up detritus below. Rea put an arm around her mother's shoulders. Ida fetched a balled-up tissue from her sleeve, touched it to her nose as she sniffed.

Ida Carlisle was a small woman, wider than she'd like at the hips, her hair lacquered in place once a week by a fey man at a city-center salon, grey roots showing through the dyed brown, the merest hint of make-up on her face. Enough to make herself presentable, never enough to be showy.

"There's always the back bedroom," Rea said. "There could be an Aladdin's cave in there, for all we know."

The door to the bedroom at the rear of the house was different from the others. The rest were panelled wood, probably hung there when the house was built a century ago. But the back bedroom door was a solid featureless white with a new handle and a lock.

The day before the funeral, a locksmith had opened the front door of the house, fitted a new tumbler and left them with a set of keys. They hadn't found the locked door upstairs until he'd gone. Rea's father had made a half-hearted attempt at putting his shoulder to it, but the door wouldn't budge. Rea had tried kicking it below the handle, like she'd seen in a police documentary, but she'd only succeeded in bruising the ball of her foot and straining her calf.

"There'll be nothing in there but old dust and air," Ida said. A tear escaped her eye. She caught it with the tissue before it could drip from her cheek.

"We'll see," Rea said, stroking her mother's back.

Neither Ida nor Graham Carlisle were comfortable with shows of affection. Hugs. Kisses. Cuddles. Such displays were for infants and television dramas. Rea couldn't remember ever being told by either of her parents that they loved her. She had no doubt that they did, but to tell her so would run against their Presbyterian grain.

At the age of eighteen, when Rea left home for university, she made a decision: regardless of whether they returned the gesture, she would tell them she loved them. And she would hug them, and she would kiss them. If that made them cringe, then tough luck. She would not live her life with her emotions tied up and hidden inside her.

"No point in worrying about it now," Ida said. "I talked to your father last night. About this place."

"Oh?" Rea asked.

"When we've got it all sorted, all the legal nonsense, we think you should have it."

The house had belonged to Raymond's wife, and she'd inherited it from her parents. When she died, Raymond had stayed on. Now, once the estate was settled, it was Ida's to do with as she pleased.

"But Mum, I can't . . . it's too much to . . ."

"It'd get you out of that shared place. You'd have a home of your own. No mortgage to tie you down. A house is too hard to buy these days, I mean for a girl on her own, even with the prices falling the way they have."

Rea shook her head. "But this place has got to be worth a hundred grand, maybe a hundred and twenty. You and Dad could have that for your retirement."

"Your father retire?" Ida smiled. "He'll not retire until he drops. Besides, he's got enough money put away to keep the both of us."

"I don't know," Rea said. "It's too big a thing. I can't get my head around it."

"Well, think about it. You'll see it makes sense. Dear knows, there's precious little left of your uncle here. Hardly anything to show for him being here at all. Whatever's in that back room, you can give it to charity, or dump it, or . . ."

She screwed her eyes shut. Her shoulders jerked.

Rea tightened her hold on her mother, brought Ida's head to her shoulder. The tears came, Rea felt the wetness through her T-shirt, and Ida seemed to melt against her. Only for a few seconds. Then it passed, and Ida came back to herself, sat upright, stiff and proper like before. Only a redness to her eyes offered any proof of what had happened. They would not mention it again, Rea was sure.

She went to speak, but Ida's mobile phone pinged.

"Och, fiddle," she muttered, reading a text message.

"What?" Rea asked.

"Your father. He's not coming. He got held up at a committee meeting."

"All right," Rea said. "I'll take the stuff to the dump. It'll take a few runs, but no matter. Why don't you go home and get some sleep?"

"Sleep?" Ida snorted. "I haven't slept for a week."

"Well, go and try. I can manage from here."

Ida smiled and stroked Rea's hand. "You're a good girl."

The closest she'd come to affection in years. Rea leaned in and planted a kiss on her mother's cheek.

"Get off!" Ida swatted her away in mock outrage.

She stood and descended the stairs. At the front door, Ida turned and regarded her dead brother's life bagged up and ready to be disposed of. She shook her head once, offered Rea a regretful smile, and left.

Rea stayed on the stairs for a time, watching the ripples of sunlight through the door's stained glass. It wasn't a bad house, and it was a nice street. A small tingle of excitement in her belly.

A house of her own.

For the last couple of years she'd shared a place with two other women in the Four Winds area, a sprawling suburb to the southeast of the city. The two housemates were younger than Rea, one of them by more than a decade, fresh out of university and working for a legal practice. They made Rea feel older than her thirty-four years. She caught herself wanting to mother them, to scold them for staying out too late, or for the clothes they wore. And she felt they regarded her as a desperate old spinster aunt, constantly trying to set her up with their work colleagues.

Once, she had reluctantly agreed to go on a blind date with one of them. He'd been a pleasant enough gentleman, not bad looking, tidy, polite. When he showed her a photograph of his youngest grandchild, Rea felt like screaming.

Three months had passed since Rea had lost her job. She'd been at the consultancy firm in the city center for almost six years, specializing in recruitment processes, devising interview strategies and aptitude tests. A good salary, too, enough for her to save a decent amount toward a deposit on a house. Since she'd been laid off, the rent on the shared place was eating into her savings, and she had been facing the horrifying prospect of having to move back in with her parents.

Rea suppressed a shudder. Now a lifeline, a chance to have a house without the burden of a mortgage. But could she take a dead man's home? And it needed work. A new kitchen, new central heating, and probably a list of things hidden beneath the surface. Rea knew from her friends' tales of buying houses that the real costs were the hundred secrets the previous owner kept from you. She doubted her savings would cover it.

But still, a house of her own.

She thought of the room upstairs. Her mother was probably right, nothing in there but dust and air. But if she was going to take this place as her own she wanted to see every room, locked or not.

Rea Carlisle decided that before the day was done, she would have the door to the back bedroom opened.

3

Detective Inspector Jack Lennon coughed and wiped his nose with an already damp tissue. The tail end of another cold, his third in as many months. The surgeon had warned Lennon he'd be prone to infections now that he was without a spleen. She'd been right.

His buttocks ached from the thin cushion on the plastic chair, the year-old injuries to his shoulder and side nagging at him. The boardroom's storage heater wheezed and clanked. The yellowed vertical blinds over the windows swayed in the air currents.

The lawyer the Police Federation had retained on his behalf sat across the table, running the tip of a pen down the page, his lips moving as he read. Fluorescent light reflected in bright spots on his scalp. Adrian Orr, his name was, and Lennon had seen far too much of him over the last year.

Orr had made a decent fist of things, but still Lennon found the heat of anger building every time he saw him. He knew he was lucky to have held onto his job this long, that if not for Orr he would have been cut adrift from the force months ago, but still.

For the first few meetings, Lennon had made an effort, tidied himself up, put on a suit. Now he didn't bother. Jeans and a shirt were fine for these dull encounters. He hadn't visited a barber for almost nine months, his dirty-fair hair hanging below his collar and over his eyes. Grey strands had worked their way in. Susan had given up telling him to get it cut. Besides, his daughter Ellen said she liked it.

"Aren't we done yet?" Lennon asked.

"Mm?" Orr looked up from the page.

"Are we nearly finished?"

"Give me a couple more minutes. Just going over these last few notes from the Ombudsman."

A heavy ache climbed from the back of Lennon's neck into his skull. The back pain would follow soon. He rolled his dry tongue around his mouth, thought of the bottle of water on the passenger seat of his car, and the strip of painkillers in the glovebox. He exhaled, an ostentatious sigh he regretted even before his chest had emptied.

Orr looked up again.

"Please, Jack, settle yourself and let me read. The sooner I get through this the sooner you can go home."

The thought of apologizing flitted through Lennon's mind, but the ugly balloon of pride that remained at his core wouldn't allow it. He shifted in the chair, buttock-to-buttock, then suppressed a grimace at the pain.

Orr set his pen down, folded his hands atop the page, and readied himself to speak as if he were delivering a speech to the Assembly up in Stormont.

"You're not going to get a medical pension, I can tell you that now."

"Fuck," Lennon said.

Orr bristled. "I told you before, Jack, I don't like that kind of language. There's no call for it."

"Yes there bloody is," Lennon said.

"You shot and killed a fellow officer—"

"Who was shooting at me. He'd have killed me and the girl if I hadn't—"

"You shot a cop." Orr's cheeks reddened when he realized his voice had risen to a near shout. He took a breath before continuing. "You helped a murder suspect flee the country. It doesn't matter what the circumstances were. Gandhi and Mother Teresa couldn't talk them into giving you a pension now."

For the last year and three months, the Ombudsman, the Policing Board, and Lennon's own superiors had been trying to find some way to sweep away the mess he'd made. Three times he'd been up in front of the misconduct panel at the PSNI headquarters on Knock Road, going over the events again and again for the Assistant Chief Constable. Orr and the Police Federation had done their best to fight his corner, but their best had achieved little.

The incident had been over a Ukrainian girl called Galya Petrova. She'd been trafficked in to work in a brothel west of the city, but she'd escaped, killing one of her captors in the process. She wouldn't have lived another day if Lennon hadn't got her to the airport that cold morning. She almost didn't make it. He had taken three bullets for her while she fled.

A young sergeant named Connolly had pulled the trigger after ten thousand pounds had been transferred into his bank account. Lennon had left his colleague's wife a widow and his twin babies fatherless. He tried not to think about them, reminding himself it was self-defense, but they crept into his consciousness anyway. Every single day.

At first, Lennon had argued that the case also revealed and brought about the capture of a killer named Edwin Payntor.

Surely that counted for something? But Payntor had committed suicide in custody, and the bodies buried in his cellar could never be formally linked to him.

The cache of dirty secrets Lennon kept was the only thing that had saved him from being slung out of the force a year ago. He could avoid formal charges if he accepted demotion and the resulting pay cut, they'd said, and serve out the remainder of his thirty-year contract behind a desk. That way, he could be seen to have been punished for his transgressions, keeping the republican politicians on the Policing Board at bay, but not so severely that it would have the unionists shaking their fists.

But Lennon couldn't afford a drop in his wage. Not now. And he certainly didn't want to spend the best part of the next decade doing paperwork. He'd offered them a choice: give him a medical pension and all the attendant benefits, or fight the case through whatever channels were available. And he'd promised them he'd spill every filthy thing he knew.

Lennon pulled open the driver's door of the eight-year-old Seat Ibiza, slumped down into the seat, and reached for the glovebox. The headache had swollen inside his skull. It pressed behind his eyes, pulsing with his heartbeat, a sickly rhythm he couldn't shake. Not without the pills.

It would be his third dose today, one more than he should have had by this time, but the session with Orr had taken it out of him. No harm in going over his self-imposed limit. Just this once.

As his hand closed on the small box, a voice said, "What happened to the Audi?"

He turned to the still-open door.

Detective Chief Inspector Dan Hewitt, hands in his pockets, his well-pressed suit jacket buttoned. To anyone else in the police station's car park, it would appear he had stopped for a friendly chat with an old colleague. Both Lennon and Hewitt knew different.

"I got rid of it," Lennon said, closing the glovebox.

He could have said it was because he couldn't afford the repairs after it was rammed by an SUV while he tried to get Galya Petrova to safety, that he'd been forced to sell, pay off the remaining balance on the finance, and buy an ageing hatchback instead. But Hewitt already knew all of that. Lennon wouldn't give him the satisfaction of hearing it said out loud.

"Audis are for posers, anyway," Hewitt said. "How've you been? You're still limping a bit."

"I don't limp," Lennon said. "There's nothing wrong with my legs."

The bullet that had passed through his flank, above his hip, and the other wound to his shoulder had left him stiff on that side, taking his balance. His gait was visibly off kilter. But it was not a limp.

"Course not," Hewitt said.

"What do you want?"

"Just to say hello."

"Then say it and fuck off."

Hewitt laughed. "Friendly as ever. You used to be good crack at Garnerville. I don't really know you any more, do I?"

"I could say the same about you."

Hewitt leaned against the car. "You could say a lot of things about me, I suppose."

Lennon watched the other man's eyes. "If I took the notion, yes, I could."

"If you took the notion. But you won't." Hewitt leaned closer. "Will you, Jack?"

"Depends."

"I know you've been snooping around," Hewitt said. "I know you've been digging out old records, making copies. You can't get up to that sort of thing without someone noticing. What are you planning on doing with them?"

"Let's hope you never have to find out."

"I can make things go easier for you," Hewitt said.

Lennon went to pull the door closed, but Hewitt blocked it.

"Or I can make things harder for you. Your choice, Jack."

Lennon looked up at him, asked, "Can you get me out of here with a medical pension?"

"No," Hewitt said, stepping back.

"Then you're no bloody use to me."

Lennon closed the door and put the key in the ignition.

4

The door fitted its frame so tight that when Rea ran her finger-tips along the edge she could barely press a nail into the gap. She pushed the door with her palm. No give at all.

Even though she knew it was pointless, she tried the handle. It was a lever type, rather than the knobs on every other door in the house, a keyhole in its plate. Rea knelt down and peered through. Nothing but black.

"Dust and air," she whispered.

Should she call out the locksmith again? His bill for opening the front door had been steep. Rea thought about her bank account. Could she spare that much? Not if she wanted to pay the rent this month.

The only option was to prise the door open with something. That would damage the frame, and the door, but if she took the house she'd want to change this door anyway. Get one fitted to match the others.

That decided it. She remembered she'd seen an old toolbox in the garage. She went downstairs. The back door that led from the kitchen to the rear garden remained locked with no key to be found, so Rea exited through the front and walked around the house.

Her uncle's battered car was still parked on the driveway, the tax and MOT discs in the window months out of date. It would likely have to be towed and scrapped.

The garage stood well back from the road, a rusted metal gate between it and the house. She slid back the bolt on the doors and allowed the light in. She looked around its walls. Asbestos cement. Having it pulled down and replaced would be another expense.

Never mind, she thought, find something to open that bedroom with.

The rusted metal toolbox lay on the floor at the back of the garage, old paint tins stacked on top. Spiderwebs skimmed Rea's skin as she went deeper into the dark. She lifted the first couple of tins from the top of the stack—almost empty, going by their weight—and set them aside.

Rea grabbed the handle of a third and pulled, but its base had been glued to the tin beneath by drying paint, and the remainder of the pile toppled to the floor. She danced back, first to save her toes from the falling tins, then to spare her shoes from the puddle of white emulsion that spread across the concrete.

"Bollocks," Rea said.

The puddle turned to a small lake.

"Shit," Rea said.

She pictured her father seeing the mess, giving her that withering stare, as if he wondered where he'd got a daughter like her from.

"Tits and arse and fuck," Rea said.

No point in worrying about it now. She edged along the rear wall to avoid the paint and hunkered down by the toolbox. Her balance wavered, and she put a hand out to keep from falling into the white puddle. The paint chilled her palm. She cursed again.

With her free hand, Rea pushed the toolbox lid up and back. Inside lay a collection of red-mottled metal and cracked plastic. Pliers and screwdrivers. A socket wrench—what her grandfather used to call a rickety—and a few loose bundles of steel wool. She pushed the smaller tools aside, digging deeper into the box.

Her fingers gripped something harder, colder, more solid. She pulled it, the screwdrivers and pliers clattering aside. It was heavy, a little more than a foot and a half long, curved at each end with fissures in its flattened blades. A crowbar. She had never used one in her life, but it looked like the right tool for the job.

She skirted the paint and headed back outside.

Across the road, a young man in a dark navy suit stood on the garden wall of the house opposite. He smoothed a sticker over the estate agent's sign, covering the words "To Let" with "Let By." He spotted her as she headed for the front door of her uncle's home.

"Excuse me," he called.

Rea paused on the doorstep and looked across.

He waved, hopped down from the wall, and jogged toward her. The garden gate creaked as he let himself through. Even younger than she'd thought, early- to mid-twenties at most. Probably just out of university. He extended his hand as he approached.

"Mark Jarvis," he said. "Mason and Higgs Estate Agents."

Rea showed him her paint-coated palm.

"Ah," he said, lowering his hand. "One of the neighbors told me your bad news. I'm sorry for your trouble."

Rea blinked at him, confused for a moment, before she said, "Oh. Thank you."

She knew what was coming, braced, instructed herself to be polite.

He gave her a broad, deferential smile. "I just wondered if you'd decided what to do with the property yet?"

"Not yet," she said. "Look, I've got a lot to—"

"I understand," he said, holding his hands up. "But I wanted to make you aware that sales are picking up in the area if the houses are priced right, and of course the rental market is very healthy right now."

He waved a hand at the house across the street.

Rea swallowed the urge to swear at him, to slap his smug face. Or to leave a white emulsion handprint on the back of his nice clean suit.

"Thank you," she said, "but this really isn't a good time to—"

"I understand," he said again. "But I just want to make sure you're aware of the services we can offer—"

Before she knew what she was doing, Rea silenced him with her palm pressed against his mouth. He stepped back, white paint dripping from his lips onto his tie.

"I told you it's not a good time." She showed him the crowbar. "Now I'd be obliged if you'd piss off and leave me alone."

He retreated along the garden path, spitting paint, fishing a handkerchief from his pocket. "Sorry for your trouble," he mumbled.

Rea stepped into the house and pushed the front door closed with her hip. She stood there for a time, her back against the wood and glass, cursing herself for being foolish enough to let the little prick annoy her. He was just doing his job, being as pushy as he was trained to be.

"It'll wash off," she said to the empty hall.

Upstairs in the bathroom she ran water over her hand, rubbed her fingers, rinsed as much of the paint away as she could. Still it remained in the creases of her skin and beneath her nails.

"Stupid girl," she scolded the mirror.

At the age of thirty-four, Rea Carlisle still considered herself a child. While everyone she'd gone to school with seemed to be enjoying glittering careers, beautiful families, or both, she felt for ever stalled in some teenager's mind.

"Grow up," she said.

The resonance of her voice in the bathroom unnerved her. She wiped her hands dry on the stained towel and retrieved the crowbar from the floor.

Back out on the landing, the locked bedroom door glowered at her. A hot and bitter swell of anger made her clench her jaw. She'd be damned if a bloody lock would keep her out of a room in what was almost certainly now her own house.

Rea pressed the blade at the straighter end of the crowbar into the gap between the door and its frame, close to the lock. It barely penetrated. She pushed harder, putting her shoulder behind it. The blade went no more than a fraction of an inch deeper. Rea leaned against the crowbar, putting all her weight behind it. She heard a scratching, cracking noise, then felt the crowbar break loose of the door frame, saw the landing carpet coming up at her.

Rea fell hard on her chest, trapping the crowbar between her ribs and the floor. She cried out as the metal jabbed into the flesh beneath her breast. The pain bloomed, and she rolled onto her back, hissing through her teeth. She slipped her hand beneath the fabric of her T-shirt, felt the offended ribcage for blood. Tender, but the skin was unbroken. She breathed in and out, expecting the pain to grow to a shriek as her ribcage expanded. Nothing broken, thank God. She imagined explaining a cracked rib to her father.

"Stupid girl," she said.

Rea grabbed the crowbar and got back to her feet. She examined the minor damage she'd inflicted on the door frame. Barely a chip on the paintwork, but it was a start.

She returned the crowbar's blade to the tiny furrow it had dug. This time, she worked the blade back and forth, widening the gap before pushing it deeper. Soon she had forced the crowbar's tip in by a quarter of an inch. Not too hard. Only a little sweat on her back.

Rea kept working, back and forth, pushing, rewarded by the grinding and cracking. The frame took the brunt of the damage, its wood softer than that of the door. When the blade had dug in almost half an inch, it met something solid. The latch plate, she thought. The crowbar would go no further.

She took her hands away. The crowbar remained suspended, wedged in place. She felt her pulse in her ears. What if she wasn't strong enough to force the door open?

"Course I am," she said.

Rea gripped the crowbar, set her feet apart, and pulled. Pressure built inside her head. Her shoulders shook with the effort.

Nothing.

She released the bar and let her hands drop to her sides. A cold line of sweat ran from her temple to her cheek. She gripped the crowbar again and leaned back, pushing with her legs, using the weight of her body.

A hard crack, and the door moved. Only a fraction of an inch, but it moved.

Rea's breath came in gulps, her heart feeling like it would force its way up her throat.

"This time," she said, taking hold of the crowbar once more.

She braced one foot against the door frame, planted the other on the floor, and threw her weight back.

Through no will of her own, a growl started deep in her chest and grew to a strained squeal. Christ, I sound like a pig, she thought. A laugh bubbled up from her belly, but before it could escape, the crowbar came loose of the frame and she fell tumbling backward.

The back of Rea's head connected with the wood of the banister and a fierce light flared behind her eyes. The world lurched and shifted. Time creased like folded paper.

Something warm and metallic in her mouth. She swallowed, felt a gnawing pain at the back of her tongue. Bitten it, probably, but she couldn't remember when. How long had passed?

Rea sat upright, rested her shoulders against the banister. She touched her fingertips to the back of her head. Tender, but her scalp was unbroken. A goose egg had already swollen beneath the skin. She turned her head from one side to the other. The muscles in her neck twitched and flickered with pain. Could've been worse, she thought. She'd known a boy at school who'd been left paralysed from the neck down after a simple fall.

What had she been thinking, anyway? She should've waited until her father was there to help. But then, she'd always been like that. Flashes of bravado followed by regret and retreat to her parents' safety net.

All to get a bloody door open.

Then she looked up and saw the empty space where the door had been. And the room beyond, dark as a cave.

5

Lennon walked through the doors of the old Presbyterian church on the Falls Road. The building had been expanded and converted into an Irish cultural center with a theatre, a cafe, exhibition rooms and galleries. He made his way upstairs to one of the classrooms and found it empty save for the Irish dance teacher packing up her gear. Lennon couldn't remember her name.

"I'm here to collect my daughter," he said.

The teacher looked up from the collection of CDs she was stowing into a bag.

"Ellen McKenna," Lennon said.

The teacher smiled. "Oh, Ellen? Her aunt came for her."

Lennon cursed under his breath. He was no more than ten minutes late, but Bernie McKenna had used those few minutes to swoop and take Ellen. She only lived a two-minute walk away, so Lennon knew Bernie had taken Ellen home, was probably preparing a meal for her.

He thanked the teacher, headed back downstairs and out onto the street.

The Irish dance classes had been Bernie McKenna's idea. Ellen had little interest, and seldom practiced, but it kept her aunt off Lennon's back. Left to his own devices, he would have allowed Ellen no contact with her late mother's family. They had wanted nothing to do with the child while her mother was alive—Marie

McKenna was a traitor for having had a child to a cop, as far as they were concerned—but ever since Ellen was made motherless, they had been trying to claw her away from Lennon.

It was Susan who persuaded Lennon to allow the McKennas this small amount of access. Ellen was their blood, Susan reminded him. It was unreasonable to keep her away from them. But Lennon knew the kind of filth that the late Michael McKenna had been involved in, and that many of his clan were still delving into. Even so, he acquiesced, and allowed Bernie McKenna to pick Ellen up from school once a week and take her to these classes. That, and a day out every other Saturday.

Lennon turned the corner onto Fallswater Parade, a narrow street, two rows of identical terraced houses, each home with a small walled garden to the front. A shallow incline led to Bernie McKenna's door at the middle of the street. Lennon knew her mother lived next door, with Bernie's sister taking care of her, and another sister across the street with her family. Ellen's mother had been raised in one of these houses.

The small iron gate squeaked on its hinges. A dog in one of the neighboring houses barked at the noise. Three paces took Lennon to the front door. He rapped on the wood with his knuckles.

The door opened almost immediately.

Bernie McKenna said, "Oh, look who decided to show up."

"I was only a few minutes late," Lennon said, irritation already blossoming into anger. "Is she ready to go?"

"I was just making her a bite to eat," Bernie said.

"She'll have dinner at home. I want to get going before the traffic gets too bad."

"Daddy," Ellen called from the hall.

She came running, grabbed her bags from the floor, pushed past her great-aunt, and out onto the doorstep. She took her father's hand in hers and pulled him along the path.

Bernie's lips thinned. "All right," she said. "But be on time in future."

Lennon stopped Ellen's retreat. "Be polite and say goodbye to your aunt."

Ellen turned and did as she was told as courteously as she could manage.

When they reached the gate, Bernie called after them.

"Here, did you think on what we talked about last week?"

Lennon stopped. "What was that?"

"Her confirmation." Bernie followed them down the short path. "You said you'd think about it."

"No I didn't," Lennon said. "I said no. You told me to think about it. Either way, it's still no."

"But she's coming ten," Bernie said. "She should be getting ready for her confirmation. If you'd sent her to a good school, not that auld Protestant place, she'd have been getting her classes and—"

"It is a good school," Lennon said. "Her friends are there. I'm not forcing any religion on my daughter, Protestant, Catholic, or otherwise. She can make her own mind up when she's old enough."

Bernie's voice rose. "How can she decide if you won't let her go to Mass? Even her mother had the decency to get her baptized."

"I'm not having this discussion with you again," Lennon said. He led Ellen away, walking back toward the Falls Road.

"That's what happens when a man raises a child," Bernie shouted after them. "It's a bloody disgrace."

Lennon ignored her and kept walking.

When they'd reached his car, and Lennon was easing into the traffic, Ellen spoke up from the back seat.

"I don't want to go to those dance classes any more."

Lennon glanced at her in the rear-view mirror. "It keeps your aunt Bernie happy."

"She's my great-aunt," Ellen said.

"Still, she's your family. I don't like it any more than you do, but that's the way it is. It's only once a week. You can stand her once a week, can't you?"

Ellen turned her gaze out of the window.

"Can't you?" Lennon repeated.

"I suppose," she said.

"Good girl," Lennon said. "It's part of growing up. There's things you don't want to do, but you go ahead and do them anyway, because it's the right thing. You understand?"

"I suppose."

Ellen remained quiet for a time before she asked, "Why does Aunt Bernie hate you so much?"

Lennon applied the handbrake at a set of lights. "She thinks I'm a bad person," he said.

"Why does she think that?" Ellen asked.

"She doesn't like policemen, for one thing. And she blames me for what happened to your mother."

Ellen shook her head. "That's stupid. You tried to help her."

Lennon could have argued with his daughter, told her he sometimes blamed himself for Marie McKenna's death, as illogical as he knew that idea to be. He could have told Ellen that her mother's fate was only one of the burdens he carried with him every day.

Instead, he said, "I love you, you know that, right?"

He heard the click of Ellen's seatbelt coming undone. She leaned over from the back seat, wrapped her arm around him. He kissed her hand. Felt her lips on his cheek. Felt clean for the first time that day.

"Seatbelt," he said as the lights changed.

6

Rea stared into the gloom for long seconds, feeling like a rodent gazing into the mouth of a silent owl.

After a while, she shook herself, swallowed blood, and said, "All right."

She got to her feet and steadied herself against the banister as a giddy wave washed through her. Her eyes adjusted to the darkness of the room, and she saw that a thin trickle of light seeped in around the edges of a closed blind. She released her grip on the banister and stepped toward the threshold. The painted doorsill creaked beneath her foot.

Inside, she could make out variations in the dark, blocks that might be furniture, patterns that could be pictures on the walls. She felt for a light switch, found it, and flicked it on. The glare of the single bare bulb made her squint, and she raised her hand as a shield.

The word 'office' appeared in her mind.

Of course, it was a home office. Just like many people had in a spare bedroom. A desk that looked as if it had been rescued from a school sat at the center of the room, along with a single chair. A cork noticeboard on one wall, bare but for the drawing pins that dotted it. A large map of the British Isles on another.

Yet it didn't make sense.

From what Ida had told her, Rea's uncle had been a manual

labourer. He had been in the merchant navy at one time, before he'd got married, but he had worked with his hands ever since. Travelled all over Britain and Ireland, wherever he could find employment. Why would he need an office in his home? And who would have an office without a computer of some kind—a laptop, or even one of those little netbooks?

"You didn't know him," she said aloud.

Rea scolded herself for talking to the empty room. She'd been doing it more and more frequently. A symptom of being single for so long. Next thing, she'd have a dozen cats.

With a creeping feeling of being an intruder, she crossed to the desk and stood by the chair. The surface of the desk was scarred with childish graffiti, slurs and insults, names of bands who'd come and gone by the eighties. The Smiths, The Jesus and Mary Chain, The Specials. In another patch, Iron Maiden, AC/DC, Dio. The kind of music middle-class schoolboys listened to while they squeezed their spots. Rea imagined this piece of furniture in some grammar school, the air thick with chalk dust, an ageing master conjugating Latin verbs while a pale young man scratched the words Echo and the Bunnymen into the wood. Raymond had probably rescued it from a skip somewhere.

Then she noticed the shallow drawer beneath the desk.

A plain brass knob at the center. Rea gripped it and pulled. Wood whispered against wood. She stared at the object within for a time before she could make sense of it.

A large leather-bound book, like a ledger, or an oversized photo album. Yes, that's it, she thought. Like a wedding album. Was it from her uncle's marriage? It didn't appear to be more than thirty years old, but perhaps it had been well looked after.

She reached into the drawer and lifted the book. The weight

of it surprised her. As it thumped onto the desk, Rea pictured Raymond sitting here, leafing through the pages, gazing at photographs of his dead wife. She felt an ache of pity for him, the latest of many in recent days.

Rea wondered what her aunt had looked like. She had to think for a moment to remember the name. Carol. Yes, Carol, that was it.

She opened the book.

Inside, wedged into the crease between the cover and the first page, was a manila envelope. Rea could tell by its fatness that it contained loose photographs. She lifted it from the book, slid her finger beneath the flap, and slipped the bundle of prints from their paper sheath. Maybe fifteen or twenty in various shapes and sizes.

The first photograph caused a moment of confused recognition. She stared at the three faces, knowing but unknowing.

Rea, her mother, and her father. A restaurant with gaudy decorations. Ida Carlisle's face and arms lobster red, Rea's the same. A family holiday, one of the very few they'd ever taken, more than a dozen years ago. Rea had just graduated from university, and Ida had insisted they go away to celebrate. Graham had resisted, saying he had far too much work to do, but eventually he gave in.

They'd gone to Salou in the Costa Dorada for a week, and it had been seven days of solid misery for Rea. If she went out to any of the bars, her parents made their disapproval clear, so she spent most nights rereading the books she'd brought while her father grumbled about the time he'd have to make up when he went back to work.

Why did her uncle have this picture? Where did he get it? As far as Rea knew, Ida and Raymond hadn't spoken in years, so it seemed unlikely they would exchange photographs.

She leafed through the bundle, examining each in turn. A few more portraits of her family, a day trip here, a birthday there, going back perhaps twenty years. A crawling sensation across her skin as she imagined her uncle alone in this room, studying these images.

Half a dozen older prints showed Raymond in his merchant navy days, two of them in formal uniform, the rest casual shots. Eating at a galley table. Bare-chested on the deck of a ship. Only one showed him smiling, and even that looked like a painful effort for him.

Rea turned over the last photograph, a Polaroid print, worn and faded. A group of six men, three in the foreground. Paramilitary flags pinned to the wall behind them. Those at the back wore military-style sweaters and trousers with camouflage patterns. Balaclavas covered their faces. They held weapons in their hands, two of which she recognized as AK-47s. The third was a pistol of some kind.

The front row, three young men, somewhere in their twenties, hunkered down, casual clothes, hands empty. On the left, Raymond Drew, his face expressionless, his eyes burning through the print. In the middle, a young man she didn't know, grinning. A tattoo on his neck.

To the right of the row, Graham Carlisle, Rea's father, smiling. The first thought in her mind: So young. Twenty-four, twenty-five?

Then she wondered what he was doing with those people, the paramilitaries. And Uncle Raymond. Had they been friends?

She touched her father's face and asked herself if she knew

him at all. So many questions, and he would answer none of them. Rea determined to take the photograph to her mother, ask her to explain it. She tucked the bundle of pictures back into the envelope, set it aside, and returned her attention to the book.

The paper was stiff against her fingers as she turned the first page. A minute or more passed as she stared, unable to grasp what she saw.

A single word, a name, cut from a newspaper headline and glued at the top of the page.

gwen.

Hair, the colour of wheat, a lock of it tied with a fine ribbon and affixed beneath the name. Without thinking, Rea touched it with her fingertip, separating the strands. Smooth and soft against her skin.

And something else. Something milky translucent, a teardrop shape stuck to the paper, ragged and stained brown at the wider end. Again, Rea touched it, finding the texture maddeningly familiar.

Then she knew, and her gut tightened. She tasted bile, swallowed, swallowed again, felt the heat in her throat as it opened.

Rea ran for the bathroom and retched over the basin. And again, her stomach convulsing, her eyes hot and stinging. She turned the taps, released a flow of water to wash the foulness away, even as more streamed from her mouth.

When it was done, her belly empty and aching, she rinsed her mouth and splashed cold water on her face. Her skin remembered the sensation of the torn fingernail, and her stomach rebelled once more, but she had nothing left.

Rea lowered herself to the floor and rested her back against the side of the bath. She twined her fingers together to subdue the tremors that ran out from her center.

"Jesus," she said.

There was no question what it had been. A human fingernail. A woman's, going by the shape. And the hair. Had they belonged to Raymond's wife? Had he kept them as a memento of her? Had he called her Gwen, some sort of pet name?

She pictured Uncle Raymond, or at least the ghost-like memory she had of him, bent over his wife's open coffin, scissors in one hand, pliers in the other.

The urge to giggle crept up on her, and she covered her mouth, kept it trapped inside. No one would hear, but even so, she would not laugh at a dead man's grief.

All right, she thought. Pull yourself together. Go back and look at it. It's gross, but it won't kill you.

Rea closed her eyes, counted to ten, and climbed to her feet. She walked back to the bedroom and paused in the doorway. The book still lay open on the desk, where she'd left it, the envelope of photographs alongside. She crossed the room slowly, quietly, as if she feared to wake it.

She stopped, told herself not to be so stupid. A bit of hair and a fingernail. That's all.

Rea stepped up to the desk and looked down at the book. What a strange and sad man, she thought, to keep such things in here. Treasures to him, maybe. Precious things to be locked away. She reached for the corner of the page, lifted it, turned it, let it fall away to the other side.

"Oh no," Rea said.

A newspaper article, cut out and pasted to the page.

MISSING GWEN FEARED ABDUCTED.

A black and white photograph of a young woman, a formal portrait taken in some studio, a reluctant smile on her pretty face. Her hair and jewellery years out of fashion.

"Oh God, no," Rea said.

The caption beneath the picture was printed in bold letters.

Greater Manchester police have expressed concerns for the safety of Gwen Headley, 23, missing since the early hours of Saturday morning.

Rea felt suddenly cold, as if the air in this secret room had crept and slithered under her clothing. She shivered as she fought the desire to flee the house.

But she wanted to know.

On the opposite page, sheets of notepaper glued in place, each one covered in line after line of neat, precise handwriting. And drawings, small, fine sketches of the same girl. And at the top of the first sheet, her name, and a date.

In spite of every shred of common sense that told her not to, Rea started to read.

Gwen Headley
MAY–JUNE 1992

I met her at the post office on Cheetham Hill Road, in the northern part of Manchester. She worked behind the counter. I was there to get a registration form for the van I'd bought while I was working on the site. She had beautiful hair. I watched her through the glass while I pretended I couldn't find the form.

I went back the next day to buy stamps. I waited and waited until there was no queue at her window. When I walked up to the glass, she smiled at me, and I shivered.

For a while I couldn't think what to say. I just stood there like a fool, staring at her.

"Can I help you?" she asked.

I opened my mouth, but nothing came out. She waited, her eyebrows raised, a little smirk on her lips, and I wanted to put my fist through the glass.

At last, I said, "Stamps."

The tag on her blouse said her name was Gwen.

"What sort?" she asked.

I kept staring at her.

"First class?" she asked. "Second class?"

"First," I said. "A dozen first class stamps, please."

She tore the stamps off a sheet while I scooped coins from my pocket. I had it exact to the penny and dropped the money into the tray. She slipped the stamps across to me.

I stood there, the stamps in my hand, for I don't know how long. Eventually, she asked, "Do you need anything else?"

I said, "No, sorry," and walked away, my face burning.

I didn't sleep that night. The old terraced house on George Street I shared with the other workers, the bunk beds occupied in shifts, all the creaking and snoring around me. I couldn't get her face out of my mind. That smirk. As if she could see right to the middle of me and tell how rotten I am inside. Judging me.

The front room of the house had once been a hairdresser's. The business had closed long ago, the owner fleeing, leaving behind three swivel chairs with their helmet-like dryers, and the mirrors on the walls. The landlord had not bothered to remove them, and

I sat in one of the chairs as I thought, watching the street outside lighten.

I decided then that I would take her.

I'd done it before, many times, but always on a whim, at random, chances and mistakes leading me to it. Boys and girls both. How many have there been? I can't be sure. More than twenty years since the first time it happened, back when I was in the merchant navy. I can't even remember what he looked like, just that it was quick and sudden, and it was over before I knew it had started.

We'd met in a bar, and he led me to a back alley. Then he wanted to touch me, and I wanted to touch him too, and I couldn't bear it.

I remember the heat of it, how quiet he became. I don't know if he really went silent, or if I went deaf for a little while. Either way, heat and quiet. Then, somehow, it was later and I went back to my ship. I told the Second Officer that I'd got into a fight at a bar. He told me to get down below or he'd have me up in front of the captain in the morning. Lots of us got into fights. A seaman coming back with blood on his clothes was nothing unusual.

I spent two weeks in terror of being caught. That a call would come over the radio to the boat, that someone wanted to talk to the crew about a dead man. After a month, the fear had gone altogether. I never worried about it again. Not once.

This time I wanted to do it right. To have a plan. A method. And Gwen would be my first.

I was lucky. Work had stalled at the site. They were waiting for some fancy kind of glass to come from Sweden, so all the men had to down tools. They put us on half-time to keep us around. Most of the boys spent their days drinking, but not me. I spent them watching Gwen.

The post office was off the main road, in a little pedestrian arcade,

next to a newsagent's. There was a cafe across the way. I went for
lunch there now and again. But not too often. I didn't want them
to notice me as I sat by the window with my fried-egg sandwich and
mug of tea, watching the post office through the glass.

Sometimes she would leave with another girl, sometimes on
her own. Sometimes I would follow her. After work, she would
walk out onto Cheetham Hill Road, with all the men in dark
suits, wide-brimmed hats and beards, and the women with their
wigs. The synagogue and the kosher shops. There, near the bank,
she waited for her bus, one of the many orange double-deckers
that streamed along the road through the day and into the night.

It took two or three times before I had the courage to join the
line behind her, climb aboard, hand the driver the coins and take
my ticket. I moved to the back with the shouting school-children.
I could see her yellow hair. She never went up to the top deck.
She'd stand rather than do that. Her stop wasn't far, after all.

I'd watch the streets change as the bus travelled further south
toward the city center. Rows of shops, family places, and greasy spoon
restaurants. Some chain stores, a McDonald's, a Kwik-Save. Within
five minutes, the buildings changed to houses, rows of old red-brick
places branching off the main road.

Eight minutes or so before she got off the bus. She'd wait at
the lights to cross. I could see her from my seat. I knew I could
follow her home from there, see where she lived. But only once.
It was almost certain she would notice me. One time might not
matter. A second time would. Then it would all be for nothing.

Six weeks and three days since the first time I'd seen her until the
day I followed her home. The site had got back to work, but I'd
called off sick more days than I'd turned up. The foreman had sacked
me a week before, kicked me out of the house, and I'd been sleeping

in my van. I'd been taking cups of tea in cafes just so I could use their toilets to wash in.

This day, I queued behind Gwen for the bus like I had a dozen times before, five people between me and her. I gave the driver my change, took the ticket, walked to the back. The schoolchildren squawking, the mothers scolding their babies, the shop workers gossiping. The noise of them all coming at me like swarms of flies. I wanted to swat at my ears, to shut them up, but I had to keep calm. Not draw attention.

I took a seat next to a fat brown-skinned man and kept one hand on the pole, leaning out so I could see her.

A young man sat across the aisle, chatting to her. A yobbish looking boy, that ugly hairstyle shaved at the sides and gelled flat at the top. A tracksuit, an earring in his ear. He was trying to make her laugh. She was trying to ignore him. I could tell.

Anger built up inside me. I wanted the boy to stop, to leave her alone. I wanted to rip that earring from his ear. To smash his face with my fists. At each of the three stops before hers, I wanted to scream at him to get off, get away, leave my Gwen in peace.

But he stayed there, kept grinning and chatting to her, and she kept ignoring him, and I remained silent while the sweat trickled down my ribs.

It probably only took five minutes to reach her stop, but it felt like hours. She stood before the bus had even halted and made her way to the front. The young man followed her. So did I.

Maybe a dozen people crammed into the aisle, waiting to step off onto the pavement. They pushed up against me, against Gwen, against the boy. I smelled them all, their sweat, their dirt, but all through it I could smell her, clean and alive.

Shoulders nudged shoulders as the bus stopped, the doors hissing open. I was carried along by the people, down onto the footpath. The huddle split, some making for the crossing at the lights.

The boy was still with her, still picking at her. I could hear him now.

"Go on, give us a chance," he said. "You might like me."

She didn't look at him. "I said, no thank you."

"Just one chance," he said, leaning close. "Just a drink."

The lights changed, the green signal to walk. She marched ahead, leaving him trailing by a few steps.

"Just one drink," he called after her. "Come on, just one drink, that's all."

She quickened her pace, making him jog to catch up. She reached the far pavement while he got snagged up in the cluster of people crossing the other way. I stayed behind him, keeping her in my sight.

When he got to the footpath, he slowed down, breathless. "All right, sod you, then. Stuck-up bitch."

If she heard, she didn't show it. She kept her head down and walked toward the corner.

The boy turned and saw me watching him.

"What the fuck are you looking at? You want some?"

I would've ripped his throat out if I hadn't wanted to avoid a scene. Instead, I stared at him, let him get a glimpse of me, of the wicked I have inside.

He went quiet and pale. He swallowed, turned, and walked away. One animal knows another. It knows when to stand, and when to run.

Gwen had turned the corner. I followed. She was halfway along the street by the time I got her in my sight again. Terraced houses, bay windows, small front yards. Dogs barking, the grumble of traffic from the main road. The dim grey time between the sun fading and the street lights coming on.

She crossed the road between the parked cars, headed for a side street. I stayed across the road, twenty yards away from her. When I drew level with the side street, I watched her stop six doors down, take a key from her bag, and let herself into the house.

I stood there as long as I dared, taking in as much of it as I could. Then I walked down the side street. Not hurrying, not dragging my feet. These houses had no gardens, front doors opening onto the footpath. Paint flaking off the window frames and doors. One house was boarded up.

Two doors before the house she'd entered there was an alleyway. I saw as I passed that it cut straight through to the next street, with another alley branching off, giving access to the rear of the houses. I pictured it as I walked, yard walls, weeds in the cracks, rubbish bins spilling litter on the ground.

I turned left at the end of the street and found where the alley opened onto the road. Without pausing, I entered, kept walking, my head down like I knew where I was headed. Just a man taking a short cut between the buildings.

Counting as I went, I passed the back of her house. A family home, I wondered, her parents' or her husband's? She didn't wear a wedding ring. Or maybe the house was divided into flats. Not that it mattered.

I kept moving until I reached the back of the boarded-up house. The gate had been forced open long ago. I pressed the wood with my fingertips. The gate eased aside, and I stepped into the yard.

It felt colder between the walls, like I'd slipped into a dead thing's womb. I stood close to the brickwork, where no one could see me, and thought.

The way became clear. Grabbing her would be easy. Keeping her quiet was the problem. And the van. People notice a strange vehicle when it's parked on their street. And a street like this, where everyone knows each other. But no way could I take her without the van. Disguising it was the only option. It was a white Toyota Hiace. There'd be hundreds of them in the city. Steal a number plate, maybe one of those magnetic signs for the side.

It was dark by the time I let myself out of the yard. I saw no one until I reached the main road with its traffic and bus stops. I was back at the patch of waste ground where I'd parked the van within half an hour, and I knew exactly how to get it done.

7

With the bedroom door closed, Lennon swallowed two pills with water. He felt them in his throat, working their way down. Another mouthful from the bottle chased them to his stomach. The headache would fade soon, and the pains in his joints, replaced by that warmth in his veins, the pleasing weight to his eyelids.

Ellen was quiet in the living area of the flat, doing her homework. Perhaps he could steal half an hour's sleep before Susan came home from her office. She would pick up her own daughter, Lucy, from swimming classes on the way.

Susan had taken Ellen and him in when he was released from hospital a year ago. He had rented out his own apartment on the floor below, leaving all but his clothes behind. Susan had nursed him, cleaned his wounds, changed his dressings. All on top of caring for her own little girl, and her career, giving him the closest thing he'd ever had to a family.

No time to think of her now. He had work to do. Or what he thought of as work.

The small electronic safe was bolted to the floor of Susan's walk-in closet. He knelt down, enduring the pain it caused, and pressed a series of six numbers on the keypad: Ellen's birthday, day, month, year. A soft whirr as the safe unlocked.

Pages and pages inside, bound together in a manila file, much of it collected in the weeks before his suspension. Prints and photocopies of arrest records, memos, emails, reports to the Public Prosecutions Service. Almost thirty cases that had fallen through due to misplaced evidence, witnesses withdrawing statements, or requests from C3 Intelligence Branch to halt investigations in order to protect informants.

DCI Dan Hewitt's name was all over them.

Lennon knew in his gut that Hewitt had paid a fellow officer to try to kill him in the car park of Belfast International Airport two Christmases ago. As he had lain on the frost-covered ground, three bullets in him, consciousness slipping away, it was Dan Hewitt's face Lennon saw through the fog.

Hours later, a taxi driver and a Lithuanian businessman were executed on the road to the same airport. He had no proof, but Lennon believed that if Hewitt hadn't pulled the trigger himself, then he'd hired someone to do it for him.

Two things had got Lennon through the days and weeks in hospital, the hours upon hours of agonising physiotherapy. His daughter, the only real and meaningful thing he had in his life, and the idea of nailing Hewitt for what he'd done.

In truth, he'd made little progress toward that goal in the last twelve months, but still he sought refuge in the materials he had gathered, poring over every page, imagining the day he would bring Hewitt down. Occasionally, CI Uprichard, Lennon's only remaining friend on the force, would pass him a few relevant pages. Lennon knew it was only to appease him, to keep his anger and hatred for Hewitt from boiling over, from becoming dangerous. And it worked, to an extent.

Susan called it an obsession, and Lennon knew she was right. But that didn't necessarily make it unhealthy. She had stopped listening when he told her the grimy details he had uncovered, and eventually told him to keep his findings to himself.

Stalking, she called it. Why couldn't he let it go? she asked. Think about us, our relationship, the girls, his daughter and hers. Ellen and Lucy had become like sisters since Lennon had given up his flat and moved in with Susan.

Lennon tried. But it was Hewitt who kept him from sleep at night, kept him reaching for the pills that would close his eyes and dull his mind.

"Daddy," Ellen said.

Lennon spun toward the door.

She stood there, fingers knotted together, as if seeking his permission to enter. He held out his hand, and she approached.

"What's up, darling?" he asked.

"Nothing," she said.

He patted the bed beside him, and she climbed up. He gathered up the few pages he'd removed from the file and slipped them back inside. Ellen pretended she hadn't seen them.

Lennon asked, "Have you finished your homework?"

Ellen nodded. "It was sums. They were easy."

"Good," he said.

She leaned into him, and he put his arm around her shoulder. Her soft hair tickling his lips and nose.

"What's wrong, sweetheart?"

Ellen remained quiet, but he could feel the quandary in her. "Tell me, darling."

She inhaled once and said, "I don't want to go."

"Go where?"

"Anywhere."

He asked, "What do you mean? Who says you have to go anywhere?"

"I like living here," she said, her voice little more than an expulsion of air. "I like living with Lucy. And Susan, too. I don't want to go."

"Is this about your aunt Bernie?" he asked. "If she's bothering you, you don't have to see her any more. She won't take you away from me."

"It's not her," Ellen said.

"Has Lucy said something?"

"No."

"Did her mummy say something?"

"No."

"Then why do you think you'll have to go anywhere?"

"Just," she said, shrugging.

Lennon felt the fine bones of her shoulders through her school cardigan. Soon after Ellen came into his care, after her mother's death, he realized she saw and felt things she shouldn't, secrets she could never know, but somehow did. He wanted to call it intuition, like Susan, but he knew it was more than that. He tried not to think too much about it: to do so would be to risk his already fragile sanity, and Ellen had learned to keep such things to herself.

But now this.

As the painkillers began to dull the blade that dug into his head, Lennon said, "Well, you're not going anywhere. What would I do without you?"

He didn't dare ask himself that question too often. Ellen was the thread that kept him tethered to his own life. In the coldest hours of the night, she kept the most terrifying possibilities from his mind.

Lennon had come closest six months ago. He had built up a stock of painkillers, over-the-counter and prescription-only, enough to stop a horse's heart. He had wondered how many he could swallow with vodka, how many it would take to put him under. He had seen enough suicides over the years to know how ugly a death it could be. The idea of Ellen finding him, vomit crusting around his mouth, made him flush most of the pills away. But not all of them.

He sometimes thanked God that his personal protection weapon had been taken from him when he was suspended. Officers were only relieved of their standard issue Glock 17s when their transgressions involved firearms. That Lennon had shot a fellow policeman, albeit in self-defense, certainly qualified. Had he still possessed the pistol over the last year or so, Lennon wasn't sure he'd still be alive.

"Neither of us is going anywhere," he said.

She looked up at him. Not a word, but she didn't need to say anything.

Ellen slipped off the bed leaving Lennon to feel like a liar even though he was sure he had told her the truth.

8

Rea sat down in the chair. It creaked beneath her weight. She felt heavier than she had before, as if the words she read had crept under her skin, small leaden things to drag her to the floor.

She brought her hand to her mouth, stomach cold and slippery inside, trying to creep up to her throat once more. She took the mobile phone from her pocket and opened the contacts.

"Hello?" her mother answered.

"It's me," Rea said. "I need you to come back to the house."

"But I'm not dressed," Ida said. "I'm running a bath."

"Please. I need you to come now."

"Why? What's wrong?"

"Just come. Please."

"All right. But I wish you'd tell me what's wrong. You've got me all worried now."

"Don't be long," Rea said, and hung up.

She suddenly felt cold, air moving around her as if the house had taken a breath. How long had she been sitting here? The thin trickle of light that had slipped past the closed blind had weakened and disappeared.

Her skin prickled, the fine hairs on her hands stood on end. That cool draught again, air displaced.

Someone was in the house.

The certainty of it formed in her, hard and immovable. She

sat motionless, frozen in the chair, listening, staring at the open
doorway and the landing beyond, now cast in a strange blue-grey
by the coming evening.

A creak from below.

Absolutely, definitely a creak. No question about it.

It wasn't until Rea's head went light that she realized she'd been
holding her breath. She let it out with a hiss, sucked air back in.
Her heart bounced in her chest; she put a hand between her
breasts as if to calm it.

Well, what are you going to do? she thought. Sit here and
wait? Or go and see?

Rea stood. Her legs quivered with adrenaline.

"Hello?" she called. "Who's there?"

She listened. No reply came.

Another creak.

"Fuck," she whispered.

She walked to the doorway, treading as soft as she could on
the bare floorboards. Each footstep felt like a thunderclap. She
stopped on the threshold, listened again.

Nothing. But still that cool draught, brushing against her cheek.

"Hello?" she called again.

No answer.

She walked three paces to the top of the stairs.

"I know you're there. I've called the police. Get out now before
they come."

Her voice resonated in the stairway and hall below, coming
back to her as a hollow, frightened girlish sound.

Yep, she thought, that'll scare them off.

Them. Was she sure there was anybody? The certainty that
had taken root so firmly in her moments before now seemed to

crack and crumble. There was probably no one. It was an old house, at least a century, and old houses are draughty and creaky. Everyone knows that. Feeling more brave and foolish with each step, Rea made her way downstairs.

There'll be a cat, she thought. A cat, and it'll jump out and hiss and scare the shit out of me. Then I'll turn around, and Jason Voorhees or Freddy Krueger will be standing there with a big fuck-off knife.

By the time Rea's foot left the bottom step, all notions of intruders, armed or otherwise, had dissolved like the childish fantasies they were. She reached for the hall light switch and flicked it on. The bin bags still lay there, lined up, waiting to be taken to the dump. They'd have to wait another day.

Creak.

She gasped, spun on her heels. And then she understood.

The front door moved in the breeze, its hinges groaning. Of course. Her father had promised to see about getting it fixed, said that it needed a good shove to close it properly.

Rea went to the door, put her hip against it, and pushed. The key still in the hole, she turned it, heard the snap and clunk of the tumbler.

She walked to the back sitting room, turning the lights on as she went, and made her way to the kitchen beyond. Ugly floral linoleum on the floor, cupboards and drawers that should have been replaced twenty years ago. A fluorescent strip light on the ceiling that accentuated the worst features of the room. At the brown plastic sink, she poured herself a cup of water. She gazed out into the garden, wondering if she had the nerve to return to the book and the handwritten pages that waited upstairs.

Minutes later, she did.

She read a story about a boy called Andrew.

Andrew
27TH MARCH 1994

I never found out Andrew's second name. No one ever reported him missing. Not a single person noticed he had gone, even his companion on the night I picked him up. At least, no one who would go to the police.

He wasn't planned. There was no preparation. No following, no watching. It just happened.

Maybe I should regret it, but regret is an emotion I don't understand. I understand anger, and lust. Sometimes I think I know love, what it feels like, so big inside me that I fear I'll burst. Do you feel that, sometimes?

I never did another like Gwen Headley. The preparation, the planning, the following, the watching. I am not careful enough. I have read about men who can do those things, over and over again, one after the other. The wicked inside me wouldn't allow me to do that. I got lucky with Gwen. I would not be so lucky if I tried it again, I know that.

But Andrew.

I'd been in Leeds for three months. They were building a hotel just off the M621 motorway, the kind of place sales reps would stay at. Lonely men, like me. The contractor worked out of Dublin, bringing some men over, hiring some on the ground. They put us up in

Portakabins on the site. They were cold and damp, the cots hard, the blankets thin. Some of the boys slept in their cars or vans instead, others went into the city to see if they could pull women, as much to get a warm bed as to fornicate.

That night, I drove through the city center to Spencer Place, the road that runs north to south, all hedges and walls and tall leafy trees. Anywhere else, it'd be where the rich people lived, with its big houses and driveways. Here, it's where a man goes to buy the things he needs. Girls, boys, drugs.

I don't bother much with the drugs. I don't like losing control. You know I find it hard to hold on to myself as it is. Bad things might happen. But that night, I wanted a boy.

Not to fornicate with, at least not in that way. I am not one of those men. I know I am not, whatever anyone else says, I am not.

My uncle told me I was. When he held me down, the pillow over my face. So big, so strong. Thick arms pinning me to the bed. A nancy, he told me, a sissy. Not a boy, he'd say, not a real boy who'd grow to be a man. A real boy wouldn't let him do those things he did to me. A real boy, a someday-man, would fight back. Would say no loud enough to make it stop.

I could never say no loud enough. I was never strong enough to make him stop. Not until I was fourteen, when I hit him so hard he never so much as looked at me again.

In Leeds, I'd got rid of the Toyota van I'd had in Manchester and bought an old blue Ford Transit. That night, I pulled up beside a pair of young men in tight jeans. I could tell by the way they smoked their cigarettes, the way they fidgeted, the hollowness in their faces, that they were rattling—suffering for want of some heroin. They would work for cheap.

I wound down the passenger window and they both approached.

"How much?" I asked.

"Two for the price of one, love," the taller boy said. He had a Glasgow accent. "Both of us for fifty quid. Bargain, eh?"

Hateful animals. Nancy boys. Sissies.

"I only want one. So twenty-five, then."

"Fifty," he said. "I said two for one. You only want one, that's your lookout."

I started to wind the window up.

"Hang on," he called before I could close it.

I wound the window back down.

"Thirty," he said.

"All right."

He opened the door and went to climb in.

"No," I said. I pointed to the other one, the younger, smaller one. "Him."

The older boy stepped back and exchanged a look with his friend. The younger boy nodded, don't worry, it's all right.

He climbed up into the cabin and closed the door behind him.

I put the van in gear and said, "Close the window, there's a good lad, keep the cold out."

He did as he was told and I moved off toward the park at the northern end of the road.

"What's your name?" I asked.

"Andrew," he said, keeping his gaze on the passing houses, the cars, the other streetwalkers.

"Is that your real name?"

He didn't answer.

"Is it?" I asked.

"Does it matter?" he said.

His accent was northeast. Gateshead, Sunderland. Maybe Newcastle.

"I suppose not," I said. "How old are you?"

"However old you want me to be," he said, smiling, fluttering his eyelids, posing like a girl.

"The truth," I said, hating him.

"I'll be nineteen in a couple of weeks," he said. "But I can pass for younger."

I said nothing more until we reached the gate at the far end of the park. It stood open, even approaching midnight. I eased the van through and along the path that wound between the sports fields and open meadows. Other cars, their windows steamed, were parked along the way, weaker men having their itches scratched.

I never meant to do the boy any harm.

As much as he made me sick. Even though he waited on a corner, selling himself like a calf for slaughter, and despite all the wretched things he made me feel inside, I did not mean to hurt him. Not really.

When I found a dark, quiet place, I intended only to do what I needed with him, then take him back to where I'd picked him up. Safe and sound. More or less.

I climbed out of the van, went to the passenger side, opened the door, and let him out. He waited while I opened the sliding door at the side, saw the mattress and blankets I'd laid on the plywood floor.

"Fucking hell," he said. "It's the Ritz."

He followed me inside, and I closed the door behind us. At one time, encounters like this terrified me. The closeness, the intimacy, the shame of it. Now I know the shame is all his. He is the one who sells himself so he can afford to blot out his mind with poison. He is the one whose sordid desires brought him here. I am not to blame.

I knelt there, waiting for him to lie down, passive like a corpse, and let me get on with it. Instead, he knelt too, facing me. I knew something was wrong. He hadn't detached himself from the now, he was too much here in the present, his eyes watching and seeing.

"So, what do you like?" he asked.

"Just lie down," I said.

He smiled. "Tell you what, why don't you lie down? Let me show you what I can do."

I didn't answer, even though I wanted to strike him for such obscenity. To offer to do things to me. Like my uncle did. He was no better. I stayed still and watchful.

"Go on, then," he said, nodding down toward the mattress.

I shook my head, only a small movement, but enough to change the expression on his face from weak obedience to fiery hate.

He tried too hard to be fast, going for his coat pocket, fumbling. I knew what he was reaching for long before he had it out, slashing at the air between us.

"Give me your fucking money," he hissed.

The knife looked like it had come from someone's kitchen, small and sharp, the kind of knife you'd use for peeling a potato or cutting up an apple.

"Put it away and get out," I said.

He bared his teeth. "I said, give me your money, now."

"I'll give you one more chance," I said. "Go. Now. I won't give you another."

He lurched forward on his knees, swiping the blade inches from my face. "I'll fucking cut your face off, I—"

One hand took his wrist, the other his neck. I slammed his head against the van's inner wall, making a dull clang. He slumped, quiet, his eyelids flickering.

Five minutes later, he was tied up with strips of bed sheet, being driven out of the city toward the countryside where the stars are brightest in the sky.

Weeks later, after I'd left for better work in the south, I heard a news report on the radio saying a body had been found by the River Aire, close to the M1 motorway, hidden in the woods. As far as I know, they never identified him. I sometimes wonder what they did with his corpse. Did it lie in a mortuary somewhere, frozen, waiting to be claimed? How long would they keep it?

I shouldn't have done it. The risk was too great. I hadn't taxed the van when I took him. It didn't have an MOT. What if the police had stopped me?

I am careless. I am rash. I am wicked.

If I let the wicked take over once too often, nothing and no one will save me.

Not even you.

9

"How many's that today?" Susan asked.

"Dunno," Lennon said.

He put his palm to his mouth and tilted his head back. The pills settled on his tongue. He took a mouthful of water, swallowed, set the glass on the drainer. A cough rattled in his lungs, reminding him that the cold still lingered.

Susan sat at the table, still wearing her work suit. He'd promised to start preparing dinner for the girls before she got home. All he'd managed so far was to rummage through the freezer, looking for something he could blast in the oven or the microwave. Susan wouldn't approve. She only kept that processed stuff for emergencies, as she'd reminded him many times before.

Ellen and Lucy were watching television in the living area, giggling at some American cartoon on one of the satellite channels.

"Fish fingers?" he asked Susan. "There's beans and oven chips."

Susan pressed her fingertips to her forehead. "There's plenty of veg there. And chicken thighs. You could roast them."

"How long for?"

She placed her hands flat on the table and closed her eyes, made a begrudging decision, and opened them again.

"I'll do it," she said, standing.

"No, I can—"

"I said, I'll do it."

Susan pushed past him to the fridge. Lennon stood with his hands by his sides for a few moments, wondering how to speak without making her angry.

Eighteen months, two years ago, she had seemed quietly beautiful to him. Too good for a wastrel like Jack Lennon, so he had resisted her attention up until then. Now he could only see the resentment on her face, masking what had drawn him to her in the first place. He believed all along that he didn't deserve a woman like Susan, someone as kind and decent. But since she'd taken him in, more out of pity than want, she seemed to have realized it too.

As she cut open a pack of chicken thighs, Susan asked, "So what did you do today?"

Lennon took the seat she had just left. "I told you, I had that meeting with the Police Federation rep this afternoon. I picked Ellen up from her dance class on the way back."

"She told me you were late," Susan said.

"Ten minutes. I had the meeting, I couldn't move it."

"The meeting took, what, an hour?" She set the knife down on the worktop, kept her gaze away from him. "Another ten minutes to bring Ellen home. You were barely out of bed when I left here this morning. What did you do with the rest of the day?"

Lennon ran his fingertips across his chin. He was surprised for a moment to find it smooth to the touch. Then he remembered he had shaved that morning. The first time in nearly a fortnight.

The girls fell silent, stopped watching their television show, studied their hands instead.

"Well, there wasn't much I could do."

Susan turned to face him. "Did you do the laundry?"

"No."

"I've been asking you for weeks to sort out what stuff you can give to the charity shop. Did you do that?"

"No."

"Did you chase up that appointment with the psychologist?"

"No."

Her eyes glistened with moisture, her cheeks reddening. "So you sat around here most of the day and did sweet fuck all?"

Without a word, Ellen and Lucy slipped away, heading for the bedroom they shared.

Lennon had a ridiculous urge to laugh. It turned to a cough as he choked it back. "Well, I—"

She slapped the worktop with her palm. "While I went out to work, you pissed about all day long."

Lennon spoke louder than he'd intended. "I'm not going to—"

"I am not your mother, Jack. You're not a child. You're a grown man, and I wish you'd start acting like one."

He walked toward the living area. "I'm not going to argue with you."

"And how many of those pills did you take?"

He grabbed the remote control from the coffee table. "I told you, I don't remember."

"You shouldn't be taking any at all. You don't even have a prescription for them. Christ knows where you—"

"I need them for the pain."

"Bollocks." She spat the word at him. "You use them for a crutch. Just like you use me for a crutch."

He gave no answer as he sat down and flipped through the channels. They did not speak as Susan fetched the girls from their room and served them dinner at the table. Lennon sat and listened to the clank of cutlery on plates. Neither Lucy nor Susan said goodnight to him as they went to bed. Only Ellen embraced him before she left him alone, and he was glad of her touch.

10

Rea sat on the stairs, in the same spot where she had said goodbye to her mother that afternoon. When Ida let herself in, it must have looked as if her daughter hadn't moved in all that time.

"Right, what's wrong?" she asked as she closed the door behind her. She looked like she'd dressed in a hurry. A breeze made the door sway inward again. Ida tutted and shoved harder. This time, it latched.

"You said you didn't really know your brother," Rea said.

Ida frowned. "That's right."

"Well, what *did* you know about him?"

"What I told you. More or less."

"How did his wife die?"

Ida came to the bottom of the stairs and leaned on the banister. "It was awful sad. Turned out she had a wee bit of a drinking problem. She'd had a bellyful of sherry the night she died. She fell down these stairs and cracked her head open."

Ida looked down at her feet as if realizing she stood on the very tiles that had crushed Carol Drew's skull.

Rea asked, "Was there ever a question?"

"About what?"

"About how she died. That there might've been more to it."

"What, you mean, something suspicious?"

"Yes."

Ida shook her head. "No, no, nothing like that, not at all. Why? What's going on?"

Rea didn't answer. Instead, she asked, "What about when you were kids? What was he like then?"

"I don't know," Ida said, lowering herself to sit two steps below Rea. "I didn't really see that much of him. He was only my half-brother, remember. He spent some of the time with an aunt of his, his own father's sister. She was a hard auld bissum, didn't have a good word for anybody. She never forgave my mother for marrying again so quick after Raymond's father died. Raymond lived with us on and off, but him and my father never saw eye to eye. And then there was that bit of trouble with the police."

Rea leaned forward. "The police?"

Ida looked down at her hands, knotted them together, like she'd set free some terrible secret. "Well . . . there were a few times, actually."

"What for?"

"The first couple of times, it was silly stuff. Lifting things out of shops. Sweets, cigarettes, anything he could fit in his pocket. Then there was that tramp he gave a beating to. He swore to our mother this tramp had attacked him. He might've gone to prison that time, only the case fell through when the tramp wouldn't talk to the police, and Raymond was only a teenager, so they couldn't make it stand.

"My father put him out then, told him he could go back to his aunt's and never darken our door again. Except she wouldn't have him either and he wound up living on the streets. After no one had heard from him for a few weeks, my mother made my father take her out in the car looking for him. They found him out by the gasworks living in cardboard boxes."

"So they took him back?" Rea asked.

"Well, Mummy didn't give Daddy much choice in the matter. Either Daddy let Raymond come back or she'd go, and take me with her. So he came back, and he was good for a while. That was the closest we ever got to being a family. But then the burglaries started. A square mile around our house, there was one or two break-ins a week. Hardly anything taken, but the drawers would be gone through, all the private things would be pulled out and thrown around the place. Sometimes, whoever broke in would do their business in the beds."

Rea almost laughed, but choked it back. "What, you mean shit in them?"

Ida gave her a hard stare. "Language. You're not too big for a clip round the ear. But yes, that. And other things."

Rea didn't want to think what the 'other things' might be.

"Anyway," Ida continued, "this went on for weeks, maybe a dozen houses were broken into. Then some big fella who worked at the shipyard caught your uncle Raymond climbing over his back wall. He gave Raymond an awful doing. Put him in the hospital. Then, of course, Raymond was off to borstal. It broke Mummy's heart, and Daddy was finished with him. He was never back in our house again. He joined the merchant navy the week after he turned sixteen."

They sat quiet and still for a while, Ida worrying at the tissue she'd pulled from her sleeve, Rea searching for a way to tell her mother the awful thing she had discovered. Eventually, there was nothing for it but to take a breath and say it out loud.

"I got into the back bedroom."

Ida looked up from her tissue. "Oh? How?"

"I broke in," Rea said. "I took a crowbar from the garage and forced the door."

"Och, Rea, who's going to fix that? Why didn't you wait and get the locksmith out again?"

Rea dropped her gaze. "I found something in there."

"What? For goodness' sake, will you just tell me what you called me back here for?"

"I did a search on my phone for her name," Rea said. "Gwen Headley. She went missing in Manchester in 1992. All they ever found of her was some clothing in an alley behind the house where she shared a flat with another girl. According to the old news reports I dug up, it rained very heavily the night she disappeared, so the police never found anything useful. Just this one scrap of clothing, it didn't say what it was. A van was seen in the area. They eventually found out its number plates were stolen off a van of the same make and colour, and a plumber's sign was taken off another van.

"This girl, Gwen, she was from Wales. She had a music degree, played clarinet. She'd stayed on in Manchester after university and got a job in a post office until she could get her music career going full time. Her parents never found out what happened to her. But *I* know."

Ida reached up, put a hand on her daughter's knee. "Rea, love, I don't understand. What's this girl got to do with us?"

"It's all up there, in a book, like a wedding album. Like a scrapbook. He wrote it all down, kept pictures, press cuttings, there's even a lock of hair and a fingernail."

Ida stared at her, shaking her head. "I don't understand."

"That girl, Gwen Headley," Rea said. "Uncle Raymond killed her."

Ida closed the book and sat back in the chair.

"I can't read any more," she said. "Is it all like that?"

"I couldn't read much more of it," Rea said. "Not in detail. A boy in Leeds, a homeless man in Dublin, a prostitute in Glasgow. And on and on. Some of them have names, some of them don't. I counted eight altogether. Some of it's just ranting at nothing. There are pages that make no sense at all. It reads like he was kind of coming and going. Out of his mind on one page, completely lucid the next. It's as if he's talking to himself sometimes. But all those people . . ."

Ida stared at some distant point, perhaps a memory of her brother, the stranger that shared her mother.

Rea leaned against the door frame. "How do you want to handle it?"

Ida looked up at her with a lost expression on her face. "What do you mean, handle it?"

"I mean, when we call the police. I suppose Dad will want to be careful it doesn't affect his standing in the party, and—"

"We can't call the police," Ida said, shaking her head.

"What are you talking about? We have to call them."

"No," Ida said. "Not without talking to your father. It could ruin him. He'd never hang on to his seat in Stormont, let alone get the Westminster candidacy. They'd drop him like a stone."

"Why?" Rea took a step into the room. "It's not his fault. He's not even really related to Raymond. They can't hold this against him."

"They can and they will. Doesn't matter that he hadn't seen Raymond in years, he barely spoke two words to him since Carol died, it doesn't matter at all. He'll be finished if this gets out."

Rea approached the table.

"But what about Gwen's parents? They never knew what happened to her. They never got to bury her. There, at the end of that section, he says what he did with her body. How can we not let them bury their daughter?"

Ida's voice became shrill and quivery. "What good will that do them? It'll not bring her back, will it? Do you really want them to know what this person did to their wee girl? Do you even know if they're alive?"

"This person," Rea echoed. "You mean Raymond. Your brother."

"My half-brother," Ida said. "He was no more a brother to me than the man in the moon."

"Then why not report it?"

"Because we can't. Your father won't allow it."

"I really don't think it's up to him." Rea leaned on the table, closer to the book than she cared to be. "I asked you how to go about it to make this easier on the two of you. But I can't keep this secret. It's not just that girl's parents who are suffering. Look through those pages. How many more of them are there? Women and men, names, places, the things he kept."

Ida stood up and moved away from the table. "I don't know. I don't want to know. I need to call your father."

She took the mobile phone from her handbag, the one Rea had bought her for Christmas, and fumbled at the buttons until she found the number she needed. She closed her eyes as she held it to her ear and waited.

"Hello? I know . . . I know you're busy, but . . . Stop . . . Stop and bloody listen."

Ida glanced at Rea, blushing at the vulgarity that had passed her lips.

"It's important. You have to come to Raymond's house straight away . . . No . . . No, not later. Right now . . . You'll see when you get here . . . You'll see . . . Tell them whatever you like, just get here . . . All right . . . Don't be long."

She hung up.

Rea said, "He'll say the same as you, won't he? Not to call the police."

Ida nodded. "You know he will."

Rea had an answer for that hidden in her pocket.

Graham Carlisle paced the room, hands clasped at the small of his back. He had worn one of his best suits to the committee meeting, charcoal grey with a pale pinstripe, a well-pressed shirt with French cuffs and a stiff collar. Rea pictured her mother ironing it that morning, feeling like the great woman behind the great man.

He'd kept in decent shape for a man his age—even a reasonable amount of hair remained on his head—and Rea vaguely remembered that his hard features had once been handsome. Graham had been a lawyer specializing in conveyancing for most of his career. He'd come from as rough a background as Belfast could offer, but he'd clawed his way to a grammar school and university education, unusual for a boy with his upbringing when such opportunities were the preserve of the middle classes.

His journey into politics began at the time when Rea moved from primary to grammar school. Somehow, Rea had sensed that his standing for election to Belfast City Council had been dependent on her passing her Eleven-Plus exams and getting into the right school. She often told herself that was a foolish idea, but she remembered the morning the results arrived in the post bringing to a climax the months of crushing pressure and tension, the after-school sessions with private maths and English tutors, one mock test after another.

When her mother opened the envelope she had sat quiet for a few moments, then burst into tears. Rea had stood there watching, waiting, an eleven-year-old child in pyjamas, the future course of her life having been decided by the piece of A4 paper in her mother's hands. She remembered needing the toilet badly, afraid she might not be able to hold it but terrified of walking away before her mother revealed the result. The tears meant she'd failed, surely. She felt heat in her own eyes, her lip beginning to tremble. There was nothing worse in the world than to fail.

The first fat, hot drop of salt water had rolled down her cheek when her mother said, "You got an A, love. You passed."

Rea's tears flowed freely then, but good tears, tears of relief. Ida came over and embraced her. Yet Rea could not stop crying.

Graham had come in from the other room where he had been hiding until he knew it was good news. He patted Rea's head and took a twenty-pound note from his wallet. Rea accepted it, thanked him, understanding this was as much of himself as he would give.

The following Monday, her father started making calls to his friends and colleagues in the party. He got the nomination for the next council election and comfortably won his seat.

For twenty-three years, Rea had told herself the timing was a coincidence, though she never quite believed it in her heart.

Now the Assembly at Stormont; next, Westminster.

Graham Carlisle had been a man of liberal views, but Rea had watched him turn into one of the grey men of unionism, moulded by the party, becoming more and more conservative as he progressed through the ranks. He had allowed his own beliefs to wither under the shadow of his ambition, no longer a man of principle but a company man, toeing the line set down by his superiors.

When a party leader had expressed the most archaic homophobic views on a late night BBC news panel, her father had been among the first to defend him the following morning. He trotted out the party policy on gay marriage, said it was against the moral beliefs of the majority of Northern Ireland's citizens. Rea had watched Graham on the lunchtime news, truly ashamed of her father for the first time in her life. It gave Rea an ache in her breast to see him turning so stony and cold that she barely remembered the man who had held her close as an infant.

"Well?" Rea asked.

"I'm thinking," Graham said, not slowing his step, back and forth, back and forth. He took his glasses off, the fine-framed pair he thought made him look sophisticated, and tapped the tip of the leg against his teeth.

Rea leaned against the wall, next to the map of the British Isles. Ida had taken the seat at the desk as soon as Graham had vacated it. She had moved it to the other side of the room, as far away from the book as she could manage.

Graham paused halfway across the floor. "How do we even know this is real? What if it's just some sick fantasy of Raymond's? Maybe it was all in his head. You said yourself, some of it sounds like he's away with the fairies."

"It's real, Dad," Rea said. "I looked up Gwen Headley's name online. It's all there, how she went missing, all of it."

Graham snorted. "Oh, it's on the Internet, so it must be true."

"It's on every newspaper website that has an archive going back that far. All the papers reported it at the time. It's real. And her parents are still wondering what happened to her."

"If they're alive," Graham said.

Ida leaned forward in the chair. "That's what I said. Didn't I say that? They could be dead and buried, for all we know."

Rea shook her head. "They'd be in their sixties by now, maybe their seventies. Not that much older than you. They're probably still alive. Still wondering. And it's not just them. There are other people in the book. Men and women. They all had families, they all had mothers and fathers."

"Well, I don't see how this is our problem," Graham said. "They have my sympathy for what they've gone through, but it's not our place to find answers for them."

Rea fought to keep the anger down. "What do you mean it's not our problem? How can it be anyone else's? Look at the information we have. It's been our problem since the moment Raymond died."

Her father approached the desk, and the book that rested there. He reached for the leather-bound cover and closed it.

"We'll destroy it," he said.

"What?" Rea stepped away from the wall, the anger pushing up and out of her.

"We'll make a fire in the back garden and burn the book."

"No." Rea's nails dug into her palms. "No, we can't. How could you do that to them?"

"I'm not doing anything to anybody. Raymond's dead. He can't hurt anyone now, and nothing's going to help that poor girl's family."

"What if it was me?" Rea asked.

"Don't," Ida said, looking up from her hands.

"But what if it was? You'd want to know what happened to me, wouldn't you? You'd want my body back."

Graham's face hardened. "But it's not you. Look, that girl's parents are no worse off tonight than they were yesterday. Or last week, or last year. Are they?"

"No," Rea said, "but that's not the—"

"Maybe they'd get a little comfort from burying their daughter, but I'd lose my career."

"You don't know that."

"Yes, I do. You know how the party's run. Any hint of a scandal, anyone who gets tainted, even if it's not their fault, they're done. If this gets out, I'll be finished. I'd be lucky if they let me go back to a council seat. I can't afford to lose my salary from the Assembly." He paused, looked straight at Rea. "We'd have to sell this house, for a start."

"What, you're going to bribe me with the house? Do you think I want to live here after finding that book?"

"I'm not trying to bribe you," he said. "I just want you to know what this would cost me. What it would cost us as a family."

Rea's hand went to her back pocket, felt the Polaroid print between her fingers. "What exactly are you afraid of people finding out about you?"

She approached the table and dropped the picture face up. It spun on the surface, came to rest in front of her father.

Graham's face reddened. He stared at the photograph. Ida got to her feet and came to her husband's side. She looked down at the picture and bit her lip.

"You and Raymond were tied up with the paramilitaries," Rea said. "What are they? UDA? UVF? Are you afraid that's going to come out now?"

"I was never a member," Graham said, bristling as if he'd been insulted. "I have contacts in those groups, yes, but I was never a member."

"Contacts," Rea echoed. She did not try to keep the scorn from her voice. "So that's all right, then. You just have contacts with these murdering bastards."

A little of Graham's calm slipped away. "That's right, they're murdering bastards. But who do you think was there negotiating with them when they called the ceasefires, eh? Who helped to guide them into the peace process? Judge all you want, but those people live and die in the same world we do, and they have as much at stake as the rest of us."

He reached for the photograph, but Rea grabbed it first. Graham watched her hand as she tucked the picture back into her hip pocket. She asked, "And what about Raymond? Was he one of them?"

"No," Graham said. "He was like me, he just knew a few people who were involved. He never joined, no matter how many times they asked him."

Rea shifted her gaze between her parents. "I thought you hardly had any contact with Raymond."

Ida spoke up. "He got back in touch when he came out of the merchant navy. Just for a year or two. That's how I met your father."

Rea shook her head. "God, you two are full of surprises. But none of this solves the problem of what to do with this book."

"There's no problem," Graham said in a tone he hadn't used on Rea since she was a teenager. "We're not going to the police, and that's that."

Rea took a step closer, raised her finger. She forced calm into her voice. "You can't stop me going to them."

"No police. And I'm destroying that book."

"You'll be destroying evidence," Rea said. "As bad as you think this looks for you, it'll look a hundred times worse if you destroy evidence."

Graham frowned at that thought. "That's a point. All right, the book can stay here until I figure out what to do with it—but no police. Now, I've got to get back to that meeting. I've no time for this carry-on."

"Please, Dad, you can't—"

He came close to her, put his hands on her shoulders, the first time he'd touched her in years.

"Listen to me, sweetheart. I've worked so hard all these years, ever since you were a wee girl. Think of everything I've sacrificed to get where I am, to get this chance. Think of everything your mother's done to support me. All those nights I spent away from the both of you for one meeting or another, all the weekends I was out working for the party instead of being with my wife and daughter. Do you really want me to throw everything away now?"

Rea shook her head. "But it's the right thing to do."

"Maybe so, but there's another way. There's always another way. Your uncle Raymond has gone to answer for what he did, and he's met whatever justice was waiting for him. But, yes, that poor girl's parents deserve better. As well as the rest in that book. And I'll figure out a way to make that happen. Please, trust me, I'll find a way to handle this right for everybody."

Rea closed her eyes and breathed out the last of her anger. "I wish I believed you."

Graham gave her a sad smile. "I'm telling you, I will find a way to make this right. A way so that no one has to suffer."

Rea studied his face, noticed new lines she hadn't seen before. "You promise?" she asked.

11

Lennon swallowed more painkillers with a mouthful of lager. Cheap stuff from the supermarket that came in a can with gaudy lettering. He used to buy good quality stuff, the bottled craft beers made by Whitewater in Kilkeel, or the Hilden brewery in Lisburn, but he could no longer afford the luxury. Not every day, anyway. This was some sort of made-up Czech brand that tasted of metal and sour fruit. The sort of thing the alcoholics bought along with their fortified wine and extra-strong cider.

He'd started going to a different shop every day, just so the staff wouldn't recognize him and note that his visits were becoming a habit.

Becoming? It had been a habit for more than six months now. And Susan had certainly noticed. She didn't say much, but she no longer wanted to sit with him on the couch in the evenings. Instead, she went to bed, leaving him to drink his cheap beer alone. She was less forgiving of the painkillers.

Earlier, when he had been alone for an hour, Lennon had gone to the table to find his meal cold on its plate. He reheated it in the microwave and ate it along with the first beer of the night.

Two hours ago, now.

He took another swig of lager and focused on the television. He realized the programme he'd been watching—a repeat of a motoring show—had ended, and some eighties comedy film had started in its place.

The silence in the flat around him felt cold and heavy. How much longer could it go on? He had told Susan he loved her after she had asked him to move in. It had been a lie, and he knew she didn't believe it, but he had honestly thought he could grow into their relationship, given the time. Instead, resentment had flourished. Eventually, she would want to talk about their life together. He would avoid it as long as possible, but he wouldn't dodge it for ever. And they would sit at the table, and she would tell him how much she loved Ellen but that they couldn't go on living there.

Maybe not tomorrow, or next week, or next month—but before long the conversation would come. And Lennon had no clue what he would do then.

For six months after his release from hospital, Susan had continuously emailed him links to articles she'd found about post-traumatic stress disorder. He rarely read them. She badgered him to seek counselling, whether it be with a psychologist, a psychiatrist or a cognitive behavioral therapist. Anything at all, just so long as he talked to somebody about what had happened to him.

Lennon still dreamed about that cold morning, the airport car park, everything blanketed in dense freezing fog. As the memory played out, as his experience regenerated itself in his sleeping mind, he would reach for his weapon and find it missing, or caught in its holster, or his hand would lose its ability to grip.

As Sergeant Connolly took aim, dream-Lennon might find his pistol's trigger too stiff to pull, or the weapon too heavy to lift, or its rounds no more than cylinders of gunpowder, no bullets to stop his attacker.

The dreams always ended the same way. Lennon on his back, holes torn out of his body, his life leaking out onto the frost-jagged ground. Connolly entering his narrowing vision, the pistol ready to end everything.

Lennon always woke before he died, heart stuttering, paralysed by fear. The painkillers and the alcohol had dulled the edges of the dreams, but less so recently.

He turned his attention back to the television. Chevy Chase and some actress he didn't recognize, sitting by a country club tennis court drinking—

Lennon's heart leapt in his chest as he felt movement against his leg. He swatted at it, felt something hard through the denim of his jeans.

Christ, his phone. It had been so long since anyone had called him that the vibration had felt alien. His fingers dug into the pocket and pulled the phone out. He read the number on the display, didn't recognize it. The time said it had just gone eleven. He slid his thumb across the touchscreen to accept the call and brought the phone to his ear.

12

Rea had toured the house, opening doors, turning on lights. She had gone from corner to corner, haunting the doorways like a ghost, looking for signs of Raymond Drew's life. A photograph, a letter, anything at all personal. She and her mother had been over the place countless times and found nothing, but still she looked.

An hour had gone by, and the building remained as empty of life as it had been the first time she crossed the threshold. She went to the stairs and sat on the same step she had earlier that evening when she had decided to open the back bedroom. Tiredness crept into her legs and arms and dried her eyes. Her jaw creaked as she yawned.

Her father had said he'd find a way to make it right. He'd promised. And she did not believe him.

Rea loved her father dearly, but she knew Graham Carlisle was not a man who kept his word. He would put his ambitions first, as he had always done. The matter of his brother-in-law's crimes would be swept aside, buried.

Perhaps the easiest thing would be to allow him to destroy the book as he'd wanted. Then it would be done, and she and her parents could forget about it.

Except Rea would not forget about it. She had seen the girl's smiling face. She had read her family's names, seen their pleas for their daughter's safe return.

Rea brought her hands to her face, shut out the light. But the images behind her eyes remained. Gwen Headley's open, happy expression. The crude sketches of her. The small photograph of the young woman's parents on a couch, clutching at each other's hands.

She couldn't keep it to herself. She had to tell someone. Christ, someone had to stand up for poor dead Gwen Headley.

There was one person she knew. Or rather, used to know.

It had been perhaps five years since she'd spoken to him, and they had parted on bad terms. She wondered if she still had his number on her mobile. And if she did, would it still be his? She had left it on the kitchen counter.

Beyond the kitchen window the back garden was a dark, layered black. Little light from the street found its way past the house.

Rea reached for the phone and opened the contacts. Scrolling through, she found the number she wanted.

A movement in the black outside distracted her. A shape, darkness upon darkness. Had it been there before?

She blinked three times to clear the dry fatigue from her eyes. The shape remained. It watched her through the glass.

Watched?

How can a shadow watch anything?

"Stupid," Rea said aloud.

She looked back to the contacts list, and the phone number she had sought. Would he remember her?

One way to find out.

13

Lennon listened to shallow breathing for a moment before he said, "Hello?"

"Jack?"

A woman's voice.

"Who's this?" he asked.

"Is that Jack Lennon?"

"Who is this?" he asked again, his voice firmer.

"Rea," she said.

He searched his memory for the name, came up with one answer, but it couldn't be right. Not now. Not after all this time, out of nowhere.

"Rea Carlisle," she said, confirming what he couldn't quite believe.

Lennon stared at the television but saw nothing other than the woman he had left in a bar five years ago. She had tears in her eyes as she fought the anger. He had known she wouldn't make a scene there, wouldn't scream or throw a drink at his head. That was why he had chosen that place to end things with her. You're too young for me, he'd told her, and I'm too old for you. He'd made it all seem logical and fair and not the callous disposal of her that it really was.

I'm not like that any more, he thought. Then he remembered Susan, and the frayed threads of their relationship, and knew that, yes, he was still like that.

For want of a better question, he asked, "How are you?"

"I . . . I've been better."

He waited for her to elaborate, but all he heard was a hiss on the line. "I'm a little surprised to hear from you," he said when the silence had gone on longer than he could bear.

A hint of a nervous laugh in her voice, she said, "Well, Jesus, when I got up this morning, I didn't expect to wind up calling you. I'm sorry it's so late."

"I wasn't asleep," he said.

"Good."

Another quiet pause before Lennon asked, "Are you going to tell me why you called?"

"Oh," she said, as if she had forgotten the reason herself. "There was no one else I could call. Not with this."

"What's up?" he asked. "What can I do for you?"

"I can't tell you over the phone," she said. "Can you meet me?"

He hesitated, then said, "Sure."

"Can you get away from work tomorrow?"

"I'm on a break. Sort of. So, yes."

"The lounge in the Errigle. Around twelve?"

"Okay," he said. "Can you tell me what—"

She hung up before he could finish the sentence.

"Who was that?"

For the second time in a few minutes, Lennon almost jumped out of his skin.

Susan stood at the hallway that led to the bedrooms, her dressing gown wrapped tight around her, arms folded across her chest.

"No one," Lennon said.

"Chatty for no one," she said.

He had the lie ready in seconds. "It was an old friend from

the force. He retired a few years ago. He just wanted to catch up. I said I'd meet him tomorrow for lunch."

"Oh? Where?"

"In town."

She tilted her head to one side. "Where in town?"

"Just in town. We'll go to Nando's or somewhere."

Susan watched him as the seconds dragged by, daring him to tell the truth. He couldn't hold her gaze for long.

When he thought he couldn't take her staring for another moment, she said, "Lucy's sleeping in with me. She said Ellen's talking in her sleep again. To that man she used to talk about. When you've had quite enough beer, you can sleep in Lucy's bed."

The tall thin man. She didn't need to say it. Lucy had been disturbed from her sleep many times by Ellen's voice. Ellen had described the man to Lucy, told her how he had died alongside her mother. The tales had frightened Lucy to the point of tears, so Lennon had to tell Ellen to keep her dreams to herself. But he knew exactly who Ellen spoke to in the night. He would never forget.

"All right," Lennon said. "I'll sleep in with Ellen."

Susan left without another word. He heard her door whisper closed.

Three empty beer cans stood aligned on the coffee table. Plus an almost empty one in his hand. He wasn't sure what Susan considered "quite enough," and in truth he didn't much care, but the painkillers had thrown a blanket of drowsiness across his brow. He downed the last swallow of lager, gathered up the cans, and took them to the recycling bin. When he'd toured the flat, switching off appliances and lights, he made his way to the girls' bedroom. He crept in and lay down on Lucy's empty bed, his feet hanging over the end.

Ellen's blonde curls spilled out over the top of her duvet. He saw her eyes, reflecting the night-light, looking back at him.

"Hiya," she said, her voice muffled by the bedding.

"Hiya," he said.

"Where's Lucy?"

"With her mum. She heard you talking."

Ellen said nothing.

"Was it him again?"

Quiet.

"Was it?"

"Mm-hm."

Lennon propped himself up on his elbow. "What did he want?"

"Just to talk."

"About what?"

"Stuff," she said, as if that explained everything.

"What sort of stuff?"

"Dunno."

"Don't you want to tell me?"

"No."

"All right. Go to sleep, love."

She burrowed down into the bedclothes, leaving only the crown of her head visible.

Lennon had tried to press her on these conversations before. He'd tried being friendly, or getting cross, or playing on her guilt. Still she had said nothing except that she had been talking to him. She would never have admitted even that, if not for Lucy telling tales of the tall thin man in the night.

He had convinced himself it was nothing more than a dream,

Ellen's mind making sense of the trauma that had damaged her and taken her mother. To imagine the alternative would break him.

Lennon rested his head on Lucy's pillow, filled with the scent of his daughter and her best friend, clean and free of the stains that blighted his soul. He did not fear dreams of the tall thin man. Far uglier monsters lurked in the darkest places of his sleep.

14

Rea waited at one of the old-fashioned circular glass-topped tables in the Errigle Inn's lounge bar, a nearly empty tumbler of sparkling water in front of her. The bar had a comforting gloominess, dark walls and flooring, the kind of intimate dimness that let you think your conversations remained private, no matter how close the next table was. A scattering of lunchtime drinkers occupied the seats around her, young office workers on their break, older men whose day's drinking started here.

The door swished open every few minutes, bringing with it a tide of cool air. She looked up each time, expecting to see the man who had parted ways with her five years before.

She checked her watch again. Twenty minutes late, now. How long would she give him? She should hardly have been surprised. He'd never been on time in all the months they were together.

The door opened again, and she looked up once more.

A middle-aged man, scruffy, hard-worn features. He walked with a limp.

She turned her attention back to her phone, and an old news article about Gwen Headley. She set about reading it for the tenth time. A shadow fell across her.

"Can I get you another water?" the man with the limp asked.

She glanced up at him. "No, thank you, I'm waiting for . . ."

She looked again. The sand-coloured hair, now shaggy and

laced with threads of grey. The same broad frame, somehow diminished, the lines on his face deeper than they should be.

"Jack?" she said.

"Do you need another?" he asked, indicating her glass.

She shook her head.

"All right, I'll just grab a pint," he said.

She watched him limp toward the bar. Except it wasn't really a limp. One side of his body seemed stiff, leaving his gait off kilter. He did his best to hide it, but it was plain as day.

It had been five years since she'd seen Lennon, but he looked like he'd aged twenty. What had happened to him in that time?

They had met while Rea was working on recruitment processes for the Police Service of Northern Ireland. She had interviewed a string of serving officers, from constables to chief inspectors, hitting them with standard multiple-choice questions, figuring out what separated the street cops from those that rose through the ranks.

Jack Lennon had been her last interview of the day. He had flattered her, charmed her, and even though she knew it was risking her job, she agreed to go for a drink with him that evening.

Soon, they were a couple. At least, Rea believed so. Lennon seemed less convinced. It was nothing he said or did, but in the six months they were together, Rea never lost the feeling that she was hanging on to the relationship by her fingernails. Three times she invited him to come to her parents' home for dinner. The first two times, he refused, saying he had work commitments. The third time he agreed, but she wished he hadn't.

After an hour of waiting, her mother had gone ahead and served dinner without him. Rea barely touched her food, excused herself, and went back to the flat she shared at the time. She got drunk on white wine, and whatever else she could find in the cupboards, and swore she would never darken his door again.

The following morning, he disturbed Rea's hangover with a phone call, telling her he'd been summoned to the scene of a serious assault the previous night. He couldn't get out of it, he said, apologizing once again.

She should have learned. It took another month for him to finally break things off with her. Oddly, in a place not unlike this bar. Over a quiet drink. No fuss. No scene made. Like grown-ups.

Lennon noticed her gaze on him as he returned with a pint of lager in his hand. His lips thinned at the effort of disguising his limp.

Rea felt a sadness in her breast, sharp like a scalpel in her flesh. Not that he deserved her sympathy. He sat down opposite.

"So, how've you been?" he asked.

"Okay," she said. "I lost my job a few months back. But I'm muddling through. What about you?"

"I'm all right," he said.

Jack Lennon was a good liar, Rea had learned that to her cost, but he couldn't sell this one.

"You don't look it," she said.

He gave a short laugh. "Thanks."

"Sorry, I didn't mean to be rude, but you don't look well. Have you been ill?"

He took a sip of beer and said, "I had a bit of trouble last Christmas."

"What sort of trouble?"

He hesitated, clearly debating with himself how much to say. "I managed to get myself shot. But I'm getting better."

"Jesus," she said. "While you were on duty?"

"Sort of," he said. "It's complicated. I'm on the mend now, which is all that matters."

In other words, leave it alone, she thought.

"Well, thanks for coming. I know it's a bit strange, calling out of the blue like this."

"No worries," he said. "It's not like I've much else to do these days. So, what did you want to talk to me about?"

How to say it? She chewed on a nail while she searched for the words.

"What's wrong?" he asked. "Are you in some sort of trouble?"

Rea placed her hands flat on the tabletop, closed her eyes, made her decision, and opened them again. "It'll be easier to show you than to tell you."

"Show me what?" Lennon asked.

She stood and said, "Come on. It's not far."

Rea knew someone had been in the house as soon as she stepped through the front door and into the hall.

Lennon had spoken little as they left the Errigle, crossed the Ormeau Road, and made their way through the side streets to Deramore Gardens. She watched him from the corner of her eye, looking for signs that the walk caused him problems. His limp grew more pronounced as they went, but his face showed no indication of pain. She considered asking if he was all right, but sensed that the question would offend him. Instead she kept her silence alongside his.

He entered the hall behind her, asked, "Shall I close this?"

Rea did not answer. Instead, she examined the row of black bin bags that still lay on the floor. The day before, she and her mother had tied each of them at the top using the yellow draw-strings. And now something wasn't right.

She looked at each one in turn, the yellow bow at the top, the black plastic creasing and bulging with the contents. Some of them had been opened and retied. She was certain of it. But how could she be so sure? It wasn't as if she had taken pictures of the bags so she could compare then and now. Really, it was nothing but a feeling. A notion. That was all, wasn't it?

"What's the matter?" Lennon asked.

Rea shook her head, felt her certainty dissolve. "Nothing," she said, and turned toward the staircase. "Come on. It's up here."

"What is?" he asked.

She stopped on the third step. "You'll see. Just come with me. Please."

He hesitated, nodded, and followed.

"Whose house is this?" he asked as they climbed.

"My uncle's," she said. "He died last week. Me and my parents have been clearing it out."

They reached the landing, and the door to the back bedroom.

"This was locked," Rea said. "I had to force it."

She indicated the crowbar, still lying on the landing floor where it had fallen a few days before. Lennon grunted as he stooped to pick it up, tested its weight in his hand.

Rea pressed the door with her fingertips, let it swing back, and reached in to flick on the light. Lennon returned the crowbar to where he'd found it.

The room remained as she had left it the night before. The map on the wall. The desk.

The empty space where the book had been.

Cold, cold, cold. All she felt was cold.

Lennon said something, maybe her name, but she didn't hear. "It's gone," she said.

A hand on her back. She stepped away from it, into the room, toward the desk. The bare top seemed so big, like a sea of scarred wood.

"I left it here," she said. "But it's gone."

Lennon spoke again, questioning, dull noises in the air between them.

Rea reached for the drawer, opened it. Empty as the hollow place inside her chest.

"Bastard," she whispered. "The bastard took it."

She went to the window and pulled hard on the cord to open the blind. Daylight broke through the dust that coated the glass. She rubbed a patch clear with her sleeve and peered through, looking for a burnt scar where a fire had been lit, and saw nothing but the poorly tended lawn.

"Fucking bastard," she said, anger choking in her throat, sending heat to her eyes. She grabbed for her pocket, dragged her mobile phone from it and fumbled at the touchscreen, looking for his number. The dial tone burred in her ear as Lennon waited across the room, his face blank.

"This is Graham Carlisle's voicemail. Please leave your name, number, along with a brief message, and I'll get back to you as soon as I can."

"You fucking bastard," Rea said, unable to hold the furious tears back any longer. "I can't believe you did that. After you promised me. You piece of shit."

She thumbed the end-call button and threw the phone to the floor. It bounced across the room, clattered off the skirting board. Lennon let out a grumph of discomfort as he bent to pick it up.

"Maybe you'd better tell me what's going on," he said.

Rea covered her eyes with her shaking hands and said, "Give me a minute."

She turned away, sniffed hard, wiped at her wet cheeks, breathing as deeply and steadily as she could manage with the rage sparking and crackling inside her. When it finally settled to a dim smoulder, she turned back to Lennon.

"So what is it you want me to see?" he asked.

"Maybe you should sit down," Rea said.

Lennon gave her back her phone then put his hands in his pockets. "No, I'm all right."

Rea took another quivery breath. Swallowed. "When I first opened this room, there was a book in the drawer of that desk. Like a big photo album, or a scrapbook."

Lennon went to the desk, reached down and opened the drawer, looked inside, and slid it closed again.

"It had newspaper cuttings, handwritten notes, and . . . other things inside."

Lennon stared back at her. He already thinks I'm crazy, Rea thought. Just say it.

"It was a book about all the people my uncle had killed."

Lennon's expression did not change. He lowered himself into the chair and said, "Go on."

15

They talked through the afternoon.

Several times, Lennon thought of standing, making his excuses, and leaving Rea to her delusions. But he stayed and listened to it all without comment.

Lennon had dealt with enough crazy people during his years on the force. He had heard hundreds of implausible stories driven by paranoia, schizophrenia, alcohol, drugs, or any number of sicknesses. He had listened to spouses accusing each other of murder plots, to grandmothers convinced their grandchildren were robbing them, to drunkards who claimed to have witnessed the most spectacular of crimes.

But the way Rea talked was different. She started at the start and ended at the end. She didn't go in circles or contradict herself. She spoke with a calm, clear voice, leaning against the wall, her arms folded, not acting out the drama of it all with waves and gesticulations.

Not that he believed her story. But he didn't think she'd lost her mind.

When she'd finished, Lennon watched her for a moment, then said, "What was the first victim's name again?"

"Gwen Headley," Rea said, and she spelt the surname.

Lennon took his phone from his pocket, opened the web browser, and entered the girl's name. He scanned the list of results:

old news headlines about the young woman's disappearance and presumed murder.

"She was real," Rea said as Lennon raised his eyes to meet hers. "She really disappeared. They don't know what happened to her. But I do."

Raymond Drew had buried Gwen Headley in the foundation trench of the building site he'd been working on, Rea explained. Her remains lay beneath the concrete footing of an office building.

"There's no way to prove that," Lennon said. "Without the book, it's just your word."

"You don't believe me," she said.

"It doesn't matter if I believe you or not," Lennon said. He considered going easy on her, but there was no point in sugar-coating the truth. "No one else will. All you can do is cause more distress to this girl's family."

Rea covered her face with her hands as she slid down the wall and hunkered near the floor. Her shoulders trembled.

Lennon crossed the room to her. He wondered if he should comfort her in some way, perhaps put an arm around her. Something told him no, don't touch her. He crouched down, clenching his jaw at the pain it caused, but kept his hands to himself.

He opened his mouth to speak, but she cut him off.

"Don't call me a liar," she said.

"I'm not calling you any—"

"The book was here. I saw it. I touched it."

Lennon took a breath before he said it. "What book? Rea, there is no book."

He saw the hate on her face and knew he deserved it.

"Get out," she said. "Go. Please."

He put a hand on her shoulder. "I want to make sure you're all right."

"Fuck off." She spat the words at him, her eyes threatening tears. "Look, just go and leave me alone."

Lennon hoisted himself to his feet. "All right," he said. "But I'll be in touch tomorrow. Just to see how you're doing."

She nodded and brought her hands to her face once more. "Thank you, but I'll be fine."

"Okay," he said. He searched for some reassurance he could give her, but he knew all she wanted was for him to be gone. His footsteps reverberated in the stairway as he descended.

"Wait," she called.

Lennon turned and looked up to her.

"I have a photograph," she said, taking something from her hip pocket.

He climbed the stairs, halting a few steps below her. She handed him a Polaroid print. Two rows of three men, the back row in paramilitary garb. To the right of the front row, a young Graham Carlisle.

Lennon said nothing.

"You recognize my father," Rea said. "That's my uncle, Raymond Drew, on the left. There's one thing you can do to help me."

"What's that?" Lennon asked.

"Find out if my father was ever suspected of anything . . . bad."

"I'll ask around," Lennon said. "Can I hold onto this?"

Rea nodded. "I'm sorry for getting angry. I appreciate you coming. I really do."

"I know," he said, tucking the photograph into his jacket pocket, and left her at the top of the stairs.

He had to slam the front door three times to get it to close behind him, cursing as he did so. Across the street, a fussy-looking man of late middle age stopped washing the windows on his house and watched him. An estate agent's sign said it was newly let.

Lennon stared back, an ugly flare of anger in his chest, daring the man to say something. The man dropped his gaze and went back to his cleaning.

As Lennon walked back toward the Ormeau Road, he took the phone from his pocket and dialled the direct line to Ladas Drive station. When the duty officer answered, Lennon said, "CI Uprichard."

"I'll see if he's available," the officer said. Lennon recognized the voice as belonging to Sergeant Bill Gracey. "Who's calling, please?"

"DI Jack Lennon." He listened to the duty officer's breathing for a few seconds, then said, "They haven't sacked me yet, Bill. Put me through."

A pause, then, "All right. Hold, please."

Lennon listened to something that passed for music until he heard the familiar voice.

"Jack? It's been a while. How are you?"

"I'm fucked, Alan, how's you?"

"Language, Jack, please. The wife has me on a diet again, but other than that, I'm all right. To what do I owe the pleasure?"

"I need a favour," Lennon said.

Uprichard sighed. "Why does that give me a bad feeling?"

Chief Inspector Alan Uprichard had been the only one to stick by Lennon after his suspension. The closest thing in the world he had to a real friend, but even that was stretching the point. Uprichard was a stout chap, pushing sixty, a devout

Christian whose wife fretted constantly over his health. Lennon couldn't imagine a man further removed from him in character, yet somehow their friendship endured, though perhaps begrudgingly on Uprichard's part.

"You've always got a bad feeling," Lennon said.

"True," Uprichard said. "Go on, then. What is it?"

Lennon told him. When Uprichard was done listening, he asked, "Is this going to get me into trouble, Jack?"

"I hope not," Lennon said.

"And you certainly don't need more bother hanging over you."

"No, I don't," Lennon said. "Will you do it for me?"

"All right," Uprichard said, "but you owe me."

"I already owe you plenty," Lennon said. "One more debt won't make any odds."

"True. I'll get back to you. Take care of yourself."

"You too."

As Lennon hung up, he noticed the time on the phone's display. "Shit," he said to himself.

"Forty-five minutes," Susan said.

"I know, I'm sorry."

Lennon couldn't look at her across the table. The girls ate in silence. The food on his and Susan's plates had barely been touched.

"Have you any idea how embarrassed I am that the school office had to call me?"

"It won't happen again," Lennon said. "I promise."

"Anything could've happened to them. Anyone could've taken them."

Lennon shook his head. "They know not to go with strangers."

"You put my daughter at risk." Her voice became a thin hiss, anger and hate driving her tongue. "And your own. How could you live with yourself if anything happened to Ellen? How could I live with myself for trusting you with Lucy?"

He raised his eyes to see the fury in her face. He swallowed his own anger at her words, but couldn't keep the tremor from his voice. "I'd never do anything to hurt our girls. You know that."

Lennon knew he should have told her the truth the night before. Had he done so, he could have explained that someone needed his help. That he would never have been so late, that he wouldn't have forgotten the time, if not for an old friend being in trouble. But he had lied, he couldn't take it back, and he hated himself for it.

Susan sighed. A tear made a crystalline track on her cheek. "But you'd let them stand on the side of a road, all alone, for forty-five minutes."

Lennon got up and left the table.

He slept on the couch until the phone call woke him in the early hours.

16

It took hours for Rea Carlisle to die.

Lennon had left. She had gone back to the room, sat down at the desk and wept until the tears were exhausted. Then, suddenly cold, suddenly aware that the house had darkened, she had walked to the landing. She had felt safe in the light. Now the light had burned away.

The blow felt like a sun exploding in her head, then the world turned beneath her feet. She supposed she must have fallen. A memory, vague and greying, of the stairs descending away from her vision, something cool and hard against her cheek.

Then another blow, and she couldn't see anything at all.

Rea wanted to cry out, to speak, to say something, but her tongue would not obey. It felt blunt and thick inside her mouth. Her voice rose in her chest, squeezed through her throat, out into the air.

An impact on the back of her neck silenced her. Then another, and another, more across her shoulders and back, so many she couldn't tell one from a doll she had when she was a little girl with blue eyes that closed when you laid it down and school corridors bright lights hard stares and falling cut knees and loving him madly like bitter tastes of God and Jesus and doggie can we have the doggie I never get anything I want and sand clinging stinging to my skin and . . .

Pain forced its way through the thickening clouds in her mind. The sound—no, the feeling—of things cracking and splintering inside her and bubbling breath and metal taste and sand and water and mummy tickles stop mummy stop daddy not a baby got to go got to go got to go . . .

And the pain once more, but the shower of blows to her back had stopped and she heard hard breathing, not hers, hers bubbly like chocolate and—no, come back—and someone pulling and stretching at her pockets then cursing then stepping over her and feet clumping down the stairs like a giant and the beanstalk and jack and david and goliath and a sling brought the giant down like the bible says yes jesus loves me this I know cause the bible tells me so deep and wide deep and wide there's a river running deep and wide . . .

Rea's consciousness receded and swelled like a tide on a barren shore, but her mind finally left her long before her lungs filled with blood, long before she drowned at the top of the stairs in a house that once belonged to Raymond Drew.

17

It was light outside when Lennon woke. He'd been dreaming of a madman he'd last seen in a burning house outside Drogheda, the flames eating them both.

Lennon breathed hard as his senses fell into place. He was already reaching into his pocket for his phone when it rang again. The display said the number had been withheld.

"Hello?" he said, his voice hoarse with sleep.

"Jack? It's Alan."

"What's wrong? It's not even six-thirty yet."

"That woman you told me about yesterday," Uprichard said. "The one in Deramore Gardens."

"Yeah? What about her?"

"She was Graham Carlisle's daughter?"

"Yes. Rea Carlisle."

Lennon listened to Uprichard's breathing. "Alan, what's wrong?"

"She's dead, Jack. She was beaten to death with a crowbar."

Lennon shook his head. "What are you talking about?"

"I turned the radio on when I got up this morning, and there was a report about a woman found dead in Deramore Gardens. I remembered what you'd said, so I rang the station to see what the story was. Her mother got worried because she hadn't been in touch, so she went to this house and found her there. The medical officer reckons she was killed late yesterday afternoon."

"No," Lennon said. "Couldn't be. I was with her late afternoon. I rang you when I left the house. There's been a mistake."

"No mistake, Jack. She's been identified. And a man was seen leaving the house, agitated, slamming the door. I read the description. It was you, Jack. You were seen leaving the house around the time of the killing."

Lennon thought of the man who'd been cleaning his windows across the road, who'd watched him slam the door and walk away. He stayed quiet for a moment as his sleep-addled brain tried to make sense of what he'd been told.

"She's dead? Rea's dead? You're sure?"

Exasperation hardened Uprichard's voice. "Yes, I'm sure, there's no doubt. Jack, are you listening to what I'm telling you?"

"Rea's dead," Lennon said. The idea lay there, a dull and hard fact. He didn't know how to feel. Yesterday had been the first time he'd seen her in five years. How did he feel?

"Yes, Jack, but that's not what I'm driving at."

Angry. He felt angry.

"Then what are you driving at?" Lennon asked.

"You were seen at her house around the time she was killed," Uprichard said. "It's only a matter of time before someone twigs it was you. It'll look better for you if you come in and explain yourself. Don't wait for them to figure it out and send a car for you. Are you listening to me, Jack?"

"Yes," Lennon said, but he really wasn't.

He'd left her there, tearful because she knew he didn't believe her. And now she was dead.

"Jack, get yourself down to Ladas Drive first thing. Tell them you're going to cooperate."

"Cooperate with what?"

"With the investigation." Uprichard's voice rose to a shout. "You get down there and tell them everything you know. If you don't, I'll put them on to you myself. Do you understand?"

"I understand," Lennon said.

He hung up.

18

Lennon spent most of the day in an interview room. Bill Gracey had been on the desk when he walked into Ladas Drive station, staring from behind the glass.

"Who's on the Rea Carlisle case?" Lennon asked.

"Why?" Gracey's frown made him look like the officious prick he was.

"Because I need to talk to them."

Gracey shook his head. "The ACC hasn't officially assigned the team yet, but it'll be Flanagan's crew."

"She's based in D District, isn't she?"

"True," Gracey said, "but there isn't an MIT going spare in B District right now."

"What about Thompson?"

Gracey leaned closer to the glass. "Between you and me, they're nudging Thompson toward retirement after the balls he's made of his last few cases. They'll not give him anything serious now."

About time, Lennon almost said. He'd been on Detective Chief Inspector Thompson's Major Investigation Team up until his own suspension more than a year ago, and had hated every minute under that idiot's command.

DCI Serena Flanagan was a different matter.

She was young for her rank—only a year or two older than Lennon—and ambitious. And hard as nails, Lennon had heard.

Republican paramilitaries had tried to kill her twice, the first time with a car bomb that had failed to explode, the second up close and personal with a Springfield 1911. The pistol had jammed after the first shot missed, leaving the gunman wrestling with a useless piece of metal while DCI Flanagan calmly drew her personal protection weapon and took aim. The would-be killer had been the pillion passenger on a motorcycle. The driver took off, spilling his friend off the back of the bike, already dead from holes in his heart and lung.

The bike had slammed into the rear of a bus a quarter of a mile away. As far as Lennon knew, the rider remained in a vegetative state.

It was common practice for an MIT to be assigned a case outside of its district and for the crew to be moved to the station nearest the crime they were to investigate.

"Is Flanagan here?" Lennon asked.

"I assume she's at the scene," Gracey said, "but DS Calvin's setting up an office for her. What's this about?"

"None of your business. Just let me talk to Calvin."

Gracey's frown deepened. "No need to be rude, Jack."

Lennon watched through the glass as Gracey went to his desk, lifted the phone, and spoke to somebody. When he hung up, he did not return to the partition. "He'll be a minute," he called, and made a show of busying himself with paperwork.

Lennon waited, listening to the familiar thrum of the station, the shrill telephones, the voices and footsteps from behind closed doors.

Five minutes passed before the doors opened and a young detective stepped through.

"DI Lennon?" he asked, extending his hand.

"DS Calvin," Lennon said, returning the gesture.

He guessed Calvin to be in his early thirties. Stocky with a face like a glowing light bulb, prematurely thinning hair, a suit that looked like it had come from a supermarket or a discount store.

"What can I do for you?" Calvin asked.

Lennon talked and Calvin listened.

It felt strange on this side of the table, in the interview room with its bare painted walls, the expanse of wood between the two men, the audio recorder sitting idle at one end.

Calvin scribbled in his notebook. "So how did you know about the killing?"

"A colleague phoned me this morning," Lennon said.

"Which colleague?"

"You don't need to know," Lennon said.

Calvin looked up from his notebook. "But I will do. Eventually." He closed the book, tucked his pen into his breast pocket, and stood. "I need to make a phone call. Wait here."

Lennon asked, "Are you calling Flanagan?"

Calvin paused halfway to the door. "I'm calling DCI Flanagan, yes."

"Tell her I want to talk to her."

"She's busy," Calvin said, turning back to the door. "But I'll pass it on. Don't worry, DCI Flanagan will deal with you in her own time. And if you talk to her like you talk to me, she'll cut your balls off."

"So, I should be scared of her?"

"Very," Calvin said. "She fucking terrifies me."

He opened the door.

"Grab me a coffee when you're out," Lennon said.

Calvin looked back over his shoulder, his eyebrows raised.

"Please," Lennon said.

Calvin left without replying.

19

Detective Chief Inspector Serena Flanagan sat very still in the chair by Dr. Prunty's desk, barely breathing. His face was so expressionless it looked as if it were cut from pale pink chalk. He reminded Flanagan of her late grandfather, who always smelled of cloves. They had the same feathery white hair that revealed too much of the scalp beneath. The same awkward length to the limbs, countered by an unlikely grace in their movements.

Ten days since she'd gone to her GP, her hands trembling even as she told herself it was nothing, nothing at all, stop worrying.

The GP—a girl so young Flanagan wondered how she could know anything—had examined her, pushed, squeezed, pulled, while Flanagan fought to suppress a giggle. When Flanagan went to her car, locked herself in, an appointment with the clinic made, she wept until she couldn't see.

And now Dr. Prunty, who was so terribly nice, and clean, and had such a kind voice matched with cold eyes and hands.

But oh fucking God, the children are so small.

Stop it.

She told herself to stop it, grow up. She had held her nerve with guns pointed at her. By Christ, she would hold her nerve through this.

Flanagan had arrived at the Cancer Center early that morning, thirty minutes before her appointment. Built as an annexe to Belfast City Hospital only a few years ago, the center's lobby sparkled like no medical facility she'd visited before. She had to stop herself from checking for her passport as she entered, as if she was running to catch a flight.

At ten minutes past ten, Flanagan found out exactly how cold Dr. Prunty's hands were. This time, she had no urge to giggle as he examined her. She stared at the ceiling, listening to his breath whistling in his nose. He moved from her breasts to her armpits, seeking abnormalities in the lymph nodes. She listened harder, waiting for a telltale pause in his breathing. None came.

Then the mammogram. The nurse said it might be a little uncomfortable, but Christ, as the perspex plate squashed her flat, she had to bite down on her lip to stifle a cry. Then an ultrasound scan, like she'd had when she'd borne her children, except the gel was slathered on her chest instead of her belly.

Suddenly, from nowhere, she had remembered the breaking of her heart when she'd failed to breastfeed her second baby. Two weeks of tears, anger, frustration at the thrashing infant squealing with hunger because she couldn't give him what he needed. At four in the morning, defeat crushing both of them, her husband Alistair had driven to the nearest twenty-four-hour supermarket and bought baby formula. Flanagan and her husband both sobbed with regret as tiny Eli drew deep on the bottle, calm for the first time in days.

This morning, finally, after all the feeling, squashing, prodding, they took a biopsy. A local anaesthetic, Dr. Prunty said, a needle, a little pressure, then it would be done.

They sent her away for two hours while the sample was analysed. She wandered along the Lisburn Road, southward past the bars and cafes, past the student digs, toward the art galleries and closer to the exclusive clusters of houses at Balmoral.

Flanagan stopped at the window of a lingerie shop. The mannequins draped in sheer lacy things, staring back at her. She studied the lines of their bodies, perfectly plastic, not a lump or abnormality between them. Her hand went to her right breast, the feeling coming back as the local anaesthetic wore off. She remembered Alistair's lips there, warm, gentle, like he'd found the sweetest of all manna. Flanagan wondered if he would ever want to taste her there again.

She had not told him. She didn't know how. Dozens of opportunities to share her terror with him had been allowed to slip by. The first few times she lied to herself that she was sparing him something, but she realized the keeping of such a secret was entirely selfish. She dreaded that conversation, inevitable as it was, and avoidance was the easier course.

When Flanagan returned to the Cancer Center, stinging and itching beneath the cotton wool and sticking plaster they'd covered the puncture with, she waited in a room with a dozen other women. Some had their partners with them, worried, fidgety men, or mothers, or sisters, or best friends. Flanagan sat alone, suddenly ashamed to have no one.

A nurse called her name, led her to Dr. Prunty's room. At the door, the nurse asked, "Did you come on your own, love?"

Flanagan nodded, ignored the pity on the nurse's face.

She noticed the box of tissues on Dr. Prunty's desk, one bursting up and out, waiting to be plucked like a flower.

I won't cry, Flanagan thought. A command to the frightened little girl that still lived inside her despite all the rotten, ugly things she'd seen.

The nurse sat on the seat beside her, took her hand. Flanagan had the urge to pull away, she didn't need mollycoddling, but she remained still, not even a tremor.

"Well," Dr. Prunty said. "The result came back as C5."

The nurse's fingers tightened around Flanagan's.

"C5? What does that mean?"

Dr. Prunty did not blink. "The lump is malignant. It's cancer."

"You're sure?" she asked.

"Absolutely sure," he said.

Flanagan stopped listening.

The doctor spoke about early diagnosis, stages, grades, high survival rates, surgery, appointments, radiotherapy, chemotherapy, options, possibilities, scenarios. The chain of surgeons, radiographers, consultants, with Flanagan to be passed between them like a parcel in a children's game. She heard little of it.

When he finished talking, Flanagan pulled her hand away from the nurse's and stood up. Her skin tingled from her scalp to the soles of her feet.

Dr. Prunty scribbled on a notepad as he spoke. "I'll call with the surgeon's appointment before end of business on Monday. Don't worry, the lump will be removed within a fortnight."

"Don't worry?" Flanagan said.

He looked up. "The NHS still runs like clockwork when it really matters."

"Don't worry?" she said again.

He looked to the nurse. "Colette here will give you some literature you might find helpful. I'll be in touch on Monday."

Dr. Prunty gave her a joyless smile. The nurse opened the door, guided her by the elbow, out and into the corridor, pulled the door closed behind them.

Placing a hand on Flanagan's shoulder, the nurse said, "We have on-site counsellors, if you'd like a quick chat."

"No," Flanagan said, walking away.

The nurse followed. "Well, I can give you some leaflets, phone numbers, and—"

Flanagan quickened her pace. "No, please, leave me alone."

"Mrs. Flanagan," the nurse called.

She kept walking, her head down, through the corridors, through the lobby, the exit, across the road through the queue of cars, her step turning to a jog, her chest heaving as she climbed the stairs to the car park's top level, into the open air, Belfast's sky grey above her. She ran to her Volkswagen Golf, thumbing the button on her key, opened the door, and got in behind the wheel.

Quiet like an empty church.

Wild tremors in her hands. She brought them to her mouth. The children. Oh Jesus, the children. How would she tell them?

It's not a death sentence. She had read that a thousand times as she'd scoured websites over the last week. It can be treated. I can survive this. I *will* survive it.

Calm, she thought. Be calm.

Flanagan closed her eyes, lowered her hands to her lap, and breathed deep. The rumble and hiss of city traffic seeped into the car. She opened her eyes and reached down into the footwell where she'd dropped her key. It slipped into the ignition. The car park ticket was in her pocket.

She'd forgotten to pay it.

"Fuck," she said. "Fuck. Shit."

Anger erupted, blinding hot, a torrent. She screamed every foul word she knew, slammed the steering wheel with her fists, the car horn blaring with each impact, cursed every kind of god, slapped her palms against the windscreen.

And then the rage was gone, leaving a cold and hollow mourning inside her.

Once Flanagan had gathered herself, gone back to the pay station, then returned to her car, she drove to Deramore Gardens. To the house where the woman's body still lay.

She had work to do.

20

Ida Carlisle sat alone and silent in the good room, the room with the pale wool carpet, silk upholstered suite and no television. If she'd ever had any grandchildren, they wouldn't have been allowed in this room. This room was for important visitors only.

Graham bought the house not long after Rea was born. A nice place in a cul-de-sac off Balmoral Avenue, in the BT9 area, where the hoity-toits lived, as Ida's mother would have said. A 1930s detached villa with a detached garage and a driveway, five bedrooms if you counted the one Graham used for his office, two receptions plus a dining room. Ida had felt a delicious thrill when they viewed it for the first time more than thirty years ago, knowing they could afford such a home. Such luxury, such a beautiful place to raise their daughter.

And all for nothing.

Ida held her hands together in her lap, her coat still buttoned over her nightdress since she'd come home an hour and a half ago. The phone had rung almost constantly. She'd switched her mobile off, but the landline kept trilling like a demented bird. The newspapers. The radio stations. The television reporters. They all had the number, ready to get a comment about whatever stories they thought Graham Carlisle would have an opinion on. Now they were scratching at the doors like hungry dogs, looking for scraps of grief to devour.

Ghouls, all of them.

Worry had got the better of Ida at eleven the night before. She had called Rea's mobile half a dozen times, left three messages, and no reply. One of the girls Rea shared a house with answered the landline there, told her sleepily that Rea wasn't in her room, that no one had seen her all evening. Graham had dismissed Ida's concerns, said Rea was probably out on the town somewhere, but their daughter had given up that kind of carry-on years ago.

So, at one-thirty in the morning, when Graham was asleep, Ida had gone downstairs, put shoes on her feet and her coat on over her nightdress, and then went out to her car.

Raymond's semi-detached house stood as quiet as it was dark. When Ida saw Rea's little Nissan wasn't parked outside, she almost drove back home. But instead, she pulled in, shut her engine off and got out of the car.

Thinking about it now, she remembered the soft sound of distant traffic as she approached the front door. The whisper of it spilling over the rooftops to this peaceful little road. And she thought how lovely a place this would be for Rea to live, if she could get over what was in that awful book.

The key opened the lock without resistance, just the smooth rotation of the tumblers, but Ida had to put her shoulder against the door to push it open. All was grey and black. She kept her fingertips on the wall as she made her way down the hallway, her leg brushing against the bin bags and boxes that still lay there, until they found the light switch.

Ida blinked against the glare of the bare bulb overhead.

"Rea?" she called.

Realizing her voice rang through the street, she went back to the door and pushed it closed. She turned and looked up the stairs.

Rea stared back down, her head resting on the top step, trickles of red falling away.

It felt to Ida that her mind had split in two at that moment. One half wondering why Rea was just lying there, why didn't she get up out of that paint she'd spilled? The other knowing beyond all certainty that her daughter was dead. She had stood there, trapped between her two selves, unable to move or speak for a minute or a lifetime, she couldn't be sure.

The following hours bled into one hellish smear. Ida could only recall them as a series of still images, tableaux of the end of the world. She couldn't remember whom she'd called first—Graham or an ambulance—but the paramedic arrived before anyone else. A man wearing green and yellow high visibility overalls. Ida saw the SUV with its fluorescent decals as she opened the door to him. The paramedic saw Rea over her shoulder, said almost nothing, and climbed up to her.

Ida watched him crouched on the steps, feeling, listening, shining a tiny torch into Rea's eyes. Then he stayed quiet and still for a while before taking a phone from his pocket and calling someone.

Graham arrived at the same time as the ambulance.

The crew entered first. The paramedic looked down at them and shook his head.

It was then that Ida fell.

The rest was a stream of flashing lights and questions, policewomen with notepads, offers of water, cups of tea, assurances, whispers, a hundred secrets being kept from her by the seemingly thousands of people who came and went in those hours.

Graham had driven Ida home.

He stopped outside an off-licence, got out of the car, and went inside. Graham had given up alcohol more than thirty years ago. Not a drop, not even a glass of sherry at Christmas.

While she sat there waiting, Ida realized two things. First, that Graham had barely spoken to her in all the hours since his arrival at Raymond's house. Second, that she had not gone to Rea, had not touched her, had not held her. She hadn't even put a foot on the stairs.

"What kind of mother am I?" she asked the empty car.

It came at her then, all of it, as one great wall of fear and grief and regret and pain, every piece falling on her at once. She howled until her throat burned.

Then Ida felt the car rock on its suspension as Graham climbed in, felt a bottle drop at her feet, and heard the engine cough into life. She had recovered herself by the time the car was moving through the traffic. Searching her pockets, she found a crumpled tissue and dabbed the tears from her cheeks.

She and Graham didn't speak as he parked in their driveway, as they climbed out of the car, as he unlocked their door, as they entered their home. Already the phone was ringing.

Graham went to the kitchen, the bottle of whiskey in his hand. Ida went to the good room, the tissue in hers.

And here she sat, quiet and still, a rage burning in her like a bright electric filament, an anger like she'd never felt before.

21

Flanagan walked toward her temporary office, a bundle of files under one arm, her jacket under the other. They'd stuck her away in the darkest corner of the station, her only view the gravel-covered roof of the adjoining block and a string of utility buildings. God-awful sixties architecture, all straight lines and concrete.

A suited man stood waiting at her door, leaning on the frame, his arms folded. His head tilted as he watched her approach, like a predator unsure whether to eat or play with its victim. She stopped several feet short of him.

"DCI Flanagan, I presume," he said.

"Yes," she said, not taking his extended hand. It dropped back to his side.

"DCI Dan Hewitt," he said. "C3."

Her mind stumbled in confusion. *But Dr. Prunty told me it was C5*, she almost said, *malignant*. Then she understood. He was C3, Intelligence Branch. Confusion gave way to suspicion.

Flanagan swallowed and took a breath, hoping she hadn't revealed too much of herself.

"What can I do for you?" she asked.

"Jack Lennon's downstairs in an interview room, waiting for you," he said.

"That's right. I'm just dropping off some things, then I'm heading down there."

She had been standing at the top of the stairs in Deramore Gardens, leaning over Rea Carlisle's devastated skull, when a constable had called from below, "Ma'am, DS Calvin's been trying to reach you."

"My phone's off," she had replied. "I'll call him back."

"He says it's urgent, ma'am."

So she had left the body and returned to the station.

"Maybe we could have a quick chat before you do," Hewitt said.

"What about, exactly?"

Hewitt shrugged. "Jack and me go back a long way. Personally and professionally. I can give you some background that might be useful. If you want."

She looked him up and down. He wore a charcoal-coloured suit, well tailored, better than most of his colleagues dressed in. And French cuffs, tasteful links binding them.

Flanagan made a dozen judgements before she opened her office door and said, "After you, Inspector."

As she followed him inside, he said, "Call me Dan."

He offered his hand once more. She dumped the files and jacket on her desk, shook his hand before gesturing toward the seat. His fingers were smooth and cool, like silken worms. Her skin itched where they had touched and she had to force herself not to reach for the bottle of hand sanitizer in the drawer.

Flanagan went to her own chair and said, "So what do you want to tell me?"

"Jack was mixed up with the woman who died last night," Hewitt said, crossing his legs. The crease of his trouser ran sharply along his thigh, over his knee, down to the hem. A watch that looked like an Oris from her side of the desk.

She wondered if Hewitt could really afford such details, or if he liked to live better than a DCI's income should allow. Even if he was C3, the force within a force.

Stop it, she thought. You're not investigating him.

"He told my colleague he saw her yesterday afternoon," Flanagan said.

"Is he a suspect?"

"Maybe. Maybe not. I'm not ruling anything out. You said he's a friend of yours."

"Yes. Well, he used to be, anyway."

"Not any more? What happened?"

"This is off the record, yes?"

"Of course," Flanagan said. "What ended your friendship with him?"

"Nothing in particular," Hewitt said. "We just drifted apart. Especially these last few years. We still speak the odd time, but he's not the same Jack I went to Garnerville with."

"Tell me about him."

"He used to be a good guy. You know, even when this was the Royal Ulster Constabulary, we were like any other police force. We had good and bad, and Jack was more good than bad. He got a commendation for bravery one time. He and his patrol were ambushed by republicans in the city center. He took a bullet to the shoulder and still saved the life of one of his colleagues. But he wasn't the same after that. I mean, he always had an eye for the girls, he chased every bit of skirt he saw—pardon the expression—but he got a bit more desperate as he got older. He had to work harder at it, and I think it made him bitter."

"Toward women?" Flanagan asked.

"The world in general, but women in particular. The way he

used to talk, sometimes. The way he saw women. I found it . . . well . . . distasteful. But he seemed to settle down for a while, with that Marie McKenna, the politician's niece. Then she got pregnant, and he cleared out. I thought that was rotten, and I told him so. He went downhill after that. Got nastier, that bitter streak coming out in him. That's when I started hearing about the backhanders."

"Bribes?"

"Small things, at first. Favours, more than anything. He got pally with some dodgy boys running prostitutes. They'd get wind of any raids that were coming, he'd get freebies from the girls. So my sources said, anyway."

"What kind of sources?"

Hewitt smiled. "The kind of sources that aren't discussed outside Intelligence Branch."

"Fair enough," Flanagan said. "Did money ever change hands?"

"Occasionally," Hewitt said. "But it was more like payment in kind, if you know what I mean?"

"What about drug use?" she asked.

Hewitt shifted in his seat.

Flanagan waited.

Hewitt shrugged and said, "It's only a whisper."

"Go on."

A high whine as he exhaled through his nose, a crease in his brow. "It's just something I heard, a friend of a friend of an informer."

Impatience made Flanagan tap her pen on the desktop. Hewitt looked at it, then back at her.

"He's never bothered with narcotics as far as I know, but since the incident last year, he's been taking prescription painkillers.

But without the prescription. It's hardly surprising. We both know cops who've suffered post-traumatic stress. We both know what it does to them."

"Where does he get the painkillers from?"

"I don't know. Presumably one of the pimps he deals with. Like I said, it's second-hand information."

Flanagan knew it was the first outright lie Hewitt had told since he entered her office. He tried to cover his deception by a smooth manner he probably thought of as charm, but she saw through it like looking through dirty glass. Everything else he'd told her had been the truth, or at least Hewitt's version of it. He'd skewed it all, made sure only to tell her what he wanted her to know. His sole fabrication had been that he didn't know Lennon's source for the painkillers. But Flanagan had learned long ago never to expect a straight answer from an Intelligence Branch officer when it came to their sources. Or any other topic, for that matter.

"I've one more question for you," she said. "And I want you to think carefully before you answer it."

"Fire away," Hewitt said.

Flanagan locked her eyes on his. "Do you believe DI Jack Lennon had it in him to kill Rea Carlisle?"

Hewitt held her gaze. Swallowed. Wetted his lips.

"Yes I do," he said.

Flanagan sat back in her chair, watching him. His eyes flicked down to her chest and back again. Then down once more, lingering there.

She felt heat rising on the skin of her neck.

Hewitt shifted in his seat. Touched a finger to his cheek, scratching some itch Flanagan knew to be a phantom. Showing his discomfort. He looked back up at her.

"You're bleeding," he said.

Flanagan glanced down, saw the red bloom on her blouse where Dr. Prunty had taped the cotton wool that morning.

"Thank you for coming by," she said. "It's been a help."

"Not at all," Hewitt said. "If you need any material on Jack, who he associates with, that sort of thing, just let me know."

He stood and left her there, her face burning red.

22

Hours had passed before DCI Serena Flanagan arrived. Lennon had drunk three coffees, eaten two rounds of toast and a bar of chocolate, and wished desperately for a cigarette, even though he didn't smoke. Not when he was sober, anyway. He thought about leaving. He wasn't under arrest, they couldn't hold him here. But still, something told him to stay put, to endure.

An ache had settled into his lower back, echoed by the joints of his shoulders and hips, and a throbbing inside his skull. He'd left the painkillers in his car. His tongue dried at the idea of swallowing codeine and the comfort that would seep through his body.

But no. He couldn't afford to dull his mind.

He thought he might feel relief when Flanagan finally entered, but the expression on her face offered none. She wore a navy blue trouser suit. Light brown hair pulled back. Pale skin that had begun to freckle with the spring sunshine.

Lennon's gaze immediately went to her left hand in search of a ring, a habit he had not been able to break. He knew she would notice, and that she would resent it. She bristled as she sat down opposite him, holding her jacket closed tight around her. She set an open notebook in front of her, along with a collection of loose A4 pages, printed side down.

Lennon had a good idea what was printed on them.

Flanagan did not introduce herself.

"Detective Sergeant Calvin told me what you said. Now, you've got one chance to convince me you didn't kill Rea Carlisle before I put you under caution."

She stared hard at Lennon across the table.

"You know I didn't kill her," he said.

"I don't know any such thing," she said. "At this moment, I've got one suspect. And that's you."

"If it was me, why would I come here to tell you what I know?"

"Any number of reasons," she said. "To cover your own arse is the most likely. To try to hide in plain view. You think by coming in with this story that you'll throw me off. But you won't."

"I'm trying to help your investigation," Lennon said. "Rea Carlisle was a friend. More than that, at one time. I want you to find whoever did this, and the sooner my being at the house stops distracting you, the sooner you can get after the killer."

Flanagan glanced at her notes. "How did you know the murder weapon was a crowbar?"

"I was told," Lennon said.

"By who?"

"A colleague."

"Who's this colleague?"

"It doesn't matter."

"It matters to me."

"I'm not going to cause grief for him unless I have to. Put me under caution, get me a lawyer, and I'll tell you then."

"I might just do that," she said. "We lifted a good set of prints from the crowbar. What if they match yours?"

Lennon swallowed. He remembered the feel of the crowbar in his hand. The weight of it.

"They could be mine."

"Oh?"

"It was lying on the floor. On the landing. I lifted it and put it straight down again."

Flanagan sat back in her chair. "This just gets better and better, doesn't it? Her mobile phone's missing. What did you do with it?"

"She had it when I left her," Lennon said. "She called someone when I was there. I assume it was her father. She left a message. And if you're still looking for her car, it'll be parked near the Errigle Inn, where I met her."

Flanagan made a note.

"Have you talked to her parents?" Lennon asked.

"No, not yet. But don't worry, I will."

Lennon slipped his hand into his jacket pocket. "When you do, ask Mr. Carlisle about this."

He dropped the photograph on the table, watched her pick it up, studied her face as she examined it. She revealed nothing.

"What's this got to do with anything?" she asked.

"Rea gave that to me. She wanted me to look into her father's history. How involved with the paramilitaries he was."

"He wouldn't be the first politician to have connections, unionist or otherwise," Flanagan said. "I don't see what bearing this has on my investigation."

"She told me she found that inside a book in her uncle's house. Something like a wedding album, or a ledger. That's what she called me about, why she wanted to see me. She said it was full of press clippings and notes."

"What about?" Flanagan asked.

"About all the people her uncle killed."

Flanagan stared back across the table, her face blank.

Lennon took the photograph from her hand, placed it on the table, and tapped his fingertip on Raymond Drew's face. "Him," he said.

Flanagan didn't look down at the picture. "And where's this book now?"

"I don't know. It wasn't there when Rea took me to the house. She said it had been taken."

"Well, that's inconvenient."

"Yes, it is," Lennon said.

"You do realize fairy tales like this aren't going to help you," Flanagan said.

"Fairy tale or not, that's what she told me. Now I'm telling you. That book will help you find whoever killed Rea Carlisle. She told her father about it, and he stopped her from going to the police. That photograph has something to do with it."

"If you're so keen on photographs, what about this?"

Flanagan turned over the first A4 page, an image covering its surface. She slid it across the table. Dark hair and a red sheen. Dull eyes open. Sprawled at the top of the stairs. Lennon would not look away.

"You left her like that," Flanagan said.

Lennon tried to keep the confidence in his voice, to keep emotion out of it. "I didn't," he said, a quiver creeping in whether he liked it or not. "She was alive when I left her."

"What happened?" Flanagan asked. "Did you try it on with her? You and she used to be an item. Did you want a quickie for old times' sake? Did she turn you down?"

"No, there was nothing like that," Lennon said, still staring at the image. "She was upset when I left her. I didn't believe what she'd told me about the book. She gave me the photo, and I left."

Flanagan placed another printed photograph on top of the last. Closer. The damage to the skull more visible.

"You got angry, didn't you? She turned you down, and you couldn't take it. So the anger got the better of you. It can happen so easily, can't it? Things are fine one minute, next thing you're seeing red. You've no control over yourself. You just lash out. I'm sure you didn't mean to do it. You didn't plan it."

"I didn't do anything," Lennon said. "Like I told you, I left her sitting in the back bedroom. She was upset. And you can't force me to look at—"

"Why were you in her bedroom?" Flanagan asked.

"It wasn't her bedroom. It wasn't even her house. It belonged to her uncle. Like I told you. She was clearing it out."

"So she took you up to this bedroom—not hers, you say—and you thought you were on to a good thing. When she didn't put out, that made you angry."

"Jesus, come on, you know that's not—"

"I know how you treat women. Yes, I've heard all about you. You fancy yourself as a bit of a ladies' man. And I know about the prostitutes."

"I haven't done that in—"

"You got suspended over a prostitute. You helped her flee the jurisdiction in the middle of a murder investigation."

"And I got three bullets in me for my trouble. She was under threat from the gang who'd trafficked her into Belfast. If I hadn't—"

"Do you know how many rape and assault cases I've dealt with? How many men have sat where you are now, telling me I had it all wrong? No, honest to God, officer, she was willing, she wanted it, she was fine when I left her. Men like you. Women and girls like Rea Carlisle."

"And how many convictions have you got?" Lennon asked. He knew it was a mistake, but he asked it anyway. Hit her where it hurts.

"More than most," she said, her eyes sparking with hate. "And I'll get you."

23

Susan was waiting with the girls when Lennon finally arrived home. He'd sent her a text message, asking her to pick them up from school, saying he'd explain later.

She had them at the table, doing their homework while she hovered, correcting their spelling, talking them through their times tables. She barely gave him a glance when he dropped his keys on the kitchen counter.

"Thanks for lifting them," he said.

She did not reply.

"I need to explain what happened."

Susan looked up from Lucy's jotter. "When their homework's done. Give us some peace until then, all right?"

Lennon nodded and went to the bedroom he shared with Susan. At least he used to. It seemed like weeks since they'd last slept together. They had lain alongside each other some nights, but not together. Not really.

He lay back on top of the duvet and studied the ceiling. Fatigue dried his eyes, weighed down his mind. His body craved painkillers, aches in his joints nagging him to swallow a couple of tablets, but he would deny himself until he and Susan had spoken.

DCI Flanagan had talked him in circles for more than an hour. Lennon knew the techniques, he'd used them himself a hundred times. The accusations turning to compassion turning

to outrage turning to disgust. Cycling through emotions, trying to get a hook into at least one so she could drag a confession out of him. Dire threats, promises of lenience. None of
it would work on Lennon, even if he were guilty.

What frightened him, however, was that she believed it. Lennon had often leaned on a suspect he knew to be innocent—all
interrogating officers did, taunting and frightening them with
suspicion in the hope that it would shake some scrap of information loose. That was not her tactic. DCI Serena Flanagan believed
he had beaten Rea Carlisle to death with a crowbar in her late
uncle's home.

She didn't have enough to formally arrest and interview him
under caution, but the moment the fingerprints on the weapon
were confirmed as his, a car would be dispatched to take him
into custody. A day at most to make the match, then she could
hold him for twenty-four hours at the Serious Crime Suite in
Antrim before either charging or releasing him; maybe ninety-
six hours if she got permission from her superiors.

By then, whoever had killed Rea would have melted away, his
trail dusted over by Flanagan's certainty that she had her man.

Lennon started and inhaled as a weight settled on the mattress.
He blinked, realized he had fallen asleep. Sitting up, he saw Susan
at the foot of the bed, looking back.

His brain seemed to grate the inside of his skull.

"So?" she said.

Lennon rubbed his dry eyes. "It's nothing to worry about."

"Oh, Jesus. Which means, start worrying."

"Honestly, it's nothing," he said. "I'll get it squared away within
a day or two."

She stared at the wall, her face slack. "Just tell me."

Lennon spoke for five minutes, gave her every detail, held nothing back.

Susan kept her silence for a time before asking, "Why didn't you tell me about her? Why did you lie to me?"

Lennon chose his words with care. "Because things haven't been good between us. I didn't want you to think there was anything going on with Rea and me. I didn't see any point in giving you anything to worry about."

Susan gave a short, desperate laugh, her gaze still locked on the wall. "Good job, Jack. You saved me all that worry. Well done."

Lennon put a hand on her shoulder. "A day or two, three at the most, and it'll be sorted."

She laced her fingers together and said, "I don't want you to sleep here any more."

Lennon nodded. "Okay, I'll stay on the couch. Won't make any—"

"No, I mean this flat. I don't want you here any more."

"A couple of days, Susan. That's all. Then it'll be sorted. I promise."

She brushed Lennon's hand from her shoulder, stood, and took a step toward the door. "What good's a promise from you, Jack? I want you out today. I don't want you around my daughter."

"What about Ellen? I can't put her in a hotel."

"She can stay with me till you get a place." Susan paused at the doorway. "Today, Jack. I mean it."

She closed the door behind her, sealing him in the silence.

Lennon took the keycard from the receptionist and rode the lift up to the fifth floor. His room overlooked an expanse of city center car park, the Baptist church on Great Victoria Street beyond that, the mix of old and new red-brick buildings, traffic streaming in and out of town.

The hotel cost more per night than he could afford, but he'd be damned if he'd go to some grotty hostel with the alcoholics and the dropouts. He had enough room on his credit card for three or four nights at best. If things worked out the way he expected them to, he'd be here no more than one.

He dropped his bag on the bed. He'd packed it with the few essentials he needed and left the flat without saying anything to Ellen. Susan agreed it was best not to cause her the upset. Lennon's daughter was used to him coming and going at odd hours. When she noticed he hadn't come back, Susan would deal with it then. Besides, Lennon wasn't sure he could bear saying goodbye to her, even if it was only for a few days. If that made him a coward, then so be it.

Lennon hadn't told Susan which hotel he'd gone to. Flanagan's team would come to Susan's flat to arrest him either late tonight or early tomorrow morning and find him missing. That would buy him half a day at least, twenty-four hours if he was lucky.

Would it be enough time to figure out what had happened in that house? Probably not, but Lennon had to try. Whatever he could learn in that time was ground recovered from Flanagan's mistake.

Nothing he could do tonight, though. Except blot out his mind, give himself a night of unconsciousness. His bag contained four cans of cheap lager and a half-bottle of supermarket vodka. Those, and the last blister strip of painkillers in his possession.

He took the ice bucket from his room, filled it from the machine at the end of the corridor, and poured the contents into his bathroom basin. He topped it up with water, then dropped the cans of lager into the basin to chill.

While he waited, Lennon broke the seal on the half-bottle of vodka. He took a swig, coughed, took another. A third mouthful washed down the painkillers he'd been craving all day.

Thirty minutes later, he relished the buzz of the alcohol and the warmth of the codeine. He suddenly wished he'd bought cigarettes. That heat in his throat and lungs, followed by the nervy tingle of the nicotine, would help smooth him out even more.

There was a newsagent's about two minutes from the hotel. Maybe he could grab some food while he was out.

His stomach grumbled at the idea.

That decided it. He reached for the keycard on the bedside locker, but the vibration of his mobile phone inside his jeans pocket stopped his hand. He checked the display. Number withheld. He pressed answer.

"Hello?"

A short silence. The non-sound of an empty room, then, "Is that Jack Lennon?"

A man's voice, soft and light.

"Who's calling?" Lennon asked, sitting down on the edge of the bed.

"I want to speak to Jack Lennon."

"I said, who's calling?"

Quiet again.

"Who is this?" Lennon asked.

"That must be you," the voice said. "Hello, Jack."

Lennon's tongue felt thick inside his mouth, a fog over his mind. "Tell me who you are or I'm hanging up."

"We have a mutual friend," the voice said with a barely suppressed tremor. "Or had, I suppose I should say."

"Okay, I'm hanging up."

"Rea Carlisle," the voice said.

Lennon kept the phone to his ear. Listened. A watery inhalation.

"Your number was on her phone when I took it. She'd called you the night before."

Lennon swallowed. The alcohol and painkillers slowed the movement of his thoughts. "That's right," he said.

"Did you take anything from her?"

"Like what?"

"Like a photograph," the voice said.

"Maybe," Lennon said. "Maybe not."

"I think you did take it. Have you shown it to anyone?"

"Maybe. Maybe not."

"Why so sneaky?" the voice asked.

"Because I don't know who you are."

"Yes you do."

"You killed Rea," Lennon said.

"Maybe. Maybe not," the voice said. "See, I can be sneaky too. Maybe I'll come and take the photograph from you."

"You should do that," Lennon said. "Come and meet me. I'd like to talk to you."

Another breath, a forced giggle, then, "Are you a policeman?"

"Maybe," Lennon said. "Maybe not."

"You talk like a policeman. Goodbye, Jack. You won't hear from me again."

"Wait, I—"

Three beeps, then silence.

Lennon wanted a cigarette more than ever.

The photograph, the one Rea had taken from the book. The same book that the caller almost certainly had in his possession. Lennon pictured him, a silhouette, a shadow of a man, hunched over the pages. Reading about spilled blood, lives long lost.

Wires
DECEMBER 2002

I dream of wires.

Every time I close my eyes to sleep, I feel them creeping up on me, into me, through my veins, all the way to my heart and to my brain. I have electricity for blood. I dream I walk the world, lightning shooting from my fingertips, my eyes, my mouth. I spit arcs as hot as the sun. My feet make sparks as they touch the ground, earthing the current that powers me.

One Christmas when I was a child, I went all alone to the pictures and saw a film about a man who wished he had never been born, and an angel made his wish come true, and showed him how the world would be without him in it. Early in the film, as a young man, he promised a girl he would give her the moon, and she would eat it and the moonbeams would shoot out from her fingers and toes and the ends of her hair.

When I saw that, I thought I could do the same. But I knew even then that I could not capture the moon. The nearest thing I knew of was the standard lamp in the living room. A tall wooden stem, a glowing bulb at the top, shrouded beneath a fabric shade. Maybe if I could eat the light, I would have beams shooting out of me like the girl in the film.

There was no one else there when I got home, so I went to the living room and switched on the lamp. I studied it for a while, then climbed on top of a chair, reached inside the lampshade, and put my hand on the bulb. It burned. I pulled my hand away, my skin tingling. I took the handkerchief from my pocket, used it as a glove, and tried again. Of course, when I took the bulb out, it died, its power lost.

After I'd put the bulb back, I thought about this for some time. I realized that the light was not the power itself, but only a manifestation of it. The power was in the wires. I found the cable that ran from the base of the lamp to the socket on the wall and knew that this thin snake held all the lightning I could ever eat. All I needed was to cut it open, put it in my mouth, and swallow.

I took the big scissors from the kitchen, with their long blades and cold metal handle. The lamp's cable was covered in braided cloth. The scissors sliced through it easily. The plastic beneath was more difficult. I had to squeeze very hard. My palms sweating. I remember the sensation of the blade touching the hardness of the bare wire.

And then someone punching me in the chest, the force of it throwing me across the room. The house went dark and so did I.

I don't know how long it was before I woke up. When I did, I felt sure I'd been blinded. But I had not. The fuse for the downstairs mains ring had blown when I cut the cable. The palm of my right hand, where I'd held the scissors, had blistered with the burn. My arm throbbed. My heart stuttered and skipped, making me dizzy.

But I was alive. In the darkness, I closed my eyes. I concentrated very hard, picturing in my mind the lightning shooting from my fingers. Crackling, searing everything it touched.

No lightning, but I felt the power of it all the same, stored in me like a battery. I still carry it with me now. The thing that gives me the strength to live with myself.

24

By the time the urge to move came upon Ida, the room had grown cold and dark. It got the sun throughout the afternoon, if there was any to be had, glowing yellow shapes creeping across the good wallpaper. No sun now.

Ida stood, went to the glass-panelled door, and brought her fingers to the handle. She froze there, a memory flaring in her mind: going to the hall, standing at the bottom of the stairs, shouting up at Rea to turn her music down. When her daughter was still a teenager, a lifetime ahead of her. Days, weeks, months, years, decades. And yet Rea was to have so few.

As her legs weakened, Ida leaned against the door, felt the cool glass against her damp cheek. She remained still for a time, her eyes closed, letting the dizziness leak away.

Finally, she opened the door and stepped through. She looked toward the kitchen. The door closed, Ida saw the shape of him beyond the rippled glass. Hunched like an old man. Well, he *was* an old man, wasn't he? He should've been a grandfather by now.

Ida opened the kitchen door. A long and wide space, room for an AGA at one end, a table and chairs at the other, real wood cabinet doors, imported Italian tiling on the walls and floor. It had been remodelled twice since they'd moved in. She had been prouder of her kitchen than any other part of the house, before, when she cared about such things. Not any more.

Graham sat at the table, a glass in front of him, the bottle of whiskey beside it. Two-thirds of it gone. She smelled its taint on the air between them. He did not raise his head to look at her. His phone lay idle on the table in front of him, silent for once.

Ida said, "We killed her."

Graham lifted the glass, took a mouthful, swallowed and coughed. He wiped the back of his hand across his eyes.

Ida took a step closer. "I said, we killed her."

"I heard you," he said.

"We should've gone to the police with her," Ida said. "If we'd told the truth, she'd be alive now."

"You don't know that." He drained the glass, opened the bottle, poured another.

"Yes I do. And you know it too. We could've told the police about the book, about Raymond."

"Raymond had nothing to do with it."

"What?"

Graham turned to look up at Ida. His eyes red and brimming. "It was a burglar. Some thief she walked in on. The book had nothing to do with it."

Ida shook her head. "How can you say that?"

He sneered, his face suddenly ugly and contorted. "What, you think Raymond came back from the grave and beat her round the head? Is that what you think?"

Ida swallowed. She wanted to scream, to tear at his face, to pound him with her fists. Instead, she said, "We have to tell the truth now. They'll be by for a statement tonight or tomorrow. When the police come, we have to stop the lies. We're going to tell them about Raymond. We're going to tell them about the book. We—"

He was on her so fast she barely registered the sound of the chair tumbling over onto the tiles. She felt his fingers digging into her arms, the heat of his breath on her face, the smell of the whiskey.

"We tell them nothing," he said, the words forced through his teeth. "Nothing."

He pushed her against the door frame. She felt the hardness of the wood between her shoulders.

"What kind of man are you?" she asked.

He gripped her jaw in one hand, forced her head against the frame. Nausea rose in her. His hand moved to her throat.

"I'm your husband. And you do as I tell you."

Ida's bladder ached. Black dots appeared in her vision.

"Please," she hissed.

"You tell them nothing," he said.

"Let me go." The words came out as a pained croak.

His hand left her throat and she filled her lungs, coughed, and dropped to her knees.

"I'll do the talking," Graham said, pacing the floor. "When the police come, you keep your mouth shut. Any contact we have with them will be through me, you understand?"

She placed her hands on the floor to keep from collapsing onto the tiles. He put a hand on her shoulder.

"Do you understand?"

She closed her eyes. Breathed deep.

"Ida, do you understand?"

She nodded.

"Good," he said. "Now, why don't—"

The chime of the doorbell froze the words on his tongue. His polished shoes disappeared from her vision as he stepped toward the hall. He gripped her upper arm and pulled.

"Get up," he said. "Get yourself tidied."

Ida reached for the table's edge and hauled herself upright. She wiped at her face before lifting the whiskey bottle and the glass. Graham watched as she put them out of sight.

She went to the sink and rested her hands on the metal. Her husband's footsteps reverberated in the hall. She heard the door open, and Graham say, "Yes?"

"Mr. Carlisle?" a voice asked. "I'm Detective Chief Inspector Serena Flanagan."

25

"Not without my solicitor," Graham Carlisle said.

Flanagan caught the scent of whiskey carried on warm air from the house. His eyes red, his cheeks flushed. He barely glanced at her identification. Nor did he acknowledge DS Calvin's presence on his doorstep.

She had guessed Carlisle would insist on having a solicitor present. He had a reputation for being litigious, had successfully sued several Irish Sunday papers for libel. A lawyer himself, he never took a significant decision without consulting another member of the Roll.

"Just a few questions," Flanagan said. "We'll be as quick as possible. I know this is a difficult time for you, but you must understand, the sooner we can get a full picture of what happened, the sooner we can find who killed your daughter."

Carlisle stood still for a few moments, his gaze fixed somewhere far away. "All right," he said. "You can come in, but I won't answer any questions until my solicitor gets here. I'll call him now."

He showed them to a living room furnished with a silk-upholstered suite, antique coffee table, a well-stocked bookcase. Flanagan couldn't imagine the Carlisles using this space for anything other than receiving visitors.

A woman waited there, perched on the edge of an armchair, her hands clasped together in her lap. A coat fastened over a nightdress. Rea Carlisle's mother, still dressed as she was when she found her daughter's corpse. She did not lift her gaze from the carpet.

"Ida," Carlisle said.

The woman did not respond.

Then louder. "Ida."

The woman looked up at him. Flanagan saw the fear on her, felt it in her own stomach.

"I've told these police officers we won't discuss what's happened without my solicitor here. Do you understand?"

Ida nodded and looked back to the floor.

Carlisle turned to Flanagan and Calvin. "Have a seat. I won't be long."

He pulled the door closed behind him.

Flanagan sat on the couch facing Ida while Calvin stood with his back to the far wall.

"I'm sorry for your loss," Flanagan said.

Ida might have said thank you, but her voice was so low Flanagan couldn't be sure. She made eye contact with Calvin, tilted her head toward the door. Calvin nodded.

"DS Calvin," Flanagan said, "I've forgotten my notebook. Would you go to the car and get it, please?"

"Yes, ma'am." Calvin slipped out of the room.

After a short silence, Flanagan asked, "Is there anything you want to tell me?"

Ida kept her eyes down as she shook her head.

"Off the record," Flanagan said. "Just between us."

Ida looked up. "Who are you?"

"DCI Flanagan. Serena Flanagan. Do you want to see my ID?"

Ida shook her head again.

"Tell me about her," Flanagan said.

"Graham doesn't want me to talk to you."

"Like I said, I forgot my notebook. I can't write anything down. I just want to get an idea of her. Of Rea. Your daughter."

A flash of anger on Ida's face. "I know who she is. Don't you think I know who she is?"

"Of course you do. But I don't. Maybe you can tell me."

Ida's shoulders slumped, her features slack. "She was a good girl. She was kind in her heart. She didn't deserve this."

"No one does," Flanagan said.

Ida looked to the door, her husband visible through the rippled glass, looking back, his mobile phone pressed to his ear.

"Some people do," she said. She turned her attention back to Flanagan. "You look tired."

"It's been a long day," Flanagan said.

"Do you have children?"

"Two. One of each."

Ida smiled. "They used to call that a gentleman's family. How old?"

"Eight and five."

"Why aren't you at home?"

"I've too much work to do. I want to find who killed your daughter."

"You'll regret it one day," Ida said. "I can promise you. You think now there's no time, but one day there really won't be any more time. You'll have wasted it, and you'll hate yourself for it."

Flanagan's cheeks burned. She felt a swell of anger, pushed it down, forced a smile onto her lips. "I don't think I'm wasting my time."

Ida locked eyes with her. "Neither did I. But what do you think I'd give now for an hour with Rea? All the things I'd tell her if I knew what an hour was worth."

Flanagan thought of Eli and Ruth, their small hands in hers. A sudden memory: Ruth clinging to her, arms wrapped around her neck, legs around her waist, the child's skin hot with fever. The feel of her breath on Flanagan's cheek.

And Eli, always managing to get dirty, his face, his clothes. Always falling off or over something. Always running, as if the world would get away from him if he didn't chase it hard enough.

She inhaled, ready to speak, but the air caught in her throat. A quiver in her chest, and a certainty that tears would come.

Flanagan swallowed hard. Blinked.

Ida asked, "What's wrong, pet?"

Flanagan shook her head. "Nothing. I'm just tired."

Heat in her eyes, in her throat.

Do. Not. Cry.

I am not this person, Flanagan thought. I am not this weak. I will hold myself together.

Even so, a tear escaped. Running down her cheek like a prisoner fleeing. She caught it with her palm, held her hand there, forced herself not to wipe, as if hiding the movement would conceal the emotion she had allowed to break free.

Ida asked, "Did I upset you?"

"No, not at all."

As Flanagan spoke, the image of her deathbed pulsed in her mind. Her children around it, watching their mother being eaten alive by her own body.

She closed her eyes, shook her head. Hard, as if to rattle the picture loose from her brain.

Ida moved to the couch, took Flanagan's hand in hers.

"What's wrong?" she asked again.

Flanagan opened her eyes, unsure whether to pull her hand away or keep hold of Ida's.

A voice from the doorway, "What's going on?"

Graham Carlisle, glaring as if he'd discovered them in some vile act.

Flanagan snapped her hand away from Ida's and shot to her feet. Dizzy for a moment, she wavered, then steadied herself. Ida remained seated, eyes cast down.

"Well?" Carlisle asked.

"I left my notebook in the car," Flanagan said.

She made for the hall, passed Carlisle without looking at him, and went to the front door. Opening it, she saw Calvin leaning against the car, looking up from his phone, the light of the display reflected on his round and quizzical face.

"Ma'am?" he said as she marched toward him.

"Go in and wait with them," she said.

"Ma'am, is there—"

"Just fucking do it."

He said no more and walked back to the house where Graham Carlisle stood in the doorway, watching her.

Tears flooded Flanagan's eyes, streamed down her cheeks, choked in her throat. She brought a hand to her mouth, ashamed, blind as a newborn. Her free hand searched for the passenger door handle, found it, pulled the door open. She lowered herself in and pulled it closed, sealing herself in the bubble of metal and glass.

"Stupid," she said. "Fucking stupid."

She wept until her ribs ached, grieving for her own life, mourning her children's futures, feeling them lost to her.

"I won't die," she said. "Not from this."

That's not true, she thought. I will die. I will die in pain and humiliation on a hospital ward with tubes and machines wired to me.

"No, I won't," she said. "Stop it. Just bloody stop it."

Flanagan slapped herself across the cheek. Not hard, but enough for the sting to cut through the clamour in her head.

"Stop it right now."

Another slap, sting upon sting, the heat lingering there.

I have to be stronger than this, she thought. Not for me. For Eli and Ruth and Alistair. I have to cope. If I can't, how will they?

And for Rea Carlisle.

A poor woman who had been blotted out of existence a day ago. Flanagan had to cope so that she could fight for Rea and take whatever justice could be had for her.

There. Calm.

She sat back in the passenger seat. Breathed deep and slow. Smoothed her emotions out. Let time slip past unnoticed.

Until the car's interior glowed white from headlights behind. She looked into the rear-view mirror, saw the lights die and a suited man climb out of a Jaguar.

David Rainey. He was not a barrister, but she had seen him lurking in courtrooms during various criminal trials, handing notes to whoever had been retained to fight for his client. Slippery as a fish, he was. She watched him lock the car and walk to the house. He did not notice her attention. Once he'd gone inside, she followed.

Graham Carlisle answered the door once again, a scowl on his face. He didn't speak as he stepped aside to let her enter.

Rainey waited in the reception room, on the seat opposite Ida. Calvin stood against the wall, a vision of discomfort.

"All right," Flanagan said. "Shall we begin?"

Graham Carlisle clammed up, gave her nothing. He'd been swimming the previous evening, he said, had arrived home late and gone straight to bed. Ida had been here alone, watching television. She had been worried that she'd not been able to reach her daughter, but her husband had reassured her she would be fine. She followed him to bed, but had been unable to sleep. She had left the house in the early hours and gone to look for Rea.

All of it perfectly reasonable. Flanagan had no cause to doubt the word of either parent. Except for the fear on Carlisle's face, and the hatred on Ida's. They sat beside each other on the couch, but might as well have been on different continents.

The solicitor contributed nothing other than to place a voice recorder on the coffee table in the middle of the room.

In her pocket, Flanagan had a photocopy of the picture Lennon had shown her that afternoon. She could produce it now, put Carlisle on the back foot, see if it would shake anything loose. But he was already antagonistic, and any hostility from her would only make him more defensive. And the solicitor would end the conversation immediately. Save it for another time, she thought.

"Do you know a police officer called Jack Lennon?" she asked.

"No, we don't," Carlisle said.

A crease appeared on Ida's brow.

Flanagan spoke to her. "Mrs. Carlisle?"

Carlisle said, "I told you, we don't know him."

"Mrs. Carlisle?"

Carlisle got to his feet. "I think I made myself clear, we don't know any—"

"I remember him," Ida said.

Carlisle opened and closed his mouth, then sat down.

"Him and Rea were an item. It was for about six months, I think. Maybe five or six years ago. I only met him the once. It was in the upper floor of Castle Court. I was out shopping and I saw them at a table, having a coffee. I went over to say hello. He looked embarrassed. He didn't say much. Rea never really talked about him until they split up. He treated her very badly."

"In what way?" Flanagan asked. "Was he violent?"

Ida shook her head. "No, nothing like that. He was just careless with her feelings. You know how some men are."

Flanagan gave her a soft smile to say, yes, I know.

"Have you seen or heard from him since that time?"

"No. Rea never mentioned him since."

"What has this police officer got to do with my daughter's killing?" Carlisle asked.

"Maybe nothing," Flanagan said. "But I know he was in touch with Rea in the last few days."

"So he's a suspect," Carlisle said.

Flanagan neither admitted nor denied his assertion. Instead, she asked, "Were you aware of a book that Rea found in her uncle's house?"

Carlisle paled. Ida looked back to the floor.

"A large scrapbook or a photo album. Possibly a ledger."

Ida inhaled, her mouth opened. Carlisle put his hand on hers. Squeezed. Ida closed her mouth.

"Mrs. Carlisle?"

"We don't know anything about a book," Carlisle said.

Flanagan kept her gaze hard on Ida. "Mrs. Carlisle?"

A pause, then Ida shook her head.

"Mr. Carlisle, did Rea leave a message on your voicemail yesterday afternoon?"

Carlisle stared for a moment, something working behind his eyes. A lie forming. "Yes. Morning or afternoon, I can't remember. Something about a locksmith. I deleted it. You can check my phone if you want."

"That won't be necessary," Flanagan said, "for now, at least. All right. I think that's enough for this evening. DS Calvin will call by tomorrow morning to take statements from both of you, if that's convenient?"

Carlisle looked to his solicitor. Rainey nodded.

"All right," Carlisle said. "No earlier than nine-thirty, no later than ten."

"Of course," Flanagan said as she stood to leave.

"They're lying," Calvin said as the street lights wafted past the car. He kept his attention on the road. Calvin seldom spoke unless he had something useful to say. That was why Flanagan kept him around.

He was a good policeman, but would never rise much higher in rank. Loyal, a hard worker. The kind of cop you wanted on your team to catch your fall. To do the legwork. Flanagan had met his wife, had gone to their baby's christening at a Church of Ireland service. She doubted he had a religious bone in his body, but she guessed they'd had the infant committed to the church to keep the grandparents happy. Some traditions are hard to break, whether you believe in them or not.

"Yes," Flanagan said. "He lied about the message. And they

know something about a book, which means Lennon was telling the truth about that, at least."

"Do you still fancy him for it?" Calvin asked.

Flanagan remained silent for a time, then said, "Take me to the house."

26

Ida Carlisle listened from the kitchen as her husband and his solicitor prepared a statement to be issued to the press overnight. The newspapers had known Rea's identity since early this morning, but had kept it quiet for the time being. They would lead with it tomorrow morning, and Graham ensured he had a few words ready for them. What a loss this tragedy was to Rea's immediate and wider family, and asking for privacy at this difficult time.

This difficult bloody time.

What a ridiculous phrase, Ida thought. She had been through many difficult times in her life, as had most people. But not this.

She supposed she should be angry, but she simply didn't have the emotion to spare. All feeling had been drained from her over the past twenty-four hours, leaving her an empty vessel of bone and skin.

As the police officers had got up to leave, Ida had one question she desperately wanted to ask. Graham gripped her arm the moment she opened her mouth, and she closed it again.

When can we have her body?

It was a simple question, now unanswered.

The young policeman had given a sad smile and mumbled that he was sorry for her loss. The woman officer had said nothing as she left. Ida could see the burden she carried, weighing on her shoulders. Something terrible had happened to that woman, just like Ida. She knew in her gut that they shared something painful, but she couldn't tell what. If she'd been allowed, if she'd had the nerve, she would have embraced the woman officer, let the pain pass between them so they could know each other.

A foolish idea.

"I'm so sorry for your troubles," David Rainey said from the kitchen doorway, startling Ida.

She said thank you, but the words barely escaped her throat. He went to the hall and conferred with her husband in whispers before exiting through the front door.

BBC, UTV, RTE, *Belfast Telegraph*, the *Irish News*, the *News Letter*—every outlet imaginable. They had it covered. Announcing to the world the family wanted privacy in this difficult time.

This difficult fucking time.

"What?" Graham asked from the kitchen doorway.

Ida's hand went to her mouth. Had she spoken the words aloud?

"Nothing," she said.

Graham went to the cupboard below the sink, reached behind the bleach and washing-up liquid, and retrieved the bottle of whiskey. He rinsed a glass under the tap and poured a generous helping. Ida could smell the drink from her seat. He removed his spectacles, tossed them on the table, sat down opposite her and took a mouthful.

She watched him for a time before saying, "You told that policewoman you went swimming yesterday evening."

Graham did not look up from his glass. "That's right."

"You told me you were at a party meeting."

Now he looked up. "I misremembered," he said.

"No you didn't. You lied."

He tilted his head. His eyes looked bluer than they had in years. "Watch what you're saying, Ida."

"Why did you lie?"

He spoke slowly and clearly, as if she were a backward child. "Like I said, I misremembered. I was confused. I told you I'd been at a meeting. But when I thought about it, I remembered I'd been to the pool."

"You didn't smell of chlorine when you got home last night. You always smell of chlorine when you come home from swimming. I can't stick it when you come to bed, that smell. Makes me feel like I'm sleeping in a toilet stall."

Graham set his glass on the tabletop. He reached across and took her hands in his. His fingers felt dry like kindling. She saw the tiny red cracks in his skin. She saw that he had been biting his nails.

"Listen to me very, very carefully," he said. "Are you listening, Ida?"

She looked up from his hands. Saw those same red lines in the whites of his eyes.

He said, "Don't ever question me again. Not in front of other people. Not when we're alone. Don't ask me where I've been or what I've done. Do you understand me?"

She swallowed before she spoke, felt heat in her eyes. "Graham, what did you do?"

His hand, hard and flat, slammed into the side of her head. She gripped the table to keep from tumbling to the floor. A storm thundered in her ear.

Graham stood and said, "Don't question me. I won't tell you again."

She didn't notice him leave and close the door. The heat of the blow swelled in her cheek. She closed her eyes and savoured it.

Ida had always known what he was. That he had violence in his heart. She hadn't known the full truth of it, the horror of his former self, until his tearful confession when they'd knelt and prayed that night a month before their wedding. The night he finally accepted Jesus Christ as his saviour. Maybe she should have run from him then, called the wedding off, braved the storm. But she was already two weeks late, Rea taking root inside her.

And he confessed his sins to Jesus. The Saviour had washed his soul clean. The Graham Carlisle who had done that awful thing had died, the new man was born in his place. They had held each other and cried.

Had that Graham, the old one, returned? Had he been hiding beneath the surface, watching, all these years?

She thought of the policewoman, Flanagan, and the card she'd left behind. The one Ida had taken from the kitchen bin, the two halves she'd hidden at the back of the cupboard.

She thought of the cold, hard black thing her husband kept locked in a safe in their bedroom.

Ida knew he kept it loaded.

27

Flanagan left Calvin in the car, pulled on white forensic overalls in the hall. The light seemed harsh now, bleaching the colour from the walls and floor. The collection of bags and boxes had been removed for inspection, making the place feel emptier than it had in the afternoon.

Her footsteps resonated on the stairs, even with the muting effect of the overshoes. Each step had been painted white over bare wood, now discoloured with age. A waterfall of red had flowed down and dried to a dark muddy brown. An empty space where the body had been, yet somehow Flanagan still felt Rea's presence, as if she haunted the air around the place where she'd died on the landing, her head hanging over the top step.

Flanagan disliked the term "victim." It was too small a word when it came to murder. One could be the victim of a pickpocket or a computer hacker. But when a life was taken, the world needed a different kind of definition, not only for the person killed, but for those left behind. The devastation of it. She had known families destroyed by the killing of a loved one. Depression, alcoholism, drug addiction, even suicide. For every life taken, many more were obliterated by the fallout.

Seven or eight years ago, as a detective sergeant, Flanagan had investigated the murder of a man by a boy he fostered, who had beaten him to death in his own bedroom. Eighteen months after the sentencing of the boy, the dead man's widow travelled to a beach on the Ards Peninsula, undressed, and walked into the sea. Her body was washed up on rocks days later. If Flanagan had her way, the boy she'd arrested and seen prosecuted for the man's killing would have stood trial again for the wife's murder.

Even through the face mask, Flanagan smelled the metallic, meaty odour of violent death. The atmosphere heavy with it. She climbed to the top of the stairway, careful where she put her feet, avoiding the red. At the top she had to hold onto the banister and swing one foot to the other side of the thickening pool, followed by the other.

Dark up here. She found the light switch, saw the spatter on the walls, turned her gaze toward the rear bedroom. The door had been forced. The blackness beyond as deep as a lake. She reached inside, searched the wall with her fingertips until she felt the switch through the thin membrane of the surgical glove.

The light filled every part of the room. The old desk at the center, the noticeboard and the map on the wall. A chair and nothing else.

Flanagan entered.

Lennon had told her about the book. Rea's parents had denied any knowledge. In spite of herself, she believed Lennon.

The desk had been salvaged from a school, by the look of it. The floorboards creaked as she crossed the room. She opened the drawer. Empty as she'd expected. She slipped her hand inside, felt the farthest corners, and underneath the desktop, searching for anything that might have been secreted there. Her fingers found nothing.

Hard to believe that a man had lived here until less than a

fortnight ago and left so little of himself behind. And this room, so glaringly empty.

Flanagan imagined the book, this journal of the dead that Lennon spoke of. She pictured a man hunched at this desk, poring over the pages, reliving the horrific acts.

Could it be true?

True or not, the desire to be away from this place surged in on Flanagan. As she manoeuvred over the bloodstains once more, she felt an urge to apologize to Rea for her intrusion, as she always did at murder scenes. Someone had died here, alone, and now Flanagan invaded that place when it was too late to do the victim any good.

She left the overalls in the hall and found Calvin waiting for her at the garden gate, her mobile phone in his outstretched hand.

"A message from Ladas Drive," he said. "Jack Lennon's been trying to reach you. He wants you to call him back."

Flanagan took the phone from him, saw that Calvin had already keyed in the number for her. All she had to do was press call.

She waited long enough to be sure she was about to be redirected to voicemail. Then he answered.

"Yeah," he said, his voice sleep blurry.

"This is Flanagan," she said.

"Who?"

"DCI Serena Flanagan. You left a message for me."

"Oh," he said. She heard the sound of his lips smacking, trying to gather some moisture in his mouth. "Yeah," he said, fumbling his words, slow as they were. "I wanted to talk to you. To tell you something. I got a phone call."

"You're drunk," Flanagan said.

"No," he said. "I mean, yeah, I've had a couple of drinks, but I need to—"

"Talk to me in the morning," she said. "When you're sober."

Flanagan hung up and put the phone in her pocket. She turned to Calvin who waited at the driver's side of the car.

"Take me back to Ladas Drive," she said.

Flanagan slipped into bed beside her husband at one in the morning, still wearing her work shirt. Alistair grumbled and pulled the duvet tight up under his chin and resumed snoring.

Exhausted when she arrived home, she had fixed herself a gin and tonic, Hendrick's with cucumber, but found after a mouthful that she didn't have the stomach for it. The ice rattled in the enamel sink as she poured it away.

They had bought the old farmhouse outside Moira twelve years ago, just before they married. It had taken eighteen months to renovate the place, she and Alistair doing much of the work themselves, learning the required skills as they went. Despite the stress of the project, she looked back on it now as the happiest time of her life. She a detective sergeant working her way through the ranks of the newly formed Police Service of Northern Ireland, and Alistair teaching history at a Lisburn secondary school. It took every penny they had, but they didn't mind the sacrifice.

As Flanagan climbed the stairs, she remembered her husband sanding the banister, proud of the blisters and calluses he'd gained. His hair pure black, not washed through with grey as it was now.

Eli and Ruth lay still and silent in their beds. They were both young enough to insist on their bedroom doors being left open a crack, and Flanagan could stand in one spot on the landing, watching them sleep. Ruth with the ugly bear an aunt had given her four Christmases ago, Eli with his legs hanging out of the bed.

Flanagan feared for Ruth most of all. She had so many things to warn her daughter of, so many monsters lurking out there in the dark places. They kept her awake at night.

The bedroom she shared with her husband was a landscape of greys and blacks as Flanagan burrowed in close to his back. She hated to close her eyes in the dark. A terror that had stayed with her since she was around Ruth's age, maybe younger.

She had gone into hospital for a small operation on her eyes— looking back, she wasn't even sure what it was for—and had drifted to sleep with a needle in her arm and her mother's soft words in her ears. When she emerged from the quicksand and tried to open her eyes, the world had remained blacker than any darkness she could remember.

She knew with complete certainty they had taken her eyes.

No one came when she screamed, not even when her voice cracked and gave in. She didn't know how long passed before a nurse—she assumed it was a nurse—put a hand on her arm and told her everything was all right.

"Where are my eyes?" she asked.

The nurse laughed, told her not to be silly, it was just the gauze pads taped over them that made her blind, and they'd have to stay on a while yet. It took almost a full day of sobbing and begging for Flanagan's mother to convince her the nurse had told the truth.

From all these years away, it seemed to Flanagan she'd come close to losing her mind in those hours. Now, for her, the dark would always have the taint of madness about it.

Flanagan shepherded her thoughts back to the present.

The book.

Lennon talked about it, though he said he hadn't seen the volume. But now Flanagan knew that was at least something he wasn't lying about. Rea Carlisle had been fixated on this book, whether it was real or not. Had she been in some sort of delusional state when she was killed? Book or not, delusion or not, that had no bearing on Lennon being the last to see her alive. It did not change his belief that his fingerprints would be on the murder weapon, the kind of evidence that convictions rested on. He was the obvious suspect, and every minute of Flanagan's experience as a police officer told her that the most obvious answer to any question was almost always the correct one.

She thought of Ida Carlisle, lost in her grief. And Graham Carlisle, belligerent, as if his daughter's killing was no more than a nuisance, that Flanagan's investigation was somehow an imposition on him. She wondered if he was violent toward his wife. Ida had that quiet fear about her. It was clear he was mentally abusive, an idiot could spot that, but had he ever laid hands on the poor woman?

God help her, Flanagan thought.

She whispered a prayer of thanks for her husband's goodness. Decent men were a rarity, of course, but more so in this part of the world. Flanagan's father had not been one of them. He had been a drunkard. An abuser. A parasite who drained the life from Flanagan's mother.

Thank God for Alistair, who had not complained when Flanagan kept her own name, who was glad to look after the children when work called her away, who was proud of his wife's achievements.

She rested her lips against the back of his neck, felt the tickle of the soft hairs there, smelled the good shower gel the children bought him for his birthday.

Jack Lennon was not a good man, and Flanagan needed to know him better. She had heard whispers about him as soon as she'd set up her temporary office at Ladas Drive station. DCI Hewitt had only reinforced what she'd already been told. His colleagues obviously didn't trust him, with the exception of CI Uprichard. DS Calvin had ferried stories to her, of how Lennon had helped out a loyalist thug with some traffic offences, how he had got embroiled in a bizarre feud that cost the life of his child's mother, how he had driven a Ukrainian prostitute—a prostitute suspected of murder—to the airport so she could escape the country on a false passport which he had lifted from a crime scene. That Lennon had brought down a killer of at least five women in the process was incidental.

Men don't attract trouble like that by sheer bad luck. Flanagan had learned this in her twenty years on the force. Back when she was in uniform, sweeping up the drunken louts from the city center on Friday nights, she had observed the same bloodied faces week after week and known that trouble doesn't go looking for anyone. So why did Jack Lennon lurch from one calamity to another? What kind of man was he?

She didn't have long to find out. In less than two weeks, she'd have surgery, and then be away from work for God knows how long. Her case would be passed to someone else, someone who might not care so much about justice for Rea Carlisle. She'd be damned if she'd let that happen.

The surgery.

As fatigue began to outweigh Flanagan's fear of the dark, she remembered the malignant lump in her breast. For the third time that day, with a knuckle between her teeth so she wouldn't disturb Alistair, she sobbed with fear.

28

He toured the city on foot, using the darkness as his cover. At night, he could go unseen by anyone that mattered. The only time he didn't feel the eyes of others on him, real or imagined.

How this place had changed. As a young man, it had seemed to him no more than a large town, its industries dead or dying, its citizens turning on each other among the ruins. People so full of hate they couldn't tell their true enemy was the poverty that should have united them. Instead they retreated to the worlds of Them and Us, put barricades between, and let the blood flow.

Now, though. Now it was a real city. Now Belfast glistened and glowed, even at this cold hour. The security barriers that had once closed off the city center were long gone. A person could enter any of the shops without having their bags searched by a security guard.

He came to the City Hall, a grand palace of a building, more than a century old, its green copper dome towering above. Built when the city flowed with money from its industries, an ostentatious symbol of a wealth that would soon evaporate. Floodlights made it seem an apparition, a ghost of stone that would fade by the morning, as fleeting as the money that had built it.

Now the money had returned. Where men and women had once constructed ships or woven linen, their grandchildren now wrote computer programs or answered telephones in call centers.

New ways. Everything changes. Nothing remains. All will burn, eventually. Even him.

He should not have hurt Rea.

All he'd wanted was the photograph. Why had he allowed his rage to decide, to take control? He remembered feeling the crowbar connect with her head. The shock of it through his wrist, up into his elbow. Sending crackles of electricity through his body. And then he couldn't stop. Even as his right mind told him no, go no further, you'll risk everything. Still he continued, the fury making him raise his hand and bring it down again.

And he had gained nothing. That policeman had the photograph.

Anger reared in him.

No. Calm.

He had felt his mind fraying since Raymond had died. His one true friend in the whole world. The one who could reach through all the madness in his life and keep him straight. Reminding him that he could keep control if he really wanted to. But he had lost control. The anger had won out and broken poor Rea who should still be drawing breath.

But now he had restored his balance. Nothing could shake him. Not if he kept the anger in its place, deep inside, where it ought to be. Until he needed it.

His breath misting on the night air, he walked west, then south, around the City Hall.

A couple came the other way, staggering, both of them drunk. A young man without a jacket, belly hanging over his jeans. A young woman with too much make-up and not enough skirt. They laughed at something, clinging to each other, her heels click-clacking in a stuttering rhythm. Heading for the taxi rank across the road from the City Hall. The wide footpath left plenty of room for them to pass.

The young man caught the watcher's stare.

"What are you looking at?"

He walked on. So calm, nothing could break his control.

"Here, I'm talking to you," the young man called after him. "Don't you walk away from me."

He kept walking, calm as still water.

"Leave it," the young woman said. "Come on."

He left the young man's coarse shouting behind him, walking through the dark, always in control.

Control would save his life. The only thing that could, now.

He thought of the book he and Raymond had shared, now hidden. The hours they had spent together, their hands sometimes touching as they reached to turn the pages. The secrets they exchanged. He remembered the confessions written there, beautiful things recorded for each other, even if to others they would seem shameful.

Raymond and he did not recognize shame. Once these things were written down, they stayed on the paper, trapped there by ink and glue. Then Raymond and he could look at it and know the shame was not theirs.

Even the worst things, the most secret things. He remembered every word, recited them as he walked.

Sickness and a Child
2ND FEBRUARY 1995

I know I am unwell.

In my body, I am sound and fit. In my mind, I am not.

Anyone can see it. I can see it on my own face when I catch my reflection in a window. That's why I have no mirrors. I don't want to see the sickness on me.

It's been getting worse. Every night is darker than the last. The hungers and thirsts that torment me become so much sharper. They are real sensations, a gnawing in my belly that no food can satisfy, sand in my throat that no water will wash away.

One day the noise will grow so loud I will not be able to keep it quiet any longer. And what will happen then? When the sun inside me explodes, when I erupt in the supernova of my final release, who can survive?

No one.

I will take the world with me. Every last man, woman and child. Child.

I took a child today.

Here, in Belfast, where I have not taken a life in twenty years. So close to home. So nearly the end of me.

The news has been all about the ceasefires for months now. First the republicans, then the loyalists. They say the killing has ended. No one will say the peace is for ever. Not the politicians or the journalists. But they say no more will die.

People are so happy. I see them on the streets, walking around as if they can start living again. As if the men with the guns could ever have stopped them.

I walked around Castle Court shopping center, aimless, going from window to window, display to display. All the people chattering, the noise digging into my head until I wanted to scream at them all to shut up.

My memory is hazy. I remember the pressure building behind my eyes, like steam in a reactor. It seemed inevitable that something would give. That I would break down there in front of everybody, pulling at my hair, screaming.

I know that feeling, the teetering on the edge, the anything-can-happen bell that rings inside me. A warning I've learned to heed.

As a younger man, I didn't heed it. Like the time I encountered that man in the alley and went back to the ship with blood on my clothes. Or the time I beat the Welshman, Aaron Pell, to death in the engine room. He had been needling me all day. Calling me poofter, queer boy, sissy, nancy, every vile thing he could think of.

Then we were alone and I took a wrench and split his head open. The feeling I had before I lifted the tool, the metal cold in my hand, that climbing force that needs to escape. I felt that today.

I stood near an escalator, very still, breathing deep, willing the feeling to pass. For calm to return. I wanted my sanity back. Once I felt the pressure leak away, I started walking again. Toward the rear of the center, to where it opens onto the ugly waste of bricks they built over the grave of Smithfield Market.

I saw a young woman hunched over a pushchair, wiping snot off a toddler's face. Another child, perhaps four years old, stood nearby. Crying, his face red. Shouting, I want it, I want it, Mummy, I want it. Over and over.

There was no conscious thought behind the act. None whatsoever. It just happened, natural as breathing.

On my way past, I took the boy's hand in mine.

"I'll get it for you," I said.

He looked up at me as we walked. He did not call out for his mother, just came along with me.

"What is it you want?" I asked.

"Thomas," he said.

"What's Thomas?" I asked.

"Thomas Tank," he said.

I knew what he meant. A train from children's books and television, with big rolling eyes and a constant smile.

"Let's go and get it," I said.

He looked back over his shoulder.

I kept walking, my pace quickening so he had to skip to keep up. At any moment, I would hear the mother call his name. And what then?

The rear exit of the shopping center was only a few feet ahead. Thirty seconds, and the boy and I would be away, gone, just like that.

And what then?

Terror cracked through my delusion.

What was I doing? I would not get away. I would be seen. They would catch me.

And what then?

Even so, I kept walking, the boy trailing from my hand.

Maybe I wanted to be caught. Maybe, after all this time, I wanted it to end.

I stopped at the door, my hand on the glass. My heart rattled in my chest like a stone in a jar.

Madness.

I let go of the boy's hand, left him there. As the door swung closed behind me, I heard the mother's voice, crying for her child, first in terror, then in relief. I walked and walked and didn't look back once.

It was on the news tonight.

Attempted abduction of a child in a busy city center shopping mall. They had CCTV footage of me leading the boy away, looking down and talking to him. Then abandoning him there at the door, and his mother running to him.

I will not leave my home for some days. The image was not clear, but it was good enough. No one will see my face for at least a week. I don't know if I will survive that time alone with myself, just my sickness and me trapped between these walls. But I have to try.

If I do survive, talk to me. Tell me not to let my mind run free like this. Help me. Make me take control, like you take control.

Promise you will keep me right.

29

Lennon drove past the triangular block of apartment buildings three times, moving through the light morning traffic, looking for police cars. On the last pass, he slowed at the entrance to the car park. No sign of anything other than residents' vehicles. He drove to the roundabout at the end of the road and circled back before pulling in.

He hadn't expected to see any cops, but was nonetheless relieved to be proven right. If they hadn't matched the fingerprints yet, they would soon, and Flanagan would come looking for him. All he wanted was to see Ellen, pick up a few things, and then get out of the way.

Lennon parked the car in his usual space and shut off the engine. Now that all was still and quiet, the hangover's oily insistence crept in on him. He had woken at seven and hobbled to the hotel's bathroom to throw up.

Once he'd recovered and drunk three glassfuls of water, he remembered speaking with Flanagan the night before. What had he said? He had only the most vague recollection of being woken from a drunken sleep and her dismissing him within a minute. Had he been sober, he might not have called. Flanagan had no reason to believe him, and he had no proof of speaking to anyone.

Maybe he'd simply needed to talk to someone, anyone, even

a woman who thought he was a murderer. And perhaps that was the same reason Rea's killer had called him.

Not that it mattered now. He got out of the car, locked it, and used his key to get into the building and ride the lift to Susan's floor.

When he entered the flat, she was sitting at the table in her kitchenette, staring at him, a forkful of scrambled egg suspended halfway between her mouth and her plate. Lucy, not dressed for school, barely looked up from her Cheerios.

He remembered it was Saturday. The last few days had smeared into one. No school today for Lucy or his daughter.

He asked, "Where's Ellen?"

Susan's fork clanked on the plate. "What are you doing here?"

Lennon took one step further into the apartment. "I wanted to see Ellen."

"Get out," Susan said. "Get out right now or I'll call the police."

"What for? They've got nothing to arrest me with." Fear grabbed at Lennon's heart. "Where's Ellen?"

"She's not here. Get out."

He took another step. Susan shot to her feet.

"Where is she?"

Susan put a hand on her daughter's shoulder. "Lucy, go to the bathroom. Lock the door and don't open it till I come for you."

Lucy obeyed without a word. Without looking at Lennon.

Lennon felt the fear break into anger. He was suddenly aware of his hands, the weight of them, the damage they could do. He willed his face to remain blank, his voice toneless.

"Please tell me where Ellen is," he said.

Susan said nothing until she heard the bathroom door close and the lock snap into place.

"Her aunt Bernie came and got her late last night."

Adrenaline hit him like an electric shock, sending tremors through his limbs and down to his fingertips, chasing the hangover from his system. "Why did you let Bernie take her? Why did you do that?"

"What was I supposed to do? I didn't know where you'd gone or when you'd come back for her. So I called Bernie. So Ellen would be with the only real family she's got."

Lennon gripped the edge of the table as rage threatened to lift him off his feet. Anger so hot it seemed to swell inside his skull, ready to split him open. Susan saw it on him and backed away. He sat down, clamped his teeth onto the back of his hand and felt the pain cut through it all.

"Jesus," he said.

Tears threatened to shame him, fury turning to salt water. He swallowed hard and ground the heels of his hands into his eyes until he saw bright red flares against the black.

When the urge died away, and his vision had returned, Lennon looked for Susan. She stood on the far side of the room, her back against the wall. Her face set hard by fear and pity.

"Please go," she said.

He sniffed and wiped his face clean.

"I'll never forgive you for this," he said. "Never."

She gave a short, sad laugh. "Why would I ever want forgiveness from you? Go on, get out."

Lennon stood. "I need to get a few things."

"All right," she said. "But be quick. And leave the keys. If you're not out of here in three minutes, I'm calling the police."

He reached into his pocket, twisted the apartment key from the ring, and dropped it on the table. He walked to the hallway, and the bedroom beyond, anger still simmering in him. What he wanted lay in the bottom of the wardrobe. The notes on Dan Hewitt, locked in the safe.

As he crossed the room, he saw movement through the window, a small convoy of cars pulling into the triangle formed by the buildings.

Two marked, one unmarked, and a van.

No flashing lights, no sirens, but they were coming for him, no question. They had matched the fingerprints and now Flanagan wanted Lennon in custody. He backed away from the window.

Maybe he could wait there for them, let Flanagan take him in. She would accept his innocence eventually. But after how long? Rea's killer would have disappeared, his trail gone cold. And Bernie would have her claws deeper into Ellen.

Lennon had to run.

He saw Flanagan emerge from the passenger side of the unmarked car, Calvin from the driver's seat. They marched toward the entrance and out of his view.

He looked at the wardrobe. Could he spare the seconds to unlock the safe and grab the file? No, he couldn't.

Run.

Out of the bedroom, along the hall, past Susan in the living area.

"I don't want you coming back here," she called after him, but he barely heard as he exited the apartment.

Lennon glanced at the lift, already on its way up, and jogged as best he could to the stairway at the end of the corridor. He paused at the door, listened, looked through the small reinforced glass window. No one there. He stepped through and started down. Descending a stairway caused Lennon more pain than climbing, the old injuries in his side and hip reminding him of their presence.

As he approached the landing on the first floor he heard a door swing open and closed below, two or three sets of footsteps on the stairs. He ducked through the door onto the first floor corridor, flattened himself against the wall, out of sight of the window, and listened to the officers pass on their way up to Susan's floor.

When they'd gone, Lennon went back through and down the stairs once more, breathing hard. On the ground floor, a fire exit opened onto the river side of the building, away from the car park.

There was no way to get to his Seat Ibiza. His only option was to walk, limping away as fast as his damaged body would allow. He headed south along the path that tracked the water's edge and rounded the end of the building. Glancing back to ensure no one was following, Lennon cut across the road and into the network of streets that led away from the river.

30

Flanagan paced the floor of the kitchenette, fury burning the very heart of her. Closing her eyes, she breathed deep, brought the anger under her control. Keep the rage where you can use it, she thought, don't squander it.

She opened her eyes and saw Susan McKee watching from the couch in the living area. Her eyes red and wet, her daughter huddled close to her.

DS Calvin hovered close by Flanagan. Two uniformed cops waited by the apartment door, another two searching the bedrooms.

"What now?" Calvin asked.

"Give me a minute," Flanagan said.

She crossed to the living area, and sat down opposite Susan.

"You know how much trouble Jack's in," Flanagan said.

Susan kissed her daughter. "Go and get some paper and pens to draw with. You can sit at the table. I'll not be long."

The little girl did as she was told without complaint. She looked like Susan, the same keen features and dark hair.

"What are you hoping to find?" Susan asked.

"I won't know until I have it," Flanagan said. "I need all of his clothes, shoes, anything that could carry any traces."

Susan locked her fingers together in her lap. She did not look up as she spoke. "Did Jack kill that woman?"

"It's early in the investigation," Flanagan said. "But right now, he's our primary suspect. Our only suspect."

Susan's tears flowed freely. She leaned forward, brought her hands to her face. Her shoulders trembled.

"Listen to me," Flanagan said. "You can't help him by keeping anything back. The only way to fix this is by telling the truth. Do you understand?"

Susan nodded. A small gesture, barely a movement.

"Good. Susan, where is he?"

She took her hands away from her face, shook her head. "I don't know. He didn't tell me. I asked him to leave last night, and he went. Just packed a bag and left. Then he showed up here this morning, asking for Ellen."

"And where's she?"

"Her aunt collected her last night. Bernie McKenna. She and Jack don't get on. He was angry with me for letting her take Ellen."

"Is there anyone else he might've gone to? Family? Friends?"

Susan shook her head. "No. His sisters haven't spoken to him in years. His mother's in care. Alzheimer's or dementia or whatever it is. He hasn't any friends I've ever met."

Flanagan watched Susan's face as she spoke, hunting the signals of dishonesty. She had spent her career listening to women lie for their men, even as they bore the bruises and cuts their love had earned them.

She asked, "What was Jack's relationship with Rea Carlisle?"

Susan remained quiet.

"Ms. McKee, please answer me."

Susan inhaled, exhaled, her shoulders slumped.

"They were a couple once, as far as I know. It was years ago, before I knew him. He told me they lasted six months. He gave me this story about a book, that she'd asked him to come over and see it, help her with it somehow, but it was gone when he got there."

"Did you believe him?" Flanagan asked.

"No."

Susan lifted her eyes to meet Flanagan's.

"He lied to me about her," she said. "When he was going to meet her, he said it was an old friend from the police."

Flanagan leaned forward. "Why would he lie to you about that?"

Susan shook her head. "I've been asking myself that question over and over. And I can't think of one good reason."

Flanagan could tell by Susan's voice that she knew her words were tightening the noose around Lennon's neck. Before she could ask another question, one of the uniformed officers called from the hall.

"Ma'am, there's a safe in the bottom of the closet in here."

She turned her attention back to Susan. "Do you know what's in it?"

"It's Jack's," she said. "He keeps information on a colleague of his. Colleague isn't the right word."

"What sort of information?"

"Evidence, he says."

"Against who?"

"His name's Hewitt," Susan said. "They used to be friends. I don't want to say any more."

Flanagan followed the constable to the bedroom. The closet door remained open.

"Have you photographed the safe?" she asked.

"Yes, ma'am."

Flanagan opened the closet and crouched down. She looked to the doorway. Susan stood there, her arms wrapped around herself.

"What's Jack's birthday?"

Flanagan tried the numbers. The safe remained closed.

"And his daughter's?"

This time, the lock whirred open.

Flanagan pulled the metal door aside and reached for the manila folder within. She stood and placed the file on the bed, opened it. Sheets of paper, printouts, photocopies. Statements. Arrest reports. Internal memos.

She thought of Hewitt's well-cut suit, his French cuffs, the expensive watch.

"Jesus," Flanagan said.

Her mobile phone vibrated. "Yes?"

A woman's voice. "Is that . . . Detective? Detective Chief Inspector? What do I call you?"

Flanagan turned away from the papers on the bed. "Who is this?"

"Ida Carlisle. I got your number off your card. I hope it's all right that I called you."

"Of course it is. What can I do for you?"

A few seconds of breathing and indecision. "Can we talk? Not on the phone. In person."

"Absolutely," Flanagan said. "I can be there in twenty minutes."

"No, not at my house. In town. This afternoon, after Graham's gone."

"All right," Flanagan said. "The new theatre, The Mac, in the Cathedral Quarter. There's a cafe there. Meet me on the upper floor. At four?"

"At four," Ida said.

31

Lennon paid the driver and got out of the taxi at the end of Fallswater Parade. He'd found a cashpoint on Stranmillis Road and emptied his current account. One hundred and eighty pounds. He had a few hundred more remaining in a savings account, but no means of accessing it quickly.

Head down, he walked along the street to Bernie McKenna's house. He hammered the door with his fist.

Voices inside. Net curtains twitched.

He hammered again, shouted, "I know you're in there."

Lennon turned in a circle. All around, faces appeared at windows. The door opposite opened. A heavy-shouldered man leaned against the frame.

Kevin McKenna, mid to late thirties. Bernie McKenna's nephew, a cousin of Ellen's late mother. A reputation known to every cop in the city. An arrest record as long as Lennon's arm. Firearms, explosives, extortion, intimidation. But never a conviction. He glared at Lennon from across the street.

Lennon turned back to Bernie McKenna's door and hammered again. And kicked.

"Open the fucking door right now."

"What do you think you're doing?"

Lennon turned to the voice. A young woman, no more than

twenty, was standing in the next garden. One of Bernie McKenna's nieces, presumably.

"Where's Bernie?" Lennon asked.

"She's out," the young woman said. "Fuck away off before I get Kevin on you."

Lennon kicked the door once more. Harder. It rattled in its frame. And again, with his weight behind it, even though it sent spasms of pain coursing through his side and lower back.

He heard a chain lock slide into place, and the door opened a few inches. Bernie McKenna's thin, pointed face slid into the gap. She stared up at him.

"What do you want?"

"You know what I want," Lennon said. "I want Ellen."

"Well, you're not getting her," Bernie said. "She's with her family now, and you won't get your hands on her again."

"I'm her family," Lennon said.

Bernie laughed. "Oh, aye? Says who?"

"She's my daughter, and you've no fucking right to—"

"Your daughter, you say." A grin spread on her face.

Lennon blinked. "What does that mean?"

"That woman you're shacked up with, she packed all of Ellen's stuff up for her. Including her birth certificate."

"So what? Just bring her out here before I kick this door through."

"I'll tell you, so what. Your name's not on the certificate. You've no proof you're anything to that child. You've no rights to her at all."

A wave of dizziness rocked Lennon on his heels.

"You get a DNA test," Bernie said, the grin still cracking her face. "You get proof you're that wee girl's father, and then maybe

you can talk to the courts about access. A man has no place raising a child, not a man on his own, and not a man like you. Now
get away from around my house and don't come back."

The door slammed shut.

Lennon heard laughter and a cheer from inside.

The young woman in the next garden said, "You heard her,
fuck away off."

He threw himself against the door, shoulder first. And again.
His body clamoured with pain. Nausea swelled inside him. He
ignored it, slammed the sole of his shoe against the wood.

A hard hand gripped his shoulder, spun him around.

Lennon hadn't realized he'd been screaming until Kevin McK-
enna slapped him hard across the face and silenced him. He fell
back against the door, but McKenna grabbed his jacket in both
hands, flung him along the path to sprawl on the pavement.

He tried to stand up, but McKenna's foot struck him hard beneath
his sternum, driving all the air from his lungs and the strength from
his legs. Lennon crawled away, spitting and coughing.

"You come back here again and I'll knock the shite out of
you," McKenna said.

Lennon used a garden wall to haul himself to his feet. He
turned, looked back.

He heard a muted voice call, "Daddy!"

Up at the front bedroom window, Ellen, her hands against the
glass, her eyes and mouth wide open.

Lennon lurched back toward McKenna.

A moment before the big man's fist connected with his jaw,
he saw Bernie McKenna snatch his daughter away from the
window. Lennon landed hard on his back, his head glancing
off the pavement. Black spots, a thunderous ache behind his

eyes. McKenna reaching down for him, dragging him to his feet, marching him onto the road, down the street.

Lennon tried to fight, tried to break away from McKenna, but he didn't have the strength. Every time he went to pull or push, or shout, or kick, meaty knuckles thumped into his temple or cheek.

McKenna shoved him all the way to the corner of the Falls Road, and threw him down onto the pavement in front of the shops, the hairdressers, the takeaways. Passers-by kept their distance, averted their eyes, hurried past. No one challenged the big man. No one offered to help Lennon.

"Now get the fuck out of here," McKenna said. "I see you again, I'll have your knees."

He turned and walked back toward his house, his arms swinging like a soldier's.

Lennon spat blood on the ground and staggered to his feet. He looked no one in the eye as he walked away.

32

Ida Carlisle waited in a booth in the cafe gallery, overlooking The Mac's concourse. All dark grey slate and cool lighting. Happy young people walked here and there, sat and drank coffee, chatted and laughed. None of them lying bleeding, their heads smashed beyond recognition.

The image would not leave Ida. Rea at the top step, the life spilled out of her.

Flanagan entered the concourse, walking slowly, looking for Ida. Ida considered waving, calling out to her, but instead she watched. The policewoman moved as if she carried a great weight, some dark thing riding on her shoulders.

How old was she? Mid forties, Ida guessed. Odd how a woman less than fifteen years her junior should stir motherly feelings in her. Since Flanagan had first entered her home, Ida had wanted to care for her, comfort her, and she had no idea why.

Perhaps the sudden vacuum that Rea had left behind needed to be filled. Maybe because Ida had no real friends of her own, only those that Graham allowed her to have, and she desired the warmth of a sister to understand her pain.

Silly notions. Ida dismissed them as Flanagan climbed the stairs. When she appeared at the top, Ida raised a hand. Flanagan saw her and smiled as she approached.

"Thank you for coming," Ida said.

"Not at all," Flanagan said as she sat down opposite. "I'm always happy to talk."

A waitress placed menus in front of them.

"Just coffee, please," Flanagan said.

Ida ordered the same.

When the waitress had gone, Flanagan asked, "So what can I do for you?"

Ida took a tissue from her sleeve, worried it between her fingers. "We've been lying to you," she said.

She watched Flanagan's face. It remained blank.

"I know," Flanagan said. "But it's never too late to tell the truth."

Ida took a breath. Then another.

"We both saw the book. Rea called me to the house and showed it to me. Then I called Graham. He said he wanted rid of it, that we couldn't go to the police. It would've ruined him, he said."

"What was in the book?" Flanagan asked.

"Terrible things," Ida said. "All the people my brother killed. He wrote it all down. And he kept stuff, like souvenirs, I suppose. Fingernails and hair."

"Where's the book now?"

"I don't know," Ida said. "It was there the day before Rea died. Now it's gone. Whoever killed her must've taken it."

Flanagan shook her head. "I have reason to believe it was taken before Rea was killed."

Ida closed her eyes, made her decision, then opened them again.

"I think my husband took it," Ida said.

"That's a possibility," Flanagan said. "Do you know where he might have—"

"I've been thinking terrible things about him. About what he might have done."

Flanagan shook her head. "Ida, we have a suspect."

"But Graham lied to you. And to me. He told you last night he was swimming when Rea died. He told me he was at a party meeting. I know he wasn't at the pool. Why did he lie about it?"

"No, Ida, listen to me. We have a suspect, I can't tell you who, but his fingerprints were found on the murder weapon. He was seen at the house around the time of the killing."

"But Graham . . ."

She almost said it. She almost told Flanagan that her husband had killed before. That he had confessed it to her before they married. Graham Carlisle had a coldness deep inside him that drove his ambition, that froze Ida and Rea out of his heart. She'd had a scene playing in her mind all day, and she could not shake it. Graham, the crowbar lifted, ready to bring it down on Rea's skull. His own daughter.

"But Graham what?" Flanagan asked.

Ida pressed the heels of her hands against her eyes. Forced the image as far back in her mind as she could. She knew it would not leave her, no matter how hard she tried to banish it.

"This suspect," Ida said. "Is it the policeman Rea used to go with?"

"I can't say."

"Have you arrested him?"

"No."

"Why not?"

The waitress returned carrying two cups of coffee on a tray. She placed them in front of Flanagan and Ida, left a bill on Flanagan's saucer.

When she'd left, Flanagan said, "He's absconded. But we'll find him tonight or tomorrow."

"What if you're wrong about him?"

"I'm seldom wrong," Flanagan said.

"But you might be," Ida said. "This time."

No might about it. Not in Ida's mind.

"I don't think so." Flanagan said. Her eyes narrowed. "Is that a bruise?"

Without thinking, Ida's hand went to her cheek. She had seen the purple-brown flare beneath her eye in the mirror that morning. A dusting of foundation had hidden it. Or so she thought.

"Just a little knock," Ida said. "I'm clumsy."

Flanagan reached across the table and took her hand.

"Ida, did something happen?"

"No," Ida said, again with no thought. "Not at all."

Stupid, she thought. Crazy. You were ready to tell this woman Graham killed Rea, but you can't bear to say he laid hands on you?

Flanagan squeezed Ida's fingers, looked her hard in the eye, and asked, "Did your husband hit you?"

Ida sat quite still, trapped between the desire to tell the truth, to be freed by it, and the need to keep her secrets. To show the world her good face, the devoted wife, the loving family not blighted by the same shameful and sordid fissures as lesser people. Still, after all that had happened, Ida's instinct was to shield herself and her family from embarrassment.

What family?

A laugh escaped from her, shrill and ridiculous, a ring of madness to it, even to her own ears.

"I think I'm losing my mind," Ida said.

"You're in grief," Flanagan said. "You're going through a terrible ordeal. There are counselling services, people you can—"

"Yes," Ida said.

Flanagan's features creased with confusion. "Yes, what?"

"Yes, Graham hit me."

"I see," Flanagan said, her face softening. "You don't have to go home. I can get you a place in a shelter this evening. He won't be able to touch you again."

"No," Ida said. "I have to go home. I have things to do. Not for him. For Rea. I won't run away from my husband. I've been a coward too long. Rea would still be alive, otherwise."

Flanagan's hand gripped Ida's harder. "Rea's death had nothing to do with—"

"What are you running from?"

Flanagan sat back, her fingers slipping from Ida's hand. "Excuse me?"

"I can see it on your face," Ida said. "In your eyes. The way you walk, I can see it weighing on you."

Flanagan's eyelids flickered. She breathed through her nose, deep, her shoulders rising and falling. Her gaze dropped.

"What is it?" Ida asked. "Here I am, telling you the worst thing I could think of telling anyone. Why do you get to keep your secrets?"

Flanagan's eyes met hers.

"I have cancer," she said.

Three words, blunt and clumsy, spat out like they carried the disease with them. Flanagan looked away, put her hand over her lips as if trying to force the confession back into her mouth, to swallow the words as if they had never been spoken.

"What kind?" Ida asked.

Flanagan shook her head, her eyes brimming. "I'm sorry. I shouldn't have told you that. It's not your worry."

"What kind?" Ida asked again.

A pause, an inhalation, then Flanagan said, "Breast cancer. Malignant, according to the doctor."

"Oh, pet," Ida said. "Can they operate?"

Flanagan nodded. "They'll remove the lump within a fortnight. And he talked about radiotherapy and chemotherapy. He said the survival rate is better than it's ever been. But . . ."

Now Ida reached for Flanagan's hand. "But you're terrified."

"I don't want to leave my babies."

Flanagan crumbled in front of her, fell into a million scattered pieces.

Ida moved to the seat beside her, put her arms around the policewoman. Rocked her back and forth, felt the warm dampness of her tears against her own cheek as she whispered, "Oh darling, oh sweetheart . . ."

33

Uprichard's wife answered the door, her dressing gown pinched tight to her bosom. She blinked at Lennon through the gap, the security chain pulled tight, her gaze picking over the bruises and cuts on his face as she struggled to remember where she'd seen him before.

He could have told her it was at her daughter's wedding reception four years ago. Lennon had drunk too much and made a fool of himself trying it on with one of the bridesmaids. Uprichard had taken him aside, gently suggested that it was time to go home.

Mrs. Uprichard didn't say a word to Lennon. She turned away from the door and called, "Alan? Alan! It's for you."

Uprichard entered the kitchen and sat down opposite Lennon. A mug of instant coffee steamed on the table.

Lennon asked, "Who goes to bed at nine o'clock on a Saturday night?"

Uprichard didn't return the smile. "We do, when I'm on an early shift the next day. She wants you away by the morning."

Lennon nodded.

Uprichard looked old. His grey hair jutted out from his temples. The pillow marks had almost faded from his cheek.

"Who did that to you?" he asked, indicating Lennon's battered features.

"Kevin McKenna."

"Michael McKenna's nephew?"

"Bernie McKenna has my little girl. I went to get her back. Kevin kicked me down the street."

Uprichard wiped a hand across his mouth. "Maybe it's the best place for her just now."

Lennon stared hard at him. Uprichard didn't back down.

"What, you're going to take a child on the run with you?" he asked. "You know, I ought to call Flanagan right now. She'd have my job for this."

"I know," Lennon said. "And I appreciate it. You've been a good friend to me." He lifted the mug of coffee. "Have you anything stronger than this?"

"What do you think?"

"All right." Lennon took the blister strip of painkillers from his pocket. One for tonight, one for the morning, then he was out.

"I suppose you've got a prescription for those," Uprichard said.

"Somewhere," Lennon said. "Did you have any luck with what I asked you about on Thursday?"

"About Graham Carlisle? A little. As far as I can gather, he was involved with loyalist paramilitaries as a young man. That's not unusual. Plenty of politicians have their hands dirty in some way or other."

"How involved?" Lennon asked.

"I don't know," Uprichard said. "I have one friend in Intelligence Branch, and she clammed up when I started asking questions. A little too quickly and a little too tightly, if you get my meaning."

"What've you heard around the station?" Lennon asked. "About me. And about Rea."

"Not much," Uprichard said. "Flanagan runs a tight crew. They don't go mouthing about what they're up to."

Lennon took a sip of coffee, wishing it were beer. "Not much is more than nothing."

Uprichard looked at his hands, fingers entwined on the tabletop. "Just that she's convinced you killed that woman."

"She's no reason to be convinced," Lennon said. "She's reaching. She wants an easy collar, and I happened to cross her path."

"Jack." Uprichard shifted in his seat.

"What? Come on, say what you want to say."

"We're talking about DCI Serena Flanagan," Uprichard said. "Not a lazy git like Jim Thompson. She's a good detective. She's smart, and she's professional, and she's thorough. She's a better cop than you or I will ever be, and she doesn't throw around accusations like a fishing line. That woman doesn't put the finger on someone without good reason."

Lennon set the mug down harder than he meant to. Dark brown liquid sloshed over the edge. "You think I did it?"

Uprichard couldn't meet his gaze. "That's not what I'm saying."

"Then what are you saying?"

Uprichard stood, his shadow spilling over the table. Lennon felt it on his skin.

"You know, I got a call from him last night."

Uprichard asked, "From who?"

"The man who killed Rea."

"Did you tell that to Flanagan?"

"I tried," Lennon said. "She hung up on me."

"Why?"

"I'd had a drink."

Uprichard indicated the blister strip. "On top of those?"

Lennon shrugged.

Uprichard shook his head. "You couldn't do without, even when you're about to lose everything. I never told you I had a son, did I?"

Lennon looked up at him. "No. Never."

"Gavin. Bright young lad. Could've done well for himself. He was studying engineering over in Warwick. He started out on cannabis, as far as I know. When I found out, I didn't make too big a deal of it. More students try it than don't, I suppose. But it didn't stop there for Gavin. He wound up getting kicked out of university. Before too long he was on the streets, shooting heroin."

"I'm sorry," Lennon said.

"I tried to help him. He was living rough in Birmingham by then. I travelled over, got him into a treatment programme, got him a place in a hostel. But he didn't last. A month later, he was back on the streets, needle in his arm. I went over again, tried to put him straight. Lasted six weeks that time. Then I got a call one night, a police station in Walsall, saying he was caught shoplifting, trying to steal stuff so he could sell it on.

"So I flew over again. I went to the station to lift him, took three months off work and stayed there with him. The magistrate let him off with community service so long as he got treatment. I got him set up. Did everything for him. Nursed him through the withdrawal. Got him a wee flat, sorted out his benefits, all of that. And we sat there in his kitchen, talked like you and me are talking now. He cried his eyes out, swore on his mother's life he'd never go back on the heroin, swore blind he'd sort himself out."

Uprichard's face reddened, his hands shaking with the memory. Lennon couldn't look at him any more, turned his gaze away.

"I left him there, happy with him, happy with myself. Sure he was on the right road. A month later, another phone call in the night. Him crying down the line to me from another police station. He'd been lifted for stealing again. A bike from someone's garden, this time. He needed to sell it to buy more heroin. I hung up the phone. I haven't heard from my son or spoken to him since. That was twelve years ago. I don't know where he is now. I don't know if he's alive or dead. I don't want to know until he's ready to stand up for himself."

"I didn't know," Lennon said. "I'm sorry. Really."

"I don't need your pity," Uprichard said. "I just need you to understand that I won't help you if you won't help yourself. You've been digging yourself into this hole for how long now? When are you going to reach the bottom? You've all but lost your career. Your daughter's gone. You've got a cop after you for murder. How much worse does it have to get for you, Jack, before you stop digging?"

He went to the door.

"You can have the couch in the front room. Me and the wife get up around six. You'll be gone by then."

Uprichard left the room without waiting for a response.

Lennon looked at the blister strip on the table. One for tonight, one for the morning. He touched his fingertips to the plastic and the foil. He swallowed, imagining the warmth the pills would bring, the comfort. Just to get through the night.

He swiped the strip away, sending it skittering across the table and onto the floor.

34

Calvin approached Flanagan, yawning.

"Go home," she said. "It's late."

He shook his head, yawned again. "It'll not be long till they're done."

They watched the team pick over Lennon's car beneath the searing workshop lights. Rubbish lay strewn around the floor—tissues, empty packets, wrappers, a few CDs, the car's tattered manuals. The clothing they'd taken from the flat had been sent to the forensics lab in Carrickfergus.

DC Farringdon finished his inspection of the well beneath the spare wheel, the carpet pulled aside.

"That's it," he said. "You want us to pull the panels out?"

"No," Flanagan said. "Let's call it a night. Thank you, everyone."

As the crew downed their tools and readied to leave, Calvin asked, "Are you going public?"

Flanagan had agonized over it all day. The press had been told she would make a brief statement outside the station at ten the next morning. Would she name Lennon as a suspect? Should she? The media and the politicians would descend like vultures on the news that a policeman was being hunted by his own. Naming a suspect was a risk at the best of times. She had to be sure.

"I'll decide in the morning," she said. "Anything from the hotels?"

"He checked into the Days Hotel on Hope Street last night. He hasn't checked out, but I doubt he'll go back there. I've got a car on the way to pick up whatever he left behind."

"Good," she said. "Now for Christ's sake, go home."

"What about you?" Calvin asked.

"I'm heading back to the office. I want to go over my notes for the morning."

That was a lie. Flanagan knew that if she went home now, Alistair would still be up. They would have one or two glasses of wine, maybe a gin and tonic, and talk about things. She would have to tell him about Dr. Prunty and his cold hands, about the surgery she would have in less than a fortnight.

Was she a coward? After all the things she had seen and done in her life, all the horrors she had witnessed, was she now finally revealed?

Flanagan couldn't imagine anything more terrifying than telling her husband about the cancer. To say it out loud to him would make it real. Their life together would be split in two for ever: the time before the words were spoken, and the time after.

If Serena Flanagan was a coward, she could remain so for another day.

35

Lennon heard an alarm clock from upstairs as he pulled the Uprichards' front door closed behind him. Darkness had begun to ease away, black sky ceding to deep blue and grey, frost touching everything. This was a decent part of East Belfast. Not the most expensive, but not bad. Good hard-working middle-class families doing the best they could. Uprichard's home stood midway along a pleasant avenue that ran between the Cregagh and Ravenhill Roads. A few lights went on and off behind the curtains and blinds of neighboring homes, but mostly the street remained Sunday morning quiet.

Lennon felt an ugly sore of resentment at the good lives these people had, and he hated himself for it.

His breath misted as he walked west, head down. Even if no residents paid attention, he risked being seen by a passing patrol car. And Ladas Drive station was less than a mile in the other direction. He tightened his jacket around him as he worked his way toward Ormeau Park, the expanse of green that stretched along the eastern side of the River Lagan.

Lennon wanted to get off the streets. A lone man on a Sunday morning, even one without battered features and a pronounced limp like his, would be noticed. The longer he stayed visible, the more likely it was that some concerned resident would put a call in to the police to report a suspicious loiterer. The park was his best bet. Lose himself among the trees and wait the early morning out.

Only one man could help Lennon right now, a man he could hardly bear to be in the presence of. And when he planned to call at his door begging for assistance, it would do him no favours to arrive too early.

Lennon checked his watch as he crossed the Ravenhill Road. Quarter past six, at least three hours to kill. He reached the iron fence that bordered the eastern side of the park and golf course. It stood no more than five feet high, and before his injuries Lennon would have been able to scale it easily. But not now.

He walked north until he found a litter bin next to a lamp post he could use to hoist himself over. A quick glance around to make sure no one was watching, and he climbed, careful of the spikes on top of the fence. He landed hard on the other side, his shoulder taking the brunt of the fall, and lay there for a while to recover. When the cold got to him, he struggled to his feet and moved.

Lennon felt exposed, almost naked, as he crossed the fairway of the golf course, heading for the clusters of trees at the other side. Once hidden within their shelter, he hunkered down, hugging himself to combat the shivers that rattled through him.

He never would have believed he could sleep in such conditions. But he did.

It had gone nine by the time Lennon was on the move again. He had woken with a start, freezing cold, his teeth chattering. A few golfers were already on the course getting an early round in, so Lennon stuck to the treeline as he headed north and out of the park. He needed a taxi to get him to Sydenham, but he saw none as he worked his way from street to street. He couldn't risk turning on his mobile phone to call one, so he relied on luck to hail a passing cab.

Tattered Union flags hung from lamp posts, marking out territory, leaving no question who these streets belonged to. Lennon had lost track of his direction, given up telling north from south, had only a vague idea of where he was. The street names didn't mean anything to him. He felt a quiet relief when he emerged onto the Woodstock Road, knowing a taxi would be easier to chance upon here, or failing that, a bus stop.

As he headed north, he heard the rumbling waves of voices from a church service. There, isolated in a sea of Protestantism and red, white and blue flags, was St. Anthony's Catholic Church. An early mass, attended by a full congregation by the sounds of it.

Lennon wondered if it was a feast day, given how early the mass was under way. Then he remembered: Palm Sunday, the beginning of Holy Week. He stopped, stared at the church doors, a strange and light feeling at his center. For no reason he could fathom, he walked toward the doors and in to where the voices swelled and resonated.

He almost passed the font before he remembered his duty. He dipped his fingers in the water, made the sign of the cross, and struggled to recall what he was supposed to say. It had been decades since Jack Lennon had attended a mass. Even the handful of funerals he'd been to in recent years had been at Protestant churches.

He found a space near the back of the congregation and squeezed in beside an elderly gentleman, who smiled and nodded at him. Others glanced at the marks on Lennon's face, judgement behind their eyes.

What am I doing here? he thought. This place had nothing for him. No belief should have drawn him into this cold building. But still he remained, standing and sitting when others did, saying, "And also with you," or "Amen," along with the faithful.

He did his best to ignore the ache in his lower back, in his shoulders and hips, and the dull throb behind his eyes. The painkillers would have eased him, but he'd left the blister strip in the bin beneath the Uprichards' kitchen sink, the two remaining pills untouched.

Lennon's mind drifted as the priest read from the Gospel of Luke, chapter twenty-two, the story of a betrayer's kiss. He thought of the wretchedness his life had become. His home and daughter gone, forced to sleep beneath a tree in a park, or beg a friend for shelter. And even that friend didn't want him around. Decent people believing him to be a murderer.

Perhaps he should have listened to Susan, gone to see a therapist. He knew all about post-traumatic stress disorder, he recognized the symptoms, but that didn't mean he had it. But it wouldn't have hurt to talk to someone. Tell them about the nightmares, the panic attacks, his inability to live with himself, let alone anyone else.

He shut out the sounds around him, the voice of the priest, its echoes rising up through the church, the coughs and sniffs and yawns of the parishioners.

In the quiet sanctuary of his own mind, Lennon began to pray. Even though he had not a shred of faith in his heart, he prayed that God would reveal a way out of the darkness that had swallowed him, some light to follow. He prayed that God would bring his daughter back to his arms, allow him the chance to be a better father. He asked that Susan would find the happiness she sought, that they could forgive each other. Finally, he prayed that Rea Carlisle's killer be found so that this curse could be lifted from him.

The congregation around Lennon said, "Amen."

He said it too.

Lennon looked up to the vaults of the ceiling, his gaze following the voices as they rose and were trapped there. He realized his prayer, too, was caught in that ceiling, like a fish trawled in a net, never to escape heavenward.

With the pain in his joints ringing louder than the worshippers around him, Lennon got to his feet and limped outside once more, the sun warming some of the church's chill from his skin.

What use was a prayer?

A taxi passed, and he raised his hand.

36

Flanagan had set her phone's alarm for seven, but she had woken long before it went off. Alistair had been lying snoring on his side of the bed, Eli sandwiched between them since he'd wandered in during the early hours. The collective heat of their bodies had caused her to sweat, her nightclothes clinging to her skin.

The children would be awake by eight. Alistair would get up with them, offer to let her sleep on, seeing as she'd worked late. When she came down for breakfast, they would talk. He would ask what was bothering her, just as Ida Carlisle had. The sickness must have shown on her, and Alistair would see it too.

He would ask in front of the children, not realizing how terrible the answer would be.

So at 6:55 she had lifted her phone from the bedside table, cancelled the alarm, pulled the duvet aside, and eased out of bed. Her bare soles made little noise on the carpet as she slipped out of the bedroom and down the short flight of stairs to the bathroom.

She washed quickly and quietly before putting on the clothes she had left there the night before, then down the stairs, closed the front door behind her without a sound. Perhaps Alistair would stir as he heard the car's cold diesel engine bark and clatter. Even if he did, he would roll over and go back to sleep, guessing she had gone to work to get an early start.

Which wasn't entirely untrue.

She found CI Uprichard in his office, watering a pot plant that perched on the windowsill.

"You're Flanagan," he said.

"That's right," she said. "Can I have a word?"

"About Jack?"

"Yes."

He pointed to the chair in front of his desk. "You'd better sit down, then."

Uprichard's office was smaller than the temporary one Flanagan had been given, and less well equipped. He must have pissed someone off, she thought as she took the offered seat, or maybe he didn't suck up to the right people. Which was probably why he had been lumbered with an early Sunday shift.

His white uniform shirt looked crisp enough to snap at the creases, his epaulettes deep black, the buttons gleaming under the fluorescent light. He touched the tip of his tongue to the center of his upper lip as he wiped each of the plant's broad green leaves with a damp cloth.

As quickly and absolutely as Flanagan had taken a dislike to Dan Hewitt, she realized she liked Uprichard. It was illogical, she knew, but her gut instincts had always served her well.

"He didn't do it," Uprichard said as he set aside the cloth. "I don't care what you've got on him. I don't care what anyone else told you. And by anyone else, I mean Dan Hewitt. Jack Lennon did not kill that woman."

Flanagan watched him as he took his seat. "What makes you so sure of that?" she asked.

Uprichard folded his hands on his desk. "I talked to him last night."

"Where?"

He hesitated for the briefest of moments. "In my home."

She sat forward. "He came to your house and you didn't call it in?"

"He stayed the night," Uprichard said, not taking his gaze away from hers.

Flanagan felt her jaw tighten, a pulsing in her temples. "You do realize what kind of trouble you could be in, don't you? The kind that ruins careers. How close are you to retirement?"

"Not bloody close enough," he said.

Flanagan leaned forward. "You'd better explain yourself before I go to the ACC with this."

"Jack and I talked last night. Not much. Just a few words, really. But enough to see the sort of shape he's in. That man's no killer."

"He killed a fellow officer not much more than a year ago, and—"

"A corrupt fellow officer who'd been paid money to kill him and the girl. Jack took three bullets to protect a young woman who'd been held captive and gone through God knows what in—"

"A young woman who was herself a suspect in a murder case."

Uprichard's face reddened. "She killed one of the bastard thugs who'd trafficked her to Belfast. She did it to save herself from being raped by him. If Jack hadn't got her out of the country, she wouldn't have lasted another day. He nearly died to save that girl. He threw away his career for her. Now you're going to tell me he battered this ex-girlfriend of his around the head just because she wouldn't let him have his way with her?"

Flanagan felt heat spread from her neck up to her cheeks. She closed her eyes and breathed deep through her nose, flushed the anger away like dirty water from a sink. When she opened her eyes again, Uprichard still stared back. He spoke before she could.

"When I left Jack in my kitchen last night I told him to be gone before the morning. I didn't sleep a wink. I lay there all night, thinking it through, looking at it from every side I could imagine. Yes, he's not always been the most noble of men. Yes, it looks bad that he was there in the house with her. Yes, he touched the crowbar that killed her. But it's all circumstantial. You sent all the clothes you took from his apartment to Carrickfergus, right? I'll bet you my house they don't find a single spot of blood from that woman. I've known Jack Lennon since he was in uniform. I know he can be a hard man to like, but I also know he's got shot on two separate occasions trying to help someone else. And I know he didn't kill Rea Carlisle."

"Everything points to Lennon," she said. "Everything. The fingerprints on the weapon, the witness who saw him leave, the history he had with the victim."

"Who are you trying to convince?" Uprichard asked. "Me or yourself?"

"If you were in my position, you'd have him for the murder too."

"Maybe I would," he said. "But I'd be wrong. And so are you. You've got a press call this morning. Are you going to name him?"

"I'm considering it," she said.

"It's a hell of a risk."

"You think I don't know that?"

"You seem to know plenty," Uprichard said as he got to his feet. He retrieved the cloth and went back to his plant. "Who am I to question a detective's judgement?"

Flanagan simmered for a few moments before she stood. "All right. Thank you for your time."

She headed for the door. As she reached for the handle, Uprichard said, "One thing to remember, though. Some people in this station can be trusted more than others."

"Is that right?" she said, looking back over her shoulder.

Flanagan thought of the file she had taken from Susan McKee's closet, the one she had decided not to store with the rest of the items taken from Lennon's home, that now lay hidden in a drawer in her office.

"It is," he said, tending to the plant's leaves. "If I was you, I'd be careful whose word you take."

She nodded, said, "I will," and left him there.

37

A one-bedroom apartment in the city center. It smelled of cheap perfume and disinfectant, but it was clean. Roscoe Patterson watched from the living area as Lennon toured the flat. Portraits of nudes on the walls. Cheap flat-pack furniture.

"It'll do," Lennon said.

"There's gratitude for you," Patterson said.

"Don't worry, I'm grateful. You know I always take care of you."

Patterson snorted. "It's a long time since you took care of me. Come to think of it, there's not much you *can* do for me. Last I heard, you were still on suspension."

Lennon had known Roscoe Patterson for coming on ten years. Their relationship was one of expediency, and neither man enjoyed being in the other's company for any longer than was strictly necessary. Patterson was respected and feared as a senior loyalist paramilitary, but he had never been overly concerned with the ideals and politics of that movement. His primary reason for belonging to such a group was profit.

Roscoe Patterson had a particular talent for managing the services of prostitutes. He was known to have strict policies about the working conditions of the women on his roster, tolerated no abuse of them by clients, and made sure they earned more with him than they would with any other pimp. And he would not have any dealings with women who were coerced into this life, or those who trafficked in them.

In their past conversations, Lennon had gathered that Patterson regarded himself more as a booking agent than a pimp. The happier his workers were, the more money he made. It was a simple formula, and he didn't like anyone or anything coming along that might disrupt his business. Thus, he had shared certain information with Lennon, and others, over the years. If a rival was getting too uppity, or rankling the human rights campaigners by mistreating the girls who worked for him, Patterson would try to smooth things out by passing leads on to the police. The alternative was to tackle such problems directly, and despite his size and appearance, Roscoe Patterson did not deal in violence if he could possibly avoid it.

Lennon and Patterson's relations had fundamentally changed when the pimp passed information about Lennon and Ellen's mother to Dan Hewitt, information that led to Marie McKenna's death. Patterson could not have known that his betrayal would have such consequences, but even so, being around him made Lennon's nerves jangle with anger and hate. If Patterson hadn't been so bloody useful, Lennon would gladly have never set eyes on him again.

So how could Patterson be trusted now? He couldn't, not really. But Lennon had given him such a beating over the last treachery that he was fairly confident Patterson would not risk doing it again.

Lennon walked back to the living area. Two cheap sofas still with plastic sheeting on them. The kitchenette had seen little use.

"What else have you heard?" he asked.

Lennon watched Patterson's face for any sign of a lie. His shaven head was darkened by a few days' growth. His expression remained closed, dead-eyed, giving nothing away. Patterson slumped onto the couch, plastic rustling beneath him.

"Not much," he said. "Are you planning on staying here long?"

"I'm not sure. Depends how things work out."

"Things," Patterson echoed with a half-smile. "Never you worry, I'll ask around. Whatever shit you've gotten yourself into, I'll find out. Anyway, I've a girl due over from Birmingham next weekend. Sexy wee thing. I've two nights' worth of punters booked in for her. That's five grand of takings. No chance I'm going to bollocks that up just to give you a place to hide."

"I'll be gone long before then," Lennon said. He sat down opposite Patterson. "But I need another favour."

"Shite," Patterson said, shaking his head. "Answering my door before noon on a Sunday should be favour enough, let alone giving you the use of this place. And now you're looking for more? Jesus."

Lennon had called at Patterson's Sydenham home, a small terraced house beneath the City Airport's flight path and less than a hundred yards from the railway line. Patterson shared the two-up two-down with a wife and three children, and Lennon wondered how the noise didn't drive him insane. The loyalist pimp could have easily afforded a nice four- or five-bedroom detached place in a better location, but not without the taxman getting curious as to how he could afford it with no other income than the benefits the family claimed.

On the drive into town, Patterson had tried to press him on how he'd got a face full of cuts and bruises but was given no answer.

Lennon took the photograph from his pocket and dropped it onto the cheap coffee table between them. He turned it with his fingertips and pushed it toward Patterson.

"Take a look," Lennon said.

Patterson lifted the picture and studied it for a time. Lennon watched his eyes move from face to face until they narrowed with recognition.

"Here, is that . . . ?"

"Graham Carlisle," Lennon said.

"I heard about his daughter. Jesus, you're not mixed up with that, are you?"

"She gave me the photo before she died. She wanted to know how involved her father was with the paramilitaries."

Patterson snorted. "Up to his neck, by the looks of this. Do you know who the others are?"

"The one on the left was Raymond Drew, Rea's uncle, Graham Carlisle's brother-in-law. You don't know him?"

"Nah," Patterson said. "Creepy looking fucker."

"You don't know the half of it. Anyway, he died a week or two ago. Rea was clearing out his house when she was killed."

Patterson tossed the photograph back across the table. "Whatever the fuck this is, you can leave me out of it. Jesus, you dig yourself into some holes, boy, and you're not dragging me into this one."

Lennon leaned forward and lifted the picture. He looked at Graham Carlisle's face, then Raymond Drew's. He thought of Rea lying at the top of a flight of stairs, the life beaten from her broken body.

"It's the one thing she asked me to do for her," Lennon said. "She's dead because I didn't listen to what she was telling me. Because I didn't believe her. I have to do this for her. Please help me."

He looked up at Patterson, who stared toward the apartment's window, the balcony beyond, his face expressionless in the light.

"Don't be getting all emotional on me, Jack. You'll have me in tears."

"Will you help me?" Lennon asked.

Patterson exhaled, his muscled shoulders falling. "All right. I'll ask around a bit, see what I can scare up."

"Thank you," Lennon said.

Patterson stood. "Is that all the favours you're going to ask? I've work to be getting on with."

Lennon smiled. "Work?"

"You know what I mean. Right, I'm off. Look after the place, all right?"

"I will," Lennon said.

"Here, I almost forgot."

Patterson reached into his jacket pocket and produced a small cardboard box, white with blue lettering, a pharmacist's prescription label stuck to it. He shook it in front of Lennon's eyes, the contents rattling within. "You'll want some of these."

Lennon looked at the box, imagined the blister strips inside, the pills in their plastic cocoons, waiting for his tongue. As if on command, pain signalled from his joints, his back, even his knuckles.

He swallowed and said, "No."

Patterson held the box out, gave it another shake. "Don't worry, you can pay me later."

Lennon shook his head. "I don't want them."

"All right, suit yourself."

As Lennon watched Patterson exit and close the door behind him, he felt a grating regret at showing so much of himself to a man he hated with all his heart.

38

He sat alone in the cafe, a cup of black tea in front of him, dry toast and a fried egg to eat. A television chattered from its place on the wall. No other customers. The owner sat at the counter, her fat chin rested on her hand, empty eyes pointed toward the screen.

The toast crunched between his teeth. He had stayed inside all morning, feeling the pressure of the walls around him. That voice in his head, telling him what a terrible mistake he'd made. How the anger had got the better of him, how he might have lost it all. He listened until he could stand it no longer. He had to get out and away.

The local news played on the television, the earnest presenter rattling off the headlines. Rea Carlisle's death was no longer the lead item, but second. He felt a mix of relief and resentment.

"And a development in the murder inquiry into the death of Stormont politician Graham Carlisle's daughter," the newsreader said. "A suspect has been named. Lauren McCausland has more."

He dropped his toast. The knife clattered from his other hand, splashing egg yolk across the plate. His gaze locked on the screen.

Footage of the house from the day before. Men and women in white overalls coming and going. He held his breath.

"The hunt for the killer of Rea Carlisle took an unexpected turn today," the voiceover said.

The air tight in his chest, pushing out against his ribs. A ringing in his ears.

Then a still image. An identity photograph, the man's face against a plain white background.

He exhaled. Stared.

"Police leading the investigation have named one of their own colleagues, Detective Inspector Jack Lennon, as a person of interest."

Jack Lennon. The policeman. The number on Rea's phone. He felt a smile twitch on his lips.

Cut to a news conference outside a police station. The woman detective. Her name flashed on the screen. Microphones and voice recorders lined up beneath her chin.

"We believe this person is still in the Greater Belfast area, and we wish to question him urgently. We appeal to anyone who knows of Jack Lennon's whereabouts, or has had contact with him in the last forty-eight hours, to call us immediately. However, we urge members of the public not to approach him as we believe him to be potentially dangerous."

Potentially dangerous. The twitch turned to a grin, died again just as quickly.

The woman cop, Flanagan, continued: "Instead, if you see him, please contact us directly. Thank you, that is all."

A flurry of questions from the reporters as she turned away from the camera.

Poor Rea. She thought a policeman could help her. No one could help her now. But the policeman had the photograph.

What to do about that?

What to do about any of it?

Perhaps he should run. Get away. Leave everything and go.

Or was that madness talking?

There was a time, long ago, when he could have chosen a different path. He'd had his chance to keep the blood from his hands, and he did not take it. The choice not taken ceases to exist once that decision is made. A person might as well regret the direction of the wind, or the shape of a cloud.

He thought of Raymond, and sadness pierced and clawed at him.

Raymond and he had never had a choice.

Not in this world.

The Driver

Do you remember the driver? How we left him there, the engine still running? Do you remember the blood slashed across the windscreen? The look in his eyes when he saw, when he knew what was going to happen to him?

That was more than twenty-five years ago. I still think about it. I dream about it. Sometimes I wonder how things would be for us if that night hadn't happened. Would we have had normal lives? Can people like us ever have normal lives?

I couldn't. I was always going to be this way.

Do you remember how we lay together that night, talking about it? You were shaking. I had to calm you, hold you tight. You cried, said you couldn't ever do it again, you'd thought you could, but it was too much, too real. Too hard to see it up close. So I had to do it for you.

We should have been born in a different place. This country was far too small for us. It still is. The minds of the people too closed. They look at us and say, "They are not the same." And they hate us.

I felt it when I was a boy. I know you felt it too. They beat everything that was different out of me. They beat me so hard, tried to bend me to their shape so often, that I didn't know what I was any more. I am neither man nor beast, fish nor fowl. I am the dark place in between. They made me that.

How can they expect me, us, to behave as normal human beings if they treat us this way? The names they called me. I pretended I didn't mind, but I did. I've stored the anger and hate up until it glows and burns in me, searching for release. Of course it shows itself. Of course others suffer. That is inevitable.

I have been indoors for a month now. I go outside to buy tinned food, bread, enough to keep me alive. The smell doesn't bother me. It's better if I stay inside. The wicked is rattling around inside me, trying to break loose. But I can't do anything here, not so close to home. It's too dangerous. I need to be away, some other place, where no one knows me. But there's no work to take me away.

One day, I'll make a mistake. It's only a matter of time. The wicked will get the better of me. I will be seen, reported, caught. What then?

Will you abandon me?

Will you pretend we never lay together in the dark, whispering our secrets? When you see the news report, will you look away as if it's some stranger's photograph? Will you become a human being like the rest of them, put the beautiful things we shared behind you?

That's the only thing that frightens me. That you will leave me alone, that you'll go and become one of them. And then who will keep me right?

I will die before that happens.

39

Ida Carlisle waited in the hall for her husband. The good wooden floor creaked beneath her feet. It had cost thousands to put down. And the wallpaper. They'd called it wall covering in the fancy shop where she'd bought it, but it was just wallpaper really. And the bevelled mirror, and the telephone table, and the ornamental crystal.

So much money squandered on things, just things, nothing that truly mattered. She remembered the feeling of pride when the sales girl had told her the price of the wallpaper—per roll, mind, not for the whole lot—and realizing she could afford it. Graham worked hard, she thought. We deserve nice things.

He was working now. Even as his only child lay on a slab with frost on her eyelashes, Graham Carlisle had gone to work. To see some people, he said. Important matters to attend to. He said he'd be back after lunch. The clock on the wall read close to three.

Ida had been standing here for an hour and a half. Waiting.

She heard the Range Rover's engine. Tires on the gravel, the engine dying. The car door opening and closing.

Ida closed her eyes and whispered a small prayer. When she opened them again, she saw her husband's silhouette through the glass of the door. He turned his key in the lock, let himself in, closed the door behind him.

Graham Carlisle froze, staring at Ida.

She raised her right hand, aimed the pistol at his chest.

He opened his mouth to speak, but no sound came. His tongue worked behind his teeth, clicking wetly.

Like most politicians, Graham was allowed to keep a personal protection weapon. He had shown Ida how to use it, proud of himself for having such a thing. And pride was a sin. The Lord was punishing them both for their sin.

She indicated the good room. Where they hosted visitors. "Go in there," she said.

He swallowed, found the nerve to speak. "Ida, what are you doing?"

"Just go in there and sit down," she said.

Graham stepped toward the open door, his eyes locked on her hand. "Please listen to me, Ida."

"No, you're going to listen to me," she said, following him into the room. "Sit down."

"No, Ida, please listen—"

"Sit down!" The words tore at her throat.

Graham dropped onto the couch, his hands raised.

"Ida, you could kill me with that."

"That's right," she said. "Now shut your mouth."

Graham went quiet, and very still. She could barely hear his breathing as he stared up at her.

"Why did you do it?" she asked.

He wet his lips. Shook his head. "Do what?"

She couldn't keep the tremor from her voice. "Why did you kill our daughter?"

His mouth opened. His eyes glistened.

"Why?" she asked.

"Do you really think I did that?"

"Don't lie to me," she said. "Not now. You've lied to me for all the years I've known you. For the love of God, don't lie to me now."

A tear rolled down his cheek. "How can you think that?"

"You've killed before," she said as she battled to keep control of herself. "You can do it again."

"That was a lifetime ago," he said. "I was a different man then. A boy, really. But you're talking about my child. My own daughter."

"Your daughter," Ida echoed. "You never treated her like your own. You never really loved her, did you?"

"Of course I did."

"Well, you never showed it. You cared more about your career than you did about her. Or me. You were never there for us. I raised her by myself."

"I was building a life for us."

"Not for us. For you."

"For us. Look at all the things you have. This house. All these things. You and Rea never wanted for anything. I slaved my guts out for the both of you."

"No, it was never for us. It was all for you. And you thought our daughter would ruin it for you, so you killed her. You bastard, you beat her to death so she wouldn't go to the police."

Graham slid from the couch, down to the floor, onto his knees. "No, I didn't, I swear to our Lord Jesus, I did not harm our Rea. Didn't you see the news this morning?"

"What news?"

"They named a suspect. That policeman Rea used to go out with. You said you'd met him. They named him this morning."

Ida took a step closer. "They're wrong. They're all wrong. I know you did it. Don't tell me you didn't."

"I didn't kill her. I swear to you."

"Then where were you when she died?"

"I told you, I was swimming."

"You weren't," she said. "I know that's a lie. Tell me the truth."

He closed his eyes for a moment, breathed deep, opened them again. "All right. You want the truth."

She kept the pistol trained on his forehead. "Go on."

"I never left the Brigade."

She lowered the pistol a few inches. "What?"

"I'm not active any more. Back then, before we married, I told them I wouldn't be involved in any actions. But they asked me to stay as an adviser."

"You're still . . ."

"Just as an adviser. On political issues. I liaise between them and the party."

"But they're criminals," Ida said. "Drug dealers. Murderers."

"We're steering them away from all that. Trying to engage them. Trying to get them to think of their communities and what they can do for them."

Ida raised the gun once more. "You've been lying to me all this time. You told me you were out of it."

"I've been working with them. Getting them away from all the sectarian nonsense, getting them to see past all the bigotry and the flags and the fear of the other side. Getting them to think about jobs, their children's education, the things that really matter."

He held his hands out before him, gesticulating to emphasize his point. Like a speech in the Assembly. Always the politician.

"That doesn't explain anything," she said. "That doesn't bring my Rea back."

"I'm trying to tell you where I was that evening, and why I had to lie to the police. I was at a Brigade meeting. In East Belfast."

Ida's hands quivered. Tears blurred her vision. "You killed her. I know you did. You were afraid she'd go to the police with that book. With that photograph. Don't you dare tell me any more lies."

He shuffled forward on his knees. "I'm telling you the truth. Do you know how hard it is for me to tell you this? Please believe me, I am not lying."

Ida stepped backward. "Don't come any closer."

He got one foot under him. Reached out a hand. "You have to listen to me, Ida. Please give me the gun."

"No," she said. Tears hot on her cheeks. Her words rising from a growl to a shriek. "No, I'm not listening to you any more. I've listened to you for thirty-five years, and you've never once told me the truth. I've taken your abuse, your putting me down, your controlling me, suffocating me, I've taken it for a lifetime and I'm not going to take it any more."

Her voice rang between the walls, consonants and vowels sharpened by hysteria.

"Give me the gun," Graham said. "Ida, give me the gun."

"No. I won't. Now you're going to listen to me," she said.

His hand swiped toward hers. She lifted the gun away before he could grab it, brought it back to aim at his chest.

"Give it to me," he said.

"Shut your mouth, you lying bastard."

He reached once more for the pistol. Once more, she whisked it away. Again, she aimed for his heart.

His face hardened. "Ida, one last time, give me that gun."

"No, I—"

He launched up and forward, grabbing. His hands locked around hers, strong and hard. He pulled the pistol toward his chest, pressed the muzzle against his sternum.

"You really think I killed Rea? Then go on. You do what you have to do. Punish me for it."

The pistol held seventeen bullets. Ida had counted every one. All she had to do was squeeze the trigger and send one ripping and tearing into his heart.

"Do it," he said.

"I hate you," she said.

Her grip softened, and her finger slipped out of the trigger guard. He removed the gun from her hands, popped out the magazine, checked the chamber, then threw the pistol to the floor.

The back of Graham's hand made fireworks explode in Ida's head. As she fell, her cheek coming to rest on the carpet, she saw the small black hole of the gun barrel, a dark tunnel disappearing into infinity.

40

The BMW M5's firm suspension did Lennon no favours. Every pothole jarred up through the wheels, through the floor, and up into his side. He tried to keep the pain from his face. If Roscoe Patterson noticed from the driver's seat, he didn't let on.

"So who's this friend of yours?" Lennon asked.

"An auld hand," Patterson said. "Dixie Stoops. He's from before my time, but there's nothing he doesn't know."

Patterson steered the car through the estates and side streets that branched off the Upper Newtownards Road, to the east of the city. Union flags everywhere, the curbstones painted red, white and blue.

Lennon had patrolled these streets back when he wore a uniform. Hatred and distrust of the police wasn't as overt as in republican areas of the city—he seldom had stones thrown at him—but cops were nonetheless unwelcome. The people were as likely to clam up when asked if they'd seen or heard anything.

"Here we go," Patterson said as he steered the BMW into a walled yard lined with sheds and a Portakabin. Timber lay stacked along one side, pallets of bricks and concrete blocks along another. The sign over the gate read MORRIS MCREA & SONS CONTRACTORS.

Patterson pulled up alongside a low prefab building where a

heavy-shouldered man waited by the door. He got out, and Lennon followed, suppressing a grunt as he hauled himself out of the car.

"You rightly?" Patterson asked the man at the door.

"Aye. Yourself?"

"Aye."

The man opened the door and stepped back to allow Patterson and Lennon to enter. The interior was lit by dimmed bulbs, the walls painted black, decorated with flags and banners, a signed Glasgow Rangers football shirt, framed photographs of loyalists who had been killed, whether by republicans, the security forces, or their own people. A dozen round tables, each with an ashtray. A pool table. A poker machine. At one end, a makeshift bar and a row of coolers filled with bottles and cans lined up behind it.

There were illegal clubs like this scattered around Belfast, all of them run by paramilitaries of one stripe or another. Places where hard drinking was done by hard men, day or night.

At one of the tables, in the darkest corner, sat a lone man. Patterson headed toward him, Lennon following. The man stared at them both as they approached, his face like red-veined marble. Pushing seventy, Lennon guessed, but still strong. He kept his thick tattooed forearms across his belly, didn't offer to shake Patterson's hand.

"This is Dixie Stoops," Patterson said. "Dixie, this is the fella I was telling you about."

Dixie let his gaze crawl from one man to the other while he lifted a can of Harp lager from the table and took a swig.

"I know your face," he said. "You were all over the news at lunchtime. They said you killed that wee girl."

"I didn't do it," Lennon said.

Dixie cracked a smile. "Funny, I said the same thing when they put me away."

Lennon felt the urge to slap the beer can from his hand, throw his weight around like he used to. Show Dixie who he was dealing with. But Lennon didn't have the strength any more. Even at his advanced age, Dixie Stoops would eat him alive.

"You arrested me one time," Dixie said.

"Oh?"

"Aye. You and some uniform boys stopped the car I was in. We had a rifle and some rounds in the boot. You gave me a hiding."

"Sorry about that," Lennon said. "I must've been having a bad day."

"Not as bad as me."

"Can I sit down?"

Dixie nodded to the chair opposite. Lennon took it as Patterson wandered off to what passed for a bar. He helped himself to a bottle of cheap import beer from one of the coolers.

"So what do you want?" Dixie asked.

"Roscoe told me you might have known someone a few years back, someone I was interested in."

"Graham Carlisle," Dixie said. "The politician."

"That's right."

"Listen, Roscoe asked me to talk to you because you're a friend of his and I owe him a few favours. I don't owe Graham Carlisle anything, but if I'd known you were mixed up in what happened to his daughter, I'd have stayed home."

Lennon held Dixie's gaze. "I didn't kill Rea Carlisle, and if I'm going to prove that, I need to find out who did. I think there's a connection to her father's past."

"Jesus, this sounds like one of them murder books the wife reads. All right, go on, ask whatever you're going to ask."

"How did you know Carlisle?"

"I was head of the Sydenham area when he joined the East Belfast Brigade. He was only a young lad, maybe still a teenager. He was odd, though."

"Odd how?"

"Well, he was at university. At Queen's, doing law. We never had many student types joining up. Any education we got was behind bars. I got a degree in political science. Wouldn't think it to look at me, would you?"

"Any idea why he joined?" Lennon asked.

"Because his mates from the neighborhood did. Same reason young men join gangs everywhere. To belong to something. To be somebody. Most of the lads round here, if they couldn't get an apprenticeship, they were fucked. They had nothing, and they knew they'd never have anything. But you put a gun in a young lad's hand, give him someone to point it at, then he feels like he's something. You know what I mean?"

"I know," Lennon said. "Doesn't make it right."

"I never said it did." Dixie shook his head. "Jesus, if I'd known then what I know now, I'd never have listened to the politi-cians—the ones who were supposed to be looking out for us—when they were getting everyone stirred up. I'd have got the fuck out and made a decent life for myself."

He leaned forward, rested his forearms on the table, making the tattoos writhe. "See, that's what was so strange about Graham Carlisle. He had the brains to pass his Eleven-Plus and get into a good school, and then on to university. He could've made something of himself, and he did make something of himself. So

I don't know what he was doing with the likes of us. Anyway, he stopped active service around the time he got married, but the command wanted him around as an adviser. Strategy, the law, whatever. And he did a good job. They didn't listen to him as much as they should have, they still don't, but things would've been worse without him."

"You sound like you admire him," Lennon said.

"Admire him?" Dixie snorted. "I hate the slimy fucker. But he's done a bit of good, here and there. See, it means we've got a direct line up to Stormont. I know by your face, you think that's not right. But if it wasn't for the likes of Graham Carlisle, people round here wouldn't have a voice up on the hill. The rest of the politicians, and I mean the Unionists, the ones supposed to be on our side, they think we're dog shit on the streets."

Lennon asked, "Exactly how involved was he, back in the day?"

"He was at the front line at one time, but not for long."

"You mean, carrying out actions?"

Dixie nodded. "Aye. But he got a sickener early on, so he backed off after that."

"A sickener? Doing what?"

Dixie's gaze flicked toward Roscoe at the far end of the room, made sure he wasn't within earshot.

"I'm guessing you're not here officially, right?"

"That's right," Lennon said.

"This is between you and me. Goes no further. You understand?"

"I understand."

Dixie cleared his throat and started talking.

"Graham had not long joined up, he'd been on a few training exercises, collected a bit of protection money, that sort of thing.

Nothing serious. But him and a couple of his mates wanted to prove themselves, show me and the Brigade commanders they had the balls for the job. So they called up one of the Catholic taxi firms, ordered a cab out of south Belfast, near the museum, I think it was. Anyway, they'd got a gun from somewhere, don't ask me where. And they waited for this taxi to show up, and pop, they shot the driver dead."

"Jesus," Lennon said.

"Well, that was enough for Graham Carlisle," Dixie said. "He didn't have the nerve to get his hands dirty like the rest of us. So he made sure he got his degree and all the rest of it."

"Who were these mates?" Lennon asked.

Dixie shook his head. "I'm here to talk about Graham Carlisle. I'm not naming anyone else."

Lennon took the photograph from his pocket and placed it on the tabletop. "Take a look at this," he said.

Dixie fished a pair of reading glasses from his tracksuit bottoms and perched them on his nose. He lifted the picture and studied it at arm's length. A sigh wheezed out of his barrel chest.

"All right. I couldn't tell you who the boys at the back are," he said, "I could be one of them, you never know. But that's Raymond Drew there on the left. Graham married his sister. Lovely wee girl, she was. Raymond was a horrible cunt, though. One of those quiet boys, you know? You can never tell what they're thinking, but you can see they're going a hundred miles an hour behind their eyes. And Howard was the same."

"Howard?" Lennon asked.

Dixie put the photograph back on the table, turned it to face Lennon, and pointed to the middle figure in the front row.

"Howard . . . Howard . . . hang on, what was his second name? Monaghan. Aye, Howard Monaghan. The Sparkle, they used to call him."

Lennon looked at the young man between Carlisle and Drew. For the first time, really. He'd been distracted by the other two and hadn't paid much mind to the man in the middle.

"Why'd they call him that?" he asked.

"Because he was an electrician by trade. A spark. Apprenticed in the shipyard, I think, but he was a bit, you know, light on his feet. What my auld da would've called a jessie, a nancy boy. So they started calling him the Sparkle in the shipyard, and it followed him around after that. He didn't seem to mind it."

"What was his relationship to Drew and Carlisle?"

"I don't know about Graham, but him and Raymond were close. They met in the merchant navy, and they were tight as anything ever since. Sometimes they'd go across the water together for work, when they could find it in the same place. Raymond was laying bricks, and the Sparkle was doing the wiring. There were a few whispers among the boys about them, how close they were."

Lennon asked, "You mean, they were gay? They were a couple?"

"No, not that. A lot of the lads didn't like queers, but they never bothered me. What a fella does in his own home is up to him, so long as he's not hurting anyone, that's what I think. But the lads in the Brigade would never tolerate it. Either way, that's not what Raymond and the Sparkle were. They just shared things, did everything together. They chased after women together, and if they couldn't get one, the lads used to say they'd settle for each other. But I never really believed that. Not after the way the Sparkle reacted."

"Reacted to what?" Lennon asked.

"We were drinking late one night in a place like this, but over on the Shankill. Raymond and the Sparkle were there. They never drank much, not like the rest of us, but they were hanging around anyway. One of the boys, Jimmy Mercer, started slagging them, you know, trying to get a bit of banter going. Asked them what they got up to when no one was looking. So Howard, the Sparkle, he lit on him. Near took the head off him before Raymond pulled him away. That's what I remember the most, Raymond with his arms around the Sparkle, whispering to him, calming him down."

Lennon looked at the photograph again, at the young man in the middle. Studied the face. Fine-boned, sharp-eyed, pretty compared to Raymond's flat features.

"Is he still around?" Lennon asked.

"I'm not sure," Dixie said. "I haven't seen him in, God, more than twenty years. That was at the funeral for Raymond's wife. I noticed him sort of hovering in the background, watching everyone."

"You didn't speak to him?"

"No. He'd been drummed out of the Brigade long before then."

"What for?" Lennon asked.

The corners of Dixie's mouth turned down in disgust. "There was a couple dealing speed and cannabis out of a flat toward Holywood. Would've been no problem, but they weren't paying anything back to the Brigade. So a few boys were sent out to have a word, nothing too rough, just let them know they had to throw a few quid our way if they wanted to stay in business. The Sparkle—Howard—he went with them. But things got out of hand. The Sparkle went mad on them, gave both of them an awful doing. Put them in hospital. One of the boys, a friend of mine, told me afterward. Said it was like he was taking something out on them, something hateful. My mate told me he'd never seen the like of it, and this boy's seen plenty. Said it scared him. He tried to stop it, but he couldn't, said the Sparkle was like a mad dog. Raymond wasn't there to calm him. I think that's what Raymond did for the Sparkle: kept him under control, stopped him going over the line. After that, no one wanted the Sparkle about the place any more. So he was cut off and told not to come back. That was maybe thirty years ago."

Lennon lifted the photograph, looked from one face to the next. His eyes were drawn back to Howard Monaghan, the Sparkle, the sharp lines of his mouth, the clear blue of his eyes.

And with a cold realisation that crackled through his mind, Lennon knew he had seen this man before.

"Roscoe," he called.

Patterson ambled back from the bar, sucking at his bottle of beer. "What?"

"I need you to drive me somewhere."

"I'm not your bloody taxi service."

Lennon looked up at him. "Please. One last favour. I need this."

Patterson and Dixie exchanged a glance.

"All right," Patterson said. "Come on."

41

Flanagan walked toward her office, a plastic-packed sandwich and a bottle of water in her hands. Her appetite had been close to nil since the diagnosis at the clinic on Friday, but after the press call, her stomach had begun grumbling. Hours later, it hadn't let up, forcing her to go out and find a newsagent's shop with a cooler.

She arrived at her door, absent-mindedly reached for the handle, and opened it. Only when the door swung inward did she remember that she'd locked it as she left.

DCI Dan Hewitt looked up from where he stood hunched over the drawers of the filing cabinet, his fingers dipped between the sheets of paper.

Flanagan froze on the threshold.

She knew what he was looking for, and that knowledge must have been clear on her face. The papers she'd taken from Lennon's apartment lay inside the locked drawer of her desk. A few more minutes, along with a little brute force, and he would have found the file.

"Can I help you with something?" she asked.

Hewitt removed his fingers from the filing cabinet drawer, pushed it closed, and put his hands in his pockets. "I was just looking for . . . uh . . . I thought I might have left . . ."

Flanagan left the door open and walked toward her desk. She

placed the sandwich and water there and waited while Hewitt desperately scrambled for a lie.

Eventually, he stopped, and his expression turned from barely concealed panic back to the smug self-confidence he'd worn the last time she saw him.

"I believe you searched Jack's apartment yesterday morning," he said.

"That's right."

She moved to the other side of the desk, kept it between him and her.

"I went through the list of items you took," he said.

"That list is none of your business."

He smiled. "I'm C3, Intelligence Branch. Everything is my business."

She did not retreat from his hard stare.

"There was one thing missing from the list," he said, circling the desk, coming closer. "I heard a whisper you'd found a file there. That you took it along with all the other stuff. But I didn't see it on the list."

"I don't know what you're talking about," she said, a tremor creeping into her voice.

"Yes you do," he said. Close, now. Close enough for her to smell his aftershave. "Let's not play games. We both know what I'm talking about. We're all grown-ups here. You know, I can be a good friend. Or I can make this a very cold place for you. I mean, just look how things are going for Jack."

Flanagan swallowed, let her gaze drop. She felt his breath on her skin.

"Come on," Hewitt said. "Do the right thing. You don't want me for an enemy, I can promise you that."

Flanagan cursed under her breath, a weak and futile exhalation. She unfixed the key ring from her belt, unlocked and opened her desk's top drawer, and took a step back. The thick unmarked file lay on top of a collection of loose papers.

Hewitt looked down into the drawer, then at Flanagan.

"Go on," she said, spitting the words at him. "Just bloody take it and get out."

He reached in with his right hand.

The high squeal he emitted as she slammed the drawer closed on his fingers caused a feeling of deep pleasure in Flanagan such as she hadn't felt for weeks.

She held it closed tight. As Hewitt scrabbled at the drawer with his free hand, she leaned her hip against the metal, applied her full weight, made him squeal again, louder and longer.

He reached for the pistol holstered at his waistband, but she was quicker. She pressed the muzzle of his own Glock 17 beneath his jaw.

"Fucking crazy b—"

Flanagan brought her lips to his ear, let him feel her teeth, and whispered, "You ever try to intimidate me again, I will cut your fucking balls off. Are we clear?"

She gave the drawer one more shove with her hip, savoured his last agonized yelp, then let him go. Hewitt staggered back against the wall, clutching his bleeding hand to his stomach, the flesh around his knuckles already swelling.

Flanagan opened the window, looked down at the gravel-covered roof of the building's adjoining wing. Hewitt's pistol bounced three times before coming to rest beside a skylight. She threw the magazine after it, then turned back to him.

"I'm sure someone in maintenance can lend you a ladder."

Hewitt stared at her, blood dripping onto his good suit.

"Go on," she said. "Be a good boy and fuck off."

He said nothing as he left, didn't glance back at her.

Flanagan slumped down into her chair and let the adrenaline rush through her, sending shakes from her center to her fingertips.

42

The BMW pulled up outside the house at Deramore Gardens. Roscoe Patterson looked at the police tape on the front door.

"Here, is this where that woman was killed?"

"Yes," Lennon said, opening the passenger door.

"You can't go in there," Patterson said.

"I'm not."

Lennon closed the door and walked across the street, watching the house with the TO LET sign still standing in its overgrown garden. The same garden from which a man had watched Lennon three days before. A man of around sixty, with fine features and blue eyes.

He heard the driver's door slam shut.

"Where you going?" Patterson called after him.

"Just wait there," Lennon said.

"I don't like it," Patterson said. "I don't need this sort of trouble."

Lennon looked back over his shoulder. "I'm just taking a look. Give me a minute."

Patterson leaned against the car, shook his head in resignation. Lennon opened the driveway gate. It turned silently on its hinge. A red-brick semi-detached house, almost a mirror image of the one Rea had inherited from her uncle.

Lennon walked across the concrete to the window. He peered

through the glass into the living room. Empty, a bare wooden floor, no furniture, nothing on the walls but ghosts of the pictures that had once hung there.

He skirted the side of the house and approached the high wooden gate that led to the rear of the property. Between the slats, he could see a dilapidated garden shed, the lawn in need of mowing, large pots overrun by weeds. Last year's leaves lay in drifts. A hole in the gate at waist height allowed his hand through to the bolt on the other side. Lennon slid it back, and the gate yawned open. He caught it before it could slam against the wall.

Stepping through, he kept a watch on the windows of the kitchen extension that stretched beyond the back of the house. Again, he went to the glass and looked inside. Again, empty, gaps where the cooker and fridge would be.

Lennon reached for the back door handle, expecting it to be immovable. Instead, it turned. The door sighed as it loosened in its frame.

He stood still for a time, unsure if he had the courage to push it open, to step inside. Then he thought of Rea and put his fingertips to the wood.

Cool air seeped from the house. Lennon entered the stillness. His feet scuffed on ancient linoleum. He advanced through the kitchen with as little noise as his lopsided gait would allow. An open door, an empty sitting room on the other side, the hallway beyond.

Lennon peered into every corner of each room. When he reached the bottom of the stairs, he looked up to the darkened landing.

No one here, he thought. No one here.

He mounted the first step. As he ascended, he became aware

of the thud in his chest, the shallowness of his breath. He paused, swallowed, waited for the straining to ease. When it did, he climbed again.

At the top, he faced four doors. To the rear, he guessed the bathroom. He pushed the door open and stood back. Nothing stirred but dust and a steady drip from the shower-head pinging on the enamel of the bath. Limescale lined the toilet bowl.

Lennon went to the next door, opened it, let it swing back into the room. A weathered and stained carpet. An old wardrobe against one wall, its doors hanging crooked from their hinges. He entered, went to the window and looked out over the back garden.

Two more rooms to the front of the house. One stood open, a box room, barely big enough to hold a single bed. Again, he went to the window. From here, he had a clear view of Raymond Drew's house. He'd be able to see anyone who came or went. Still leaning against his car, Roscoe Patterson stood smoking a cigarette.

Lennon went to the last room. He hesitated at the door, afraid of what might be on the other side, even though he had no reason to expect it to be anything but empty. He turned the handle and pushed the door open.

A large leather-bound book lay at the center of the worn carpet.

Lennon swallowed. The room had a stale smell, a man's smell, heavy with sweat and mildew. A sleeping bag in the corner, a few empty tins, some bottled water, a brown satchel, loose pencils and paper.

An iPhone, its screen black. He knew whose it was, and the knowledge chilled him.

Pictures taped to the wall, drawn in pencil. The sketches were crude, but done with enough flair for Lennon to recognize the woman rendered on each page. Most showing her at windows or in doorways, looking out, observed from a distance. Rea Carlisle reborn in slashes of grey.

He stepped over the threshold and into the tainted air. Five paces took him to the book, its cover glowering with a dull sheen. Lennon grunted with effort as he knelt down. He took a clean tissue from his pocket and kept it between his fingertips and the leather as he opened the book and turned the first page.

Just as Rea had said, the fingernail, the lock of hair. The name, Gwen Headley.

"Christ," Lennon whispered.

He would not look at it any more. Time to hand it over to Flanagan, to tell her what he knew. Let her track down the Sparkle, Howard Monaghan, the man who had killed Rea. And, Lennon believed, the man who had killed the people in this book, with or without Raymond Drew.

Lennon put a hand on the floor to steady himself as he got his legs under him. Pain stabbed at his flank as he stood upright. He went to the corner and lifted the phone, pressed and held the button at the top edge to turn it on. When it finally booted and found a signal, the battery icon showed a thin red line of remaining power. An image flickered in his mind: Rea calling him from this phone, no idea she had less than a day to live.

He dialled the number for Ladas Drive from memory.

"DCI Serena Flanagan," Lennon said.

"Who's calling?"

"DI Jack Lennon."

A few moments' silence, then, "Hold on."

He walked to the window overlooking the street as he listened to the synthetic chimes of the hold music. Patterson no longer stood by his BMW. Lennon couldn't see through the car's tinted windows, but he imagined Patterson in the driver's seat, debating whether to drive off and leave him. Once he'd spoken to Flanagan, he'd go down and tell Patterson to make himself scarce. His presence here would only complicate matters.

A click, then, "Where are you?"

"I'm in Deramore Gardens," Lennon said.

"At the house?" Flanagan asked. "Christ, you've some neck."

"No, across the road," Lennon said. He gave her the house number. "You'd better get down here."

"Are you ready to hand yourself in?" she asked.

"Just come now."

Lennon hung up and returned the phone to the corner where he'd found it. He walked back to the landing, closed the door behind him. Gripping the handrail to keep his balance, he made his lopsided way down the stairs, each step jarring his side.

He heard the choked gurgling as he neared the bottom.

From the hall, through the open doors and the rear sitting room, he saw them in the kitchen. Roscoe Patterson on his back, the hilt of what looked like a filleting knife jutting out from his chest. His breath bubbled wet in his throat, his blank eyes staring somewhere beyond the ceiling.

Crouched over Patterson, a man, the one Lennon had seen in front of this house three days ago. Small, slender, the vest he wore showing a dancer's hard and wiry body. The fine features given a suggestion of jaggedness by age. White hair greased flat to his skull. The tattoo on his neck that a shirt collar had concealed before.

He was watching Patterson's dying breaths with a kind of distant interest, like a child studying an insect impaled on a pin.

After a while, he lifted his head to look at Lennon.

The Sparkle said, "Hello, Jack."

43

The policeman took slow steps toward the kitchen, like a child coming to meet its punishment. He could not hide his limp any more than the big man on the floor could hide the knife in his chest.

"Howard," the cop said.

"No one calls me that."

"No," Lennon said. "They call you the Sparkle."

The Sparkle stood upright, took a step back from the growing puddle of deep red on the linoleum.

"That's right," he said. "Since I was a boy in the shipyard. They used to say, look, here comes the Sparkle, watch him dance along like a wee girl."

Lennon stopped at the kitchen doorway. "Did that make you angry?"

"No. I didn't like it, but names stick, don't they?" He looked down at the man who had stopped breathing. "Who's your friend?"

"His name was Roscoe. He wasn't my friend. He just helped me out sometimes."

"Roscoe." The Sparkle felt a smile on his lips. "That's a stupid name."

"Why did you kill him?" the cop asked.

"He tried to hit me. And I got angry. I can be quick-tempered sometimes. One minute I'm fine, and then it's all . . ."

He waved a hand toward the man lying at his feet, sure the policeman would understand his meaning.

"I won't hit you," Lennon said. "I won't come any closer. We'll just talk. All right?"

"Who did you call?" the Sparkle asked.

The policeman shook his head. "I didn't call anyone."

"Liar. Was it that woman cop? The one I saw on the television?"

"I told you, I didn't call anyone."

"Will she come here?"

"No," Lennon said. "No one's coming."

"I'd like to meet her," the Sparkle said. "I'd like to show her things."

"Like what?"

"Secret things."

Lennon took one step further into the kitchen. "Do you want me to bring you to her? I can do that. She wants to meet you too."

"I know you called her. I know she's coming here. But I suppose she'll bring others. Listen."

Somewhere not too far away, the high whoop of a siren.

Lennon asked, "Did you kill Rea?"

"Yes."

"Why?"

"To get the photograph from her."

"But she didn't have it."

"I know that now. I didn't mean to kill her. I shouldn't have. But I did. And now look where we are. My wicked temper. My uncle said I had a temper ever since I was a wee boy. Wicked wee bastard, he used to call me. Wicked, wicked, wicked wee bastard."

"Did you kill the people in that book?"

"Yes. Wicked, wicked, wicked, wicked . . ."

He let the words trail off into a whisper, like smoke on his breath.

"Did Raymond Drew help you?"

"No," the Sparkle said. "He never had the nerve for it. He wasn't strong like me. He didn't have the wicked in him. But he liked me to tell him about the things I did. I wrote them down for him. Sent him things. We used to look at the book together. Just the two of us. It was nice. He was my friend."

"Just a friend?" Lennon asked.

The Sparkle tilted his head. "What do you mean?"

Lennon kept his gaze hard on his. "I spoke to someone today. Someone you used to know."

"Who?"

"Doesn't matter."

"Tell me."

"Dixie Stoops. He said you and Raymond might have been more than friends."

"He's a fucking liar!" The force of the Sparkle's voice bent him at the waist, his arms tucked into his sides, spit arcing from his mouth like sparks.

"I know," Lennon said. "I didn't believe a word of it."

The Sparkle laughed and wagged a finger at the cop. "You're trying to bait me." He took one step toward the door leading to the garden. "Do you still have the photograph?"

"Yes," Lennon said. "Do you want it back?"

"Doesn't matter now." He moved closer to the door. "It's all lost. All gone. There's nothing to hold back for any more."

Lennon came further into the room. "What do you mean?"

"I've nothing to lose now. No more secrets to keep. Everyone knows, don't they? Everyone knows how wicked I am. No point in hiding it any more. Everyone knows how bad I am. How dirty. I'm a wicked boy and everybody knows it."

The Sparkle felt a giggle in his tummy, a shameful laugh, like when he'd been caught with his fingers in his pants and he couldn't help but grin.

"All the other mummies know," the Sparkle said. "They all know, and they'll point at me, and they'll say there's the dirty boy. The dirty, dirty boy, the bad boy, the wicked boy, the—"

He slapped himself hard across the cheek. Brought his mind back into focus. Don't let this cop see the madness in you, he thought. He'll think you're weak. The Sparkle slapped himself again, harder, so the cop wavered in his vision.

Perhaps he should kill this cop. Lennon was a big man, but weakened by whatever made him limp. Still, the cop would fight. The Sparkle was quick, but quick enough to take the knife from the dying man's chest before the policeman could move on him? He would not tackle the cop without a weapon.

And the sirens coming ever closer. No time.

"I should go now," he said.

"Please don't," the policeman said. "I want to talk to you."

"Do you have a gun?" the Sparkle asked.

"No. It was taken off me when I was suspended."

"Then you can't shoot me when I run."

"Don't run. Please."

"And you can hardly chase me with that limp."

Lennon came closer. "Please stay here. You're right. She's coming, the policewoman. She wants to meet you. You can show her whatever you want."

The Sparkle shook his head. "No. I should run away now. Oh, I know it's only a matter of time before you catch up with me. You or the woman cop. And I've been holding myself back for so long. And now it doesn't matter."

The Sparkle took a sharp step forward, his foot splashing in the blood. Lennon jerked back.

"But you remember this. Everything that happens now is on your head. I've spent so many years keeping this inside me, the wicked, the lightning, and now it's free. Because you set it free. When you see the bodies, you'll know they're yours as much as mine. And you can keep that book upstairs. There's no need for it now. When my end comes, everyone will know. You before anyone."

He turned, ran for the door, to the back of the garden, light on his feet like everyone always said. Light as a feather. Up and over the fence, away, riding the breeze like a floating ember, the policeman's hoarse shouts rising through the air behind him.

44

Flanagan listened to DS Calvin's hard breathing as he pushed the car through the Sunday traffic, a marked vehicle with blues flashing and siren wailing ahead of them. He's loving this, she thought, like a boy with a computer game.

The pleasant middle-class neighborhoods whipped by as they approached the Ormeau Road, Edwardian houses, bay windows, hedge-bound gardens. The good citizens looked up from their lawnmowers and secateurs to see the commotion as it passed. Flanagan was thrown against the passenger door as Calvin made the right turn onto the main road. Other road users moved aside, some braking hard as the police cars cut across their paths at traffic lights.

"Calm down," Flanagan said.

"I'm just trying to keep—"

He slammed his foot on the brake pedal to avoid a bus that pulled out from a stop. The driver waved them past.

"Fucking idiot!" Calvin shouted, despite the negligible chance of the bus driver hearing him.

"I said, calm down," Flanagan said. "This isn't *Starsky and Hutch*, for Christ's sake."

"Sorry," Calvin said, but he kept after the marked car all the same.

A left turn took them into the narrow side streets, smaller

houses bunched together. The siren echoed between the buildings. Another left into Deramore Gardens, a hundred yards along the house where Rea Carlisle died.

The patrol car skidded to a halt alongside a BMW kitted out with tinted glass, spoilers and exaggerated wheel arches. Calvin pulled in to the curb. Flanagan had the passenger door open, her foot on the ground before the car came to a rest. She looked across the street for the house number Lennon had given her.

There, the side gate ajar.

She sprinted over, along the driveway.

"Ma'am!" Calvin called from behind. "Ma'am, wait!"

Flanagan pushed the side gate back against the wall. She unholstered her Glock, kept it aimed at the ground. "Jack Lennon, show yourself."

Her voice resonated between the neighboring houses. No reply. She heard Calvin's footsteps behind her, the heavier boots of the uniformed men following him.

The kitchen door stood open. She edged toward it. Her fingertip slipped inside her pistol's trigger guard, felt the cold curve within. With her free hand, she waved at the others to stay behind.

A single concrete step at the entrance to the kitchen. She put one foot upon it, eased forward until she could see inside.

There, kneeling on the floor, his back to her, Jack Lennon. Another man, on his back, staring at the ceiling. A red pool spread around them both. Lennon's hand at the man's neck. The handle of a knife, the blade hidden in the man's chest.

Flanagan raised her Glock. "Move away from him, Jack."

"He's dead," Lennon said.

"Move away. Right now."

Lennon put his hands to the blood-slicked floor to push

himself up and away from the body, a deep groan in his throat from the effort. He got to his feet and turned to Flanagan. Red stained his knees, dripped from his fingertips.

Flanagan locked eyes with him. "Put your hands on your head."

Lennon didn't argue.

"Now step outside, slowly, very slowly."

Flanagan backed away, out into the clear air, away from the death smell. Lennon followed.

"Face down on the ground."

His face twisted in pain as he obeyed, each movement awkward and stiff.

When his cheek rested on the concrete, Flanagan said, "Hands behind your back."

One of the uniformed men had the cuffs ready, swooped down, had Lennon's wrists bound within seconds. Flanagan clicked her fingers, pointed into the kitchen. Calvin raced in to check on the man who lay in there.

The two uniformed officers rolled Lennon onto his back and pulled him into a sitting position. Flanagan slid her Glock back into its holster and hunkered down in front of him. Unshaven. Dark circles beneath his eyes. Lines a man his age shouldn't have.

"Who is that?" she asked, tilting her head toward the kitchen door.

"His name's Roscoe Patterson," Lennon said. "He's known to the police. I didn't kill him."

"Then who did?"

"Howard Monaghan. They call him the Sparkle. He also killed Rea Carlisle, and others. Upstairs in the front bedroom, there's a book. The book Rea told me about. The one I told you about. Rea's phone's in there too."

"And where is this man now?"

Lennon looked toward the fence at the rear of the garden. "He got away."

Flanagan stood upright, instructed the uniformed men to help Lennon to his feet. They rooted through his pockets, emptied the scant contents onto the ground.

Calvin emerged from the house. He shook his head.

Flanagan said, "Jack Lennon, I am placing you under arrest on suspicion of murder. You do not have to say anything, but I must caution you that if you do not mention when questioned something which you later rely on in court, it may harm your defense. If you do say anything, it may be given in evidence. Do you understand?"

"I understand," Lennon said. "But the longer you keep your focus on me, the less chance you have of catching up with Monaghan. If he kills again, it'll be your cross to bear."

"I have plenty of crosses," she said, leading him away. "One more won't break me."

45

Lennon sat on a hard plastic chair in the corner of the room, eyes closed, head back, pain resonating within his skull. He listened to Flanagan pace circles around the table that stood at its center. Upon the table, the book, open, its secrets spilling out.

"How much of it did you read?" Flanagan asked.

"Only a page or two," Lennon said, opening his eyes. "Enough to get the idea. You?"

She ceased her march, stared somewhere far away. "All of it," she said.

"How bad?"

She shook her head. "The worst I've ever seen. Not all of it is coherent. Some of it's just lunatic screeds, but there's enough detail there to get the picture."

"It could be some sort of fantasy. He might have seen reports of missing persons in the press and made up stories for himself."

Flanagan looked sideways at Lennon. "Do you believe that?"

"No," he said.

She exhaled, a long and despairing hiss from her chest. "We'll get DNA samples from a good number of the entries, mostly off fingernails. Even if the bodies can't be recovered, family members can be tested for matches. At least there'll be some resolution for them."

"But he's still out there," Lennon said. "Somewhere."

"Howard Monaghan's last passport expired two years ago." Flanagan resumed her pacing. "His driving licence a year before that. He hasn't had a vehicle registered to him for three years, hasn't completed a Self Assessment tax return in five, or paid National Insurance. No credit history, one bank account that hasn't been touched in a decade, the last time he showed up on the electoral roll was the late nineties. This man, the Sparkle you call him, has been gradually disappearing for years."

"What about the house he was in?" Lennon asked.

"Three days after Raymond Drew died, he walked into the letting agent's office with a cash deposit, three months' rent, a reference from a previous landlord who doesn't exist, and signed the rental contract with someone else's name. He showed them a counterfeit driving licence and a stolen bank statement. I have to assume he wanted to watch his friend's house, see if he could get in and take the book. Calvin had knocked on the door when he was canvassing the neighbors for witnesses, but there was no answer. He assumed the house was unoccupied."

"Did you find anything else there?"

She sat down on the chair beside Lennon.

"There was a key to the front door of the house Rea died in. It looked new, freshly cut, with a locksmith's tag on it. And that lock was changed only last week."

"So who gave it to him?" Lennon asked.

Flanagan had no answer. She stared at the window opposite, her eyes distant.

"Night before last," Lennon said, "when I tried to call you. I was trying to tell you he'd phoned me."

"You were drunk," she said.

"Even so, you should have listened to me."

"What difference would it have made?" she asked.

"Probably none," Lennon said. "Either way, he's going to kill again. And soon."

"So you say."

He turned his head. She kept her gaze forward, her face expressionless.

"That's what he told me," Lennon said. "You've seen what's in that book. You saw what he did to Roscoe. You saw what he did to Rea."

"All I saw of Mr. Patterson was you kneeling over him with blood on your hands. You're still the most direct link I have to Rea Carlisle's death. Don't kid yourself, Inspector. You haven't wriggled out of this yet. You're still a suspect."

She turned to look at him.

"You're the only person I found at the scene. Maybe this Howard Monaghan, the Sparkle, did all these things in the book. But you turn up at the scenes of two murders and I haven't seen a hair on the Sparkle's arse. I've only your word for any of this, and right now, your word isn't worth two shits."

Lennon asked, "After all that's happened today, you still think I did that to Rea?"

Before she could answer, a knock at the door.

"Come," she said, not taking her eyes off Lennon.

Gracey opened the door, a sheet of A4 printed paper in his hand. "Sorry to disturb you, ma'am."

Flanagan turned her attention to the doorway. "Go on," she said.

"You were called to Deramore Gardens this afternoon." Gracey did not look up from his page.

"That's right," Flanagan said.

"Well, just going through the incident reports for today, there was a car hijacking a couple of streets away. A young woman was getting into her Vauxhall Corsa. Someone pulled her to the ground, grabbed the keys from her hand, and took off in the car. Her head got a bit of a bang on the pavement, but she gave a pretty good description of the assailant."

Now he looked at Lennon, only for a moment.

"Small athletic build, maybe five-six, aged around sixty, wearing a vest and trousers, dark stains on the vest."

Flanagan sat silent for a few seconds, then said, "All right, thank you. I'll want to talk to the victim."

"I'll set it up," Gracey said. He nodded and left, pulling the door closed behind him.

Flanagan did not turn back to Lennon. "You're still a suspect," she said.

"I know," Lennon said. "Now, do you want to go after this piece of shit?"

Flanagan nodded. "Yes, I think I will. Where do I start?"

"With Graham Carlisle," Lennon said.

46

"You bloody bastard," Graham Carlisle said.

The Sparkle smiled. "I knew you'd be angry," he said. "That's why it had to be here."

They stood on one of the boat-like platforms that rose through the central atrium of Victoria Square, escalators and spiralling staircases all around them, rising upward to the shopping mall's glass dome and observation deck. The shops had closed two hours ago, but families, couples and teenagers milled all around them, coming and going from the cinema and the restaurants. Their clamouring voices reverberated in the cavernous space, ringing in the Sparkle's ears, eating into his skull.

A remarkable clarity had settled within him over the last few hours as he fled to his home, washed and changed. As if his life, and the world around him, had suddenly come into focus. As if cataracts had been removed from his eyes. He had never felt more rational, more purposeful.

Perhaps this wasn't the end. He had devised a plan, so simple, a way to survive. All he had to do was hold his nerve. Let everyone else fall to pieces, like Graham.

And if this was the end, the final implosion of his universe, then it wasn't so bad.

"You didn't have to hurt her," Graham said, his voice quivering with rage and sorrow. "I just wanted the photo and the book. That was all. You didn't have to do that."

When Graham had come to him with the key to the house, the Sparkle had been thrilled. He had been watching Raymond's home ever since he'd rented the place opposite. Waiting for an opportunity to go in and take what was his. Then Graham had tracked him down, given him the key, told him to get his filth out of that house, never show his face near there again, and it had seemed a gift.

But Graham was right, he hadn't had to touch Rea. Now look where he was.

"Maybe not," the Sparkle said. "But it's too late now."

Graham smelled of alcohol. His suit seemed to hang loose on him, as if it belonged to a bigger man, and his shirt needed ironing. A black shape lurked in the waistband of his trousers.

The Sparkle asked, "Are you going to shoot me?"

Graham's red eyes flickered. He wet his lips with his tongue. "I should. I should blow your bloody brains out for what you did. And I might. If you force me to defend myself."

"Here? In front of all these people?"

Graham straightened, tried to look taller. "I might."

The Sparkle shook his head. "I don't think you will. If you shoot me, everyone will see you, they'll recognize you. And you'll be finished. When it comes down to it, you're just too selfish to sacrifice yourself. Aren't you?"

"Fuck you," Graham said, stuttering over the F, his mouth seemingly unused to such dirty words. "What did you call me here for?"

"I need your help."

Graham's jaw dropped open. "Why would I help you? After what you've done, why would I lift a finger for you?"

"To return the favour."

Graham's head shook, anger turning to confusion on his face.

The Sparkle sighed. "You asked me for help. You asked me to get that book, and then the photograph. I did what you wanted. Or I tried, anyway."

Graham took a step closer, the anger rising again. "I didn't ask you to kill my daughter."

The Sparkle felt spittle on his cheeks. He looked over the railing, down to the concourse below. Two uniformed cops strolled among the people, eating frozen yogurt from paper tubs.

"All right," he said. "Let's you and me both go down there and talk to those police officers. We'll tell them what we did. We'll tell them you wanted that photograph so you could save your own skin. I can say, honest to God, officer, he didn't mean for her to die. Will we do that?"

Graham's fists grabbed at the Sparkle's clothes, pushed him back against the rail. "Shut your mouth," he hissed.

"And then we could tell them about what we did to that taxi driver when we were boys. You feel so bad about it, why not get it off your chest? Come on, let's go down there together and talk to them."

Another shove. "I said, shut your fucking mouth."

"Graham, Graham, Graham." The Sparkle put his hands on the other man's shoulders. "People are looking."

"Let them fucking look."

"They'll have phones. They might start taking pictures."

One more push, no strength behind it, and Graham backed away. "So what do you want?"

The Sparkle glanced over his shoulder. The cops were moving on. They dropped their tubs and plastic spoons in a litter bin.

"I need to run," he said. "They know who I am. They have the photograph. And the book."

"Oh, Christ." Graham's shoulders rose and fell. His face paled.

"I've no passport any more. I can't travel abroad. I need to go over the border, down south."

"They have the photo? With you and me in it?"

"That's right. And the book."

"Oh God, what am I going to do? I'm finished. Oh Jesus, I'm finished. What'll I do?" Graham went to the railing and leaned on it.

"Stop panicking, for a start. That's all they have to connect us. For all the cops know, we haven't seen each other since that photo was taken. The book's my concern. You've committed no crimes. Not unless I tell them otherwise."

"But my career. When the papers get hold of this, I'm done."

"But you won't go to prison. If I get away, the worst you'll have to face is a scandal and an early retirement. If I get away."

Graham covered his eyes with his hands. His shoulders jerked and shuddered. "My little girl died for this," he said, the words choked between sobs of self-pity.

The Sparkle had the urge to spit on him. Such a pathetic man. So weak. Had he any balls, he would have gone straight to the cops with the book, and his daughter would be alive.

"You can cry all you want when I'm gone," the Sparkle said. "Now pull yourself together and listen to me."

Graham turned his wet face to the Sparkle's. "What kind of animal are you?"

Quick as water on glass, the Sparkle reached down to Graham's waistband, seized the pistol in his right hand, hugged him around the shoulders with his left arm. He kept the gun pressed flat against Graham's soft stomach, hidden from view.

"Stop your crying and listen to me or I'll blow a hole through your gut right in front of all these people. You don't have the nerve to do it, but I do. That's the only difference between you and me. I've got the strength. You haven't."

Graham wiped his sleeve across his eyes.

"Are you listening?" the Sparkle asked.

Graham nodded.

"Good. I need money. Enough to live on for a year or two. I have a bit hidden away, sterling and euro, but it's not enough. I want fifty thousand euro in cash."

"I can't," Graham said, his jowls quivering as he shook his head. "It's too much."

"Don't lie to me." The Sparkle jabbed at Graham's belly with the pistol's muzzle. "You've got ten times that, probably more. You want me out of the way, you'll hand it over."

"Christ. All right. I'll need a few days."

"We don't have a few days. I want it here, tomorrow, at twelve. You show up a minute later, I'm going to take your gun and start shooting till the police get here. Women, children, I don't care. I've nothing to lose. And when the cops arrive, I'm going to lower the gun, like a good boy, and I'm going to tell them everything."

He leaned close, his lips against Graham's ear. "Everything," he whispered. "Every dirty little secret."

Graham whined. "I can't. I just can't."

"You know I'll do it. And every dead mummy, and every dead baby, they'll be on your head. And everyone will know you could've stopped it. And when I've told them, I will end it all."

The Sparkle looked around, slipped the pistol into his coat pocket, and stepped back.

"Tomorrow at noon," he said. "Not a minute later."

He walked away through the chattering crowd, almost tasting the clarity of it all.

The Sparkle had never felt so well. The Sparkle had never shone so bright.

47

Lennon's mobile rang. Number withheld.

"Yes?"

"Hello again, Jack."

Lennon sat down on the plastic-covered couch. After Flanagan had let him go, he'd returned to the apartment Roscoe Patterson had given him the use of. It felt strange knowing the owner was dead, the air inside somehow different, colder. Now that he was no longer being chased by Flanagan, he could use his own mobile again. The first call he'd made had been to Bernie McKenna. It had gone straight to voicemail.

Now this.

He listened to the Sparkle's breathing. After a few seconds, he asked, "What do you want?"

"Just to talk. I was a bit emotional this afternoon. I wasn't myself."

"I didn't think killing bothered you that much."

"It doesn't bother me at all." Lennon could hear the smile in his voice. "Not after all this time. But it does get my blood up. It's a dizzy feeling, like going on a fairground ride. You know. You've killed people."

Lennon swallowed. "Yes, I have. But I didn't get any pleasure out of it."

A small, childish laugh. "Oh, Jack. See, that's what people like you never understand. I didn't get any pleasure from killing all those people. I never killed anyone for fun."

"Then why?"

"Because it was . . . necessary."

"What?"

"To take what I needed from those people, to let the wicked out, it was necessary to kill them. Killing was a part of it, but it was never the point. Do you understand?"

"No, I don't. And I never will."

"Of course not. But don't worry, I'll be gone soon enough. You won't have to think about it any more."

"Gone where?"

"Far away where you can't touch me. Not you or anybody else."

"You've no passport," Lennon said. "It's too hard to fake one now. You can't get out of Ireland. You can only go south across the border. How long do you think you can hide out down there?"

"As long as I need to."

"And what happens when you want to kill again? What if you slip up? You're not a young man. How long can you keep doing this?"

"As long as I need to. Anyway. Must go. I just wanted to say goodbye."

"Maybe you'll see me again. Maybe sooner than you think."

"Oh?"

"Maybe we're getting close to you."

"And maybe not. Whichever, you'd better make your move soon or I'll be gone. Bye-bye, Jack."

Click.

Lennon dropped the phone on the coffee table. It spun away, its display dimming. He thought of Graham Carlisle and Serena Flanagan, and of Rea, and how she hadn't deserved to die that way.

He thought about the feel of Ellen's hand in his, her arms around his shoulders, and how he would kill to get her back. If it was necessary.

48

Ida Carlisle ate toast at her kitchen table, alone, in only the light that filtered through the door's glass panels. She had slathered the bread with butter, yet it felt dry and tasteless as dust on her tongue.

Graham had not come home.

No more than an hour, he'd said. Now it drew close to eleven, and he was still out there somewhere, doing whatever he did. How many secrets did he keep? How many lives did he have? One more than he deserved, she knew that much.

He had taken his gun with him. She had heard the heavy clank of the safe's door closing up in their bedroom. Once he'd left, she checked, and yes, it was gone.

Ida was relieved, in a way. She had gone up there several times today, keyed in the combination, and lifted the plastic case out. She had flipped open the latches with her thumbs and found it nestled there in the foam, run her fingertips across its flank, and felt a hateful surge low down in her belly. This afternoon, while Graham was downstairs with the solicitor, she had even lifted the pistol out of its case. She could still feel the weight of it in her hand.

Imagine it tearing through her skull. She hadn't the courage to shoot him, but maybe she had the courage to shoot herself.

Imagine if Graham and his solicitor had heard the shot and come running upstairs. Imagine if they found her lying on the bed, her brains spilling out over the Egyptian cotton.

Imagine, imagine, imagine.

What if Graham had taken the gun and driven to some dark place, beneath a bridge or behind a disused warehouse? Maybe he had parked there, turned off the engine, and taken the pistol out of the glovebox, brought the muzzle to his lips. Perhaps he had tasted oil before his existence blinked out.

Imagine.

The doorbell jangled, startling her. She sat still and quiet, her breath held tight. Through the open kitchen door, along the hall, through the frosted panes of the front door she saw the shape of a person.

Another chime, and Ida returned the piece of toast to the plate. She stood, opened the kitchen door and took slow steps along the hall.

"Who is it?" she called.

"Mrs. Carlisle, it's DCI Flanagan. Please open the door."

Ida did as she was told. Beyond the garden, the street seemed frozen like a photograph. She felt no breeze, heard no sound.

The policewoman stood alone on the step, darkness in and around her eyes.

"Where's the other policeman?" Ida asked.

"It's late," Flanagan said. "I sent him home."

"Does he have a family?"

"Yes. A girlfriend and a baby boy."

"Not married? I suppose that's the way these days."

Flanagan smiled her agreement. "Can I come in?"

Ida stepped back and allowed her to pass. Without bidding,

Flanagan headed for the kitchen, switched the light on as she entered. Ida followed.

"Did I interrupt your supper?" Flanagan asked, indicating the plate of half-eaten toast.

"Not really," Ida said. "I've not much of an appetite. Would you take a cup of tea?"

"Please," Flanagan said, sitting at the table.

Ida flipped the switch on the still hot kettle. It hissed and bubbled as she fetched a mug from the cupboard and a teabag from the caddy.

Flanagan said, "Actually, it was your husband I wanted to talk to."

"He's out," Ida said.

"Will he be long, do you think?"

Ida poured boiling water into the mug. "He said he'd be an hour. That was before eight."

"Does he often disappear like that?"

The policewoman's tone had changed. Even Ida could hear the difference between polite conversation and a question to which the answer had real meaning.

"Always," Ida said. She poured a dash of milk into the mug. "Ever since we were first married and Rea was born. I was pregnant out of wedlock, you know."

Flanagan gave a nod and a smile as Ida placed the tea in front of her. "That's not unusual these days."

"It was then." Ida sat opposite her. "Especially in this country. I never told my parents. They knew, of course, when the months didn't add up. But we never talked about it."

"So where does Mr. Carlisle go when he disappears?"

"Party business. Meetings, constituency clinics, fundraisers. That's what he's always told me."

"Do you believe him?"

"I used to."

"Used to?"

Ida held Flanagan's challenging gaze. "Now I realize I don't know him at all. I've been lying beside a stranger for more than thirty years. I used to blame myself for the way he treated me. I thought I deserved it. What a stupid woman I am."

Flanagan extended a hand, perhaps meant to comfort Ida, but she thought better of it and returned her fingers to the side of the mug.

"He made you blame yourself. He needed you to think it was your own fault. I've seen the same pattern of abuse time and time again. It's all about control. I can give you contacts, people you can talk to. People who can help."

Ida almost told her she didn't need any help, that her path was clear. Instead, she asked, "Have you told your husband about the cancer yet?"

The compassion flaked away from Flanagan's face, showing the tiredness beneath. She shook her head. "No, I haven't had the time. I've hardly been home over the last few days."

"You're afraid to tell him," Ida said. It wasn't a question.

Flanagan looked down at the mug, her hands wrapped around its warmth. "Yes."

"So you come here at eleven o'clock at night to avoid facing him. Just like Graham stays away to avoid facing me."

"It's not the same," Flanagan said, the edge of her voice sharpening. "Not the same at all. And I'm not here to talk about me."

Ida said, "You're here to talk about Graham."

"That's right." The small cloud of anger left Flanagan's expression. "How has he been since Rea died?"

"Drunk, mostly. He hadn't touched a drop since our wedding day, but he bought a bottle of whiskey the morning after she was killed. And a few more since. There's a bottle in the cupboard if you want some."

"No, thank you." Flanagan placed her palms flat on the table. "Ida, we found the book. We know who—"

The bang and judder of the front door bouncing against the wall, a wave of cool air. They both looked along the hall and saw Graham leaning against the door frame.

He blinked at them, red eyes in a redder face, and asked, "What's going on?"

49

Flanagan held the words back. She had hoped to prize some sort of truth out of Ida before her husband returned, but now it was too late. And he was drunk.

She got to her feet. "Mr. Carlisle, I need to ask you a few questions."

He slammed the front door behind him. "I told you before, I won't say a bloody word to you without my solicitor. Now get the fuck out."

Carlisle shuffled along the hall, his fists clenched. He had violence on his mind, Flanagan could tell.

Stay or go?

No, she wouldn't leave Ida alone with him.

"By all means, call your solicitor. We can talk while we wait for him."

His frame filled the doorway to the kitchen. "I said, get out."

"Mr. Carlisle, we can talk here, or I can call for a car to take you to—"

He grabbed the underside of the table, hauled upward, sent the mug of hot tea to shatter and spill on the floor along with the plate of uneaten toast. The table refused to tip over until he gave it another shove, a hoarse sob of anger in his throat.

Flanagan stepped away, pressed her back against the fridge.

Carlisle barked at his wife. "Clear that up."

Ida obeyed, her face blank, picking fragments from the floor and taking them to the sink.

"Mr. Carlisle, we have the book."

He turned to look at Flanagan. She expected shock and fear on his face. Instead, she saw hate.

"So what?"

"You lied to me. You made your wife lie too."

He lurched forward, skidded on the spilled tea, regained his balance. "It's got nothing to do with me," he said, indignant.

"And the photograph." She held his reddened gaze. "You stopped your daughter from coming forward with that book. You made her keep it secret to protect your career, and now she's dead."

He pointed at the door. "Get out."

"I know who killed Rea," Flanagan said.

"Get out now."

"Howard Monaghan," she said. "He was in the photograph with you and Raymond Drew. He killed your daughter."

Not a hint of shock or surprise on his face, only drunken fury.

He knew, Flanagan thought. The idea formed bright and hard and clear in her mind. Carlisle had known who had killed his daughter all along and had said nothing. And he knew that she knew it too.

He knew.

Carlisle shambled toward her, made a grab for her coat. She slapped his hand away.

"Mr. Carlisle, have you spoken with Howard Monaghan today?"

"Graham," Ida called from the other side of the room.

"Get out!"

Flanagan felt his breath hot on her skin. "Answer the question, Mr. Carlisle, have you had contact with Howard Monaghan?"

Ida moved closer, called again, "Graham."

He put his hand at the center of Flanagan's chest and pushed hard. The back of her head glanced off the fridge door.

"Get the fuck out of my house, I don't have to—"

Ida said, "Graham."

He spun toward her voice, his hand up and ready to strike. "What do y—"

Silence then, as if Flanagan had gone suddenly deaf, leaving only the rushing and pulsing in her head.

As Carlisle stood frozen, his mouth open, Ida moved once more, something bright flashing between her and her husband.

Too late, as the red spilled out from his belly, Flanagan understood. Again, Ida's hand withdrew the blade, drove it back, then again, and again.

A whining expulsion of air from Carlisle's mouth broke whatever bound Flanagan in place. She threw herself forward, grabbing for Ida's wrist, pushed her away.

The knife rang on the tiled floor, the blade breaking away from the hilt. Ida stumbled backward, tripped over her own feet, and fell against the cupboards on the other side of the kitchen. She dropped down and curled her knees up to her chest, staring back at Flanagan.

The patter of blood on the tiles drew Flanagan away from Ida's gaze, back to Carlisle. He remained upright, swaying. His hands went to his stomach. He looked down, saw them drenched red, then leaned against the fridge, leaving bloody smears across its polished white surface. His knees cracked on the floor and he settled back with a wheeze, facing his wife.

Carlisle's face crumpled in grief and regret.

"I'm sorry," he said. "Ida, I'm sorry. Tell Rea I'm sorry."

Ida remained still and quiet for long seconds, then screamed, "She's dead!" She threw herself forward, hands clawed and outstretched. "She's dead, you killed her, you killed—"

Flanagan grabbed her shoulders, hauled her back across the room, shaking, sobbing and kicking.

"Tomorrow," Graham said, the word thin in the air between them.

Flanagan turned to him. "What?"

"To . . . tomorrow. Howard . . . the Spark . . . the Sparkle."

She crawled across the floor, through the warm tide of blood. "What? Were you seeing him tomorrow?"

"Vic . . . Vic . . . toria . . . Sq . . ."

"Victoria Square? Were you to see him at Victoria Square? Where in Victoria Square? What time?"

His eyes widened as he opened his mouth to speak.

Then, silence.

Flanagan put her fingers to his throat, felt for life. She found none. She turned her head, saw Ida reach for the broken blade, bring the metal to her wrist.

"No!"

Flanagan dived across the floor, hands outstretched. She knocked the blade from Ida's grip before she could find a vein. Ida went after it, but Flanagan took her in her arms, gripped her tight, rocked her just as she had been rocked by Ida the day before.

50

The Sparkle woke early, his bare room lit a dim grey by the coming sunrise. He lay on the top bunk, huddled against the wall, blankets wrapped tight around him. Ordinary beds had never suited him. Too soft, like sinking in mud. He preferred the firm cots of his merchant navy days. This bunk bed had been rescued from a youth hostel in Downpatrick that was being renovated some years ago.

Most of his possessions had been acquired this way. Taking cash-in-hand wiring jobs around the country, gutting old houses and office blocks, threading new veins into their walls, collecting whatever he found useful in the site skips.

The Sparkle pushed back the blankets and lowered himself to the bare wooden floorboards. He went to the small window and pulled aside the sheet of linoleum that served as a blind.

Quiet and still on the street outside.

It had been anything but, last night. The students that shared most of the houses along this street had been drinking on the pavements until the early hours, moving threadbare couches and armchairs out to the footpaths despite the weather not being quite warm enough yet.

A few hardy types remained by their front doors, coats and hooded tops wrapped around them, two-litre cider bottles in their hands, or Buckfast fortified wine. Litter everywhere, empty beer cans, the remains of takeaway meals.

He hated them all, spoiled brats pissing their parents' money up the walls, expecting the city council to come and clean up after them. Most ordinary residents had fled, selling their homes to the property investors and landlords, leaving the streets to this invasion of vermin.

They called this part of Belfast the Holylands. Nothing holy about it.

But the Sparkle had stayed in the house he'd rented under a false name for more than a decade. He came and went quietly. The students barely noticed him. Few stayed longer than a year. He lived like a mouse behind the skirtings, watching them go about their wasteful business.

While the revellers had shouted and sung to the heavens last night, the Sparkle had packed a bag. Not much. A few changes of clothes. Some wash things. A few of his favourite drawings rolled up and bound with a rubber band. Four-and-a-half thousand pounds in sterling notes, a little over two thousand in euros.

He needed one more thing.

The pistol lay on the peeling top of the child's bedside locker. He crossed the room to it, lifted the gun in his right hand. It had been years since he'd pulled a trigger. He didn't like such weapons. Too loud, too sudden, too easy. But he liked the weight of the pistol in his hand. The cold and the hard of it, the power held tight within the metal.

The springs of the lower bunk creaked beneath his weight as he sat down to wait beside the bag. He had much to do today, but not yet. He set the gun aside, lifted a pad of lined A5 pages and a pencil, began to draw, starting with diagonal slashes, building them up until they formed the shape of a tower of boat-shaped platforms. Circles and lines representing people standing on and climbing over them. How many levels were there in the shopping mall? Three? Four? No matter.

The Sparkle would arrive at Victoria Square a few minutes before noon so that he could be there waiting for Graham. He was confident Graham would not go to the police; he didn't have the nerve. He would either come or he wouldn't.

If Graham came, all would be well. He would hand over the money, and the Sparkle would walk the short distance to Central Station, take the next train to Dublin, and all this would be over and done with. For him, at least.

And if Graham didn't come? Well, then his fate was laid out before him, just like he'd always imagined it.

He turned the page, began a new picture. A pistol, much like the one that sat on the bed beside him. A finger, much like his, on the trigger.

51

Lennon followed Flanagan to the conference room, a Styrofoam cup full of coffee in his hand. The same room he'd spent an hour fidgeting in last week while the Police Federation lawyer read notes.

He'd managed only a brief sleep, and a shower, every cell of his body craving the warm blanket of painkillers, before the call came. Flanagan looked like she'd had none at all. Lennon checked his watch as they made their way along the corridor. Ten past seven. As they approached the door, two passing officers saw him approach, surprise clear on their faces. Apart from his meetings with the lawyer, he hadn't been seen in this station for more than a year, so he could hardly blame them.

The chatter and bustle in the room ceased as Flanagan entered, followed by straggling whispers at the sight of Lennon. He felt his skin burn at their attention. Officers from E Department, Special Operations Branch. Surveillance, undercover work, often tasked with investigating their colleagues on the force. Lennon guessed some of them had been digging into his own case.

Adhering to the Regulation of Investigatory Powers Act, Flanagan had put a request to mount the operation in to the ACC at four A.M. The nine-strong team had been sent over from Palace Barracks in Holywood. Most of the men hadn't shaved. One of the three women sat applying make-up.

Flanagan took her place at the head of the room. Lennon took a seat facing DS Calvin at the far wall. Calvin nodded. Lennon returned the gesture.

"Thank you all for coming at such short notice," Flanagan said. "We don't have a great deal of time, so I'll keep this brief. As of yesterday afternoon, we have a firm suspect in the killing of Rea Carlisle. I'm sure you're aware of the case from the news reports."

The officers exchanged glances and murmurs. Calvin stood and opened the folder he'd been holding on his lap. He took out a bundle of A4 pages and handed them to the nearest cop, who took one and passed the pile along.

Lennon got the last page. A grainy blown-up image of the Sparkle's face, copied from the photograph Rea had given him only four days before.

"Howard Monaghan," Flanagan said. "This photograph is around thirty-five years old. Monaghan is about sixty now. I believe he has killed two people in the last few days, one of them Rea Carlisle, the other Roger 'Roscoe' Patterson, a career criminal who I'm sure was well known to some of you. There is also reason to believe Howard Monaghan has killed a further eight people across the British Isles since the early nineties."

Another ripple of hushed words across the room.

"Quiet, please," Flanagan scolded. "Last night, between eleven and eleven-fifteen, I called at the home of Rea Carlisle's parents, hoping to speak with Mr. Carlisle. Largely due to information brought to light by Detective Inspector Lennon, I had reason to believe there was some connection between Graham Carlisle and Howard Monaghan, dating back to their youth. Mr. Carlisle wasn't there when I called, but he arrived a short time after. There followed an altercation, and before I could intervene, Mr. Carlisle was stabbed by Mrs. Carlisle with a large kitchen knife."

More voices, louder now.

Lennon kept his silence. Flanagan had told him everything in her office half an hour before, her hands still shaking.

"Quiet. Quiet, please."

She waited, her gaze stalking the room like that of a schoolmarm.

"Mr. Carlisle was pronounced dead on arrival at the Royal Victoria Hospital just after midnight. Mrs. Carlisle is now in custody. This is being kept out of the press for the time being. It will not be mentioned outside this room. Am I clear?"

They nodded their assent.

"Good. Before Mr. Carlisle lost consciousness, he was able to speak a few words. Two of them were 'Victoria' and 'tomorrow.' It is my belief that he had been in contact with Howard Monaghan, and that he intended to meet him at Victoria Square today. I don't know where. I don't know what for. I don't know what time. But I believe Howard Monaghan will be there today."

She looked at her watch.

"It's now coming up to seven-twenty. The center opens at eight. That gives us forty minutes. We do this quietly. Everyone in radio contact, it'll be an all-informed net, recorded as per usual. Keep chatter to a minimum. Who's your comms operator?"

A slender man with dark short-cropped hair raised his hand. "Sergeant Beattie, ma'am."

Lennon recognized him, wished he hadn't. He'd noticed Beattie hanging around the hospital corridors when he'd been recovering from the shooting. Watching who came and went, using his mobile phone one time too often to cover a radio conversation, drawing the kind of attention only another cop would give.

"Okay," Flanagan said. "DS Calvin will pair with you. Stab vests are mandatory, but keep them concealed. There's an Out-of-Bounds order on the center extending to fifty meters from each exit, so no other police units will get in the way. We'll be split into pairs, one per level, including the car park underneath the main complex. You can see all the main street entrances from the platforms in the central tower, and the connecting walkways. Between the lot of us, we should be able to keep the entire center covered."

Calvin raised his hand. "What about using the center's CCTV? I'm sure the management will cooperate, let us use their control room. Surely they've everything covered from there?"

A groan went around the room.

Beattie said, "We never tell anyone an operation's in place. For one thing, we're not required to. And more importantly, if the center management know about it, their staff will be shitting bricks all day waiting for it to kick off. Your target will twig the second he sees a security guard sweating, and he'll be away."

Calvin nodded and looked down at the floor, his cheeks glowing red.

Beattie turned back to Flanagan. "And how exactly do we recognize this guy? You said this photo was thirty-odd years old."

Flanagan looked to Lennon. "Jack?"

Lennon grunted as he stood, kept a hand on the back of the chair for balance. "I saw Monaghan yesterday afternoon, up close. His hair has greyed, a little thinner on top, his face is more heavily lined, but other than that, he hasn't changed too much. He's about five-six, five-seven, slender build, wiry, very agile, despite his age."

Flanagan said, "DI Lennon will be with me, ready to confirm

Monaghan's identity if and when any of you spot him. We'll stay on the upper level to try and avoid Monaghan seeing DI Lennon."

"I thought Lennon was on suspension," Beattie said. "For shooting a colleague, no less."

He did not look at Lennon.

"DI Lennon will not be part of the arrest operation, he will be there purely to identify the suspect. I've cleared this with the ACC. I expect the full cooperation of every participant in this operation. Is that clear, Sergeant Beattie?"

The cop nodded. "Yes, ma'am."

She had told Lennon about her conversation with the Assistant Chief Constable that morning. The ACC hadn't appreciated being woken in the early hours to be spun a yarn about some mad killer who might decide to go shopping that morning. He had begrudgingly given Flanagan permission to pull together a small team to stake out the place for the day, but no more than that. He wasn't going to waste resources based on the dying whispers of Graham Carlisle, even if he was a politician.

Lennon knew that even if Flanagan had another day to prepare, rather than a few hours, the ACC still wouldn't give her the manpower she really needed. She was making do, and it showed.

Flanagan continued. "Anyone spots someone they think is Howard Monaghan, radio his exact location. Don't approach him yourself. DI Lennon and I will move as close as possible without spooking him. Once he's identified, each pair of officers will move to cover the nearest exit. DS Calvin and I will carry out the arrest. We need to do this as quietly as possible, surprise him, don't give him the chance to run. Any questions?"

No one raised a hand.

"Good," Flanagan said. "Let's try not to fuck this up."

52

The unmarked cars moved in convoy toward the city center. Flanagan sat in the passenger seat of the lead vehicle, Calvin driving, Lennon in the back. The early morning grey had burned away, leaving swatches of blue over Belfast and its good citizens. Mothers on school runs, commuters on buses.

"I meant what I said." She looked back over her shoulder at Lennon. "You identify him, then you back off."

"Don't worry," Lennon said. "I've no desire to get into it with this piece of shit."

"Even though you've a personal interest? He'll answer for what he did to Rea. You've no call to get involved."

"I said, I'll stay out of it."

Lennon returned his gaze to the window as the car crossed the Albert Bridge, the River Lagan glowering muddy brown below.

The crowds thickened as the hours passed. Flanagan's calves ached from pacing the upper floor and walkways, Lennon limping alongside her. They said little as they paused at restaurants to study menus, posing as hungry shoppers looking for a meal.

Clusters of young preschool children and their parents drifted toward the cinema, off to see whatever computer game was passing for a movie these days. Flanagan had taken her own children here many times, always feeling their excitement by proxy, the child that remained inside her filled with delight.

A place like Victoria Square couldn't have existed when she was their age, and that caused an odd resentment in her. Even twenty years ago, this place would have been irresistible for the paramilitaries. They would have called it an economic target when they claimed responsibility for whatever bomb destroyed the place. In truth, the men in balaclavas simply couldn't abide the people of Belfast having anything good. A decent cinema, a handful of good restaurants, glittering shops full of pretty things. Such indulgences could not be tolerated by those who dealt in death and fear, and they would have burned it to the ground.

These children have no idea, she thought, watching them stream up and down the escalators.

A voice crackled in her earpiece.

"What about this one? Ann Street entrance, tan trousers, dark jacket."

Lennon heard it too. Flanagan followed him to the railing edge of the gondola-like platform. She scanned the tides of people until she saw him, as described, a small trim man with white hair.

"There," she said, pointing.

Lennon stared for a few seconds, then said, "No."

"All right," Flanagan said, walking back toward the nearest walkway. "Keep looking."

Three and a half hours.

Flanagan had allowed the pairs to split, letting them take turns so that one could have a break while the other kept patrolling. The last of them had radioed in that they were rejoining their partners. She could hear the fatigue and boredom in their voices.

She lifted her wrist to her mouth and spoke into the microphone. "Calvin, do you see anything?"

"No one that looks the part," Calvin said, his voice thin in her ear.

Lennon rested his forearms on the rail overlooking the Victoria Street entrance, the restored Jaffe Fountain visible through the glass, its yellow dome glaring in the sunlight. Flanagan remembered reading about its restoration when the shopping mall was built. The fountain had originally been located in Victoria Square in the 1870s, but was later moved to Botanic Gardens in the south of the city, where it stood neglected and graffiti-strewn for decades. Much like Belfast itself, it had now been cleaned up and made respectable again.

"How much longer are you going to give it?" Lennon asked, his hand over the microphone inside his lapel.

"All day, if I have to."

Lennon reached inside his jacket, switched the microphone off. "You look tired," he said.

"Thanks," Flanagan said, doing the same. "You don't look so sprightly yourself."

Lennon shrugged. "I've felt like shit for more than a year now. Same old, same old."

"Do you think you'll ever be back on the job?"

He shook his head. "I doubt it. Even if I was fit. As soon as they figure out how to get shot of me, they'll do it."

"When we searched your girlfriend's flat—"

Lennon gave her a hard look. "She's not my girlfriend."

"Well, the flat where you were living, I found the safe. I had a look inside it."

"And?"

"I think if you brought that information to the ACC, or maybe the Police Ombudsman, Dan Hewitt would have some explaining to do. I didn't log the file with the rest of the evidence. It's in my office. You can have it back when this is done."

He turned his gaze to the crowds below. "Thank you," he said.

"I understand your anger at him," Flanagan said. "But there's a right way and a wrong way to tackle this. Whenever you make your move, I hope you choose the right way."

"I'll do what needs doing. But not until I'm ready."

"Or maybe you just like wallowing in your hate. Maybe you enjoy being angry at him. Gives you a way to avoid looking too closely at yourself."

Lennon snorted. "Christ, you sound like Susan."

"She seems like a decent woman."

"Yeah, I thought that too," he said.

Flanagan studied the lines on Lennon's face, the way he tried to disguise his lopsided stance. "I heard you were a good police officer, at one time."

"Not any more," Lennon said.

He switched his microphone back on and walked away.

53

The Sparkle stepped off the bus and onto the pavement. The high buildings of Chichester Street trapped the traffic's rumble and screech, made it feel as if he had waded into a pool of jagged noise. He hitched his bag over his shoulder and walked east, the modern enclave of the Laganside Court complex ahead, all white stone and glass, the Waterfront Hall beyond that. Pedestrians streamed past him, some heading back toward the City Hall, others following his path, to the shopping center.

He felt a strange sense of calm. Being so close to other people usually made him uneasy. He hated when their shoulders brushed against his, or they did that stupid foot-to-foot dance as they tried to avoid slamming into him. Their voices grated on his nerves.

But not today. Today, he felt at peace here. He had the sense of an ending, something final. Beyond that, he didn't know. A new life or none at all. He would take either.

Whichever, it would be glorious.

In his heart, he knew that Raymond's death was not the cause of his sickness. If he was truthful with himself, he had been unwell for some time. In his mind. The illness came and went. For weeks at a time, he could feel almost like a real human being. Reasonable. Calm. And then his hold on himself would slip, the wiser part of his mind unable to assert itself. And he became dangerous, more to himself than to anyone else.

But now, today, his mind was under his control.

The Sparkle checked his watch. Eleven fifty-four. He would have liked to have arrived earlier, but the bus was delayed by roadworks. He quickened his pace.

Less than a minute took him to the southeastern corner of Victoria Square. The doors of a department store opened onto the street. The rest of the center could be reached through the other side. He slipped in, up a short flight of stairs, into a maze of crystalline displays selling handbags, gloves, scarves. Young women with too much make-up prowled the aisles, looking for sales. He avoided them, made his way past the banks of escalators that led to the department store's upper levels, signs for menswear and home furnishings.

At the back of the store, the row of glass doors leading onto the shopping center's atrium. The Sparkle pushed one open, noted the change in sound, the soft chatter of shoppers, sales girls and piped music replaced by the voices of children and parents echoing up to the glass dome that towered above.

Rising up through the middle of the atrium was the series of boat-shaped platforms connected by escalators and walkways, and the observation deck at the top. People swarmed up and over them, an army of ants desperate to throw away their money.

Money, the only thing he needed now.

The Sparkle crossed to the foot of the spiralling staircase that rose up the side of the platforms. He ascended, checking his watch as he climbed.

Two minutes to spare. He slowed, lingered there in the stairway, waiting, watching.

54

"There," Calvin said. "Upper ground level. On the platform. Beattie and me are up at the cinema, so I only got a quick look, but I think it might be him."

Lennon spoke into the microphone on his lapel. "We're across from you. I can't see without going down there. What's he wearing?"

He headed for the escalator, Flanagan at his heels.

"Black or navy baseball cap, dark jeans, grey jacket. A red and black backpack over his shoulder, Adidas, I think."

"We're on our way down," Lennon said as he reached the second level, fighting against the crowd.

Flanagan called from behind. "Go easy, Jack. Remember what we said."

"I won't touch him," Lennon said.

Calvin's voice in his ear again. "I recommend everyone keeps their positions until we've confirmed it's him. Do you want me down there, ma'am?"

"Not yet," Flanagan said, "but be ready."

A gang of young boys who should have been in school clogged the escalator down to the first level. Lennon shoved them aside, ignoring their curses. Flanagan did the same, followed him to the next escalator.

She skidded into Lennon's back as he stopped on the upper

ground level platform. Clusters of people, all ages, jostled between the lifts and the stairs. He looked for the baseball cap.

"I don't see him," Lennon said into the radio.

"By the elevator bank," Calvin said, "right hand side, against the railing."

Lennon saw him. A thin man, his back to them, white hair showing beneath the cap.

"Is it him?" Flanagan asked.

"I don't know," Lennon said, walking toward the man. "I can't see his face. It might be him. I need a closer look."

Flanagan grabbed his arm. "We can't afford to spook him. We can't give him a chance to run."

They went to the railing, twenty feet along from the white-haired man. Lennon edged toward him, Flanagan at his side.

"Is it?" she asked, her voice barely audible above the crowd.

"I don't know," Lennon said, leaning out over the railing, trying to see more of the man's profile. "I think . . . I don't know."

"Shit," Flanagan said. "Hold on."

She took Lennon's arm again, spoke into her microphone. "Calvin, make your way down to us."

"Have you ID'd him?" Calvin asked.

"Not yet, not positively, but I want you close when we do."

"Yes ma'am," Calvin said.

55

The Sparkle checked his watch one last time.

A minute past the hour.

Graham Carlisle had not come. He would not come.

The Sparkle felt a small ache of sadness for himself. A grieving, almost.

This emotion surprised him. He had always thought, as he had written, that he would welcome the end with a joyous heart. That the final eruption of his light would be his own personal rapture. Maybe he had been wrong. Too late to think of that now.

With no money, he could not run. He didn't want to end things like this, but that was Graham's choice, not his. He couldn't have made things clearer. The money here at noon, or he would do a terrible thing.

He sighed, a long expulsion of air that left him empty of more than his breath. He thought of Raymond and all the dark and secret pleasures they had shared. Raymond, alone amongst all humans, had some understanding of him. Had the Sparkle believed in God, in places above or below this one, he might have hoped to see Raymond again. They could find some corner of hell to lie together and whisper to each other through the eternal night.

But he did not believe in those things. He did, however, believe in keeping his promises. The bag slid to the ground, between him and the railing. He hunkered down, unzipped it, reached inside. The pistol felt good between his fingers. Like a promise in his hand.

The Sparkle stood and looked around.

Who?

In this final sin, who would he silence?

Then he saw.

56

Flanagan unholstered her Glock, held it by her side, muzzle pointed at the floor.

Now, she thought. It has to be now.

"Howard Monaghan," she called.

The man did not respond.

"What happened to waiting?" Lennon asked.

"Just stay back," she said.

She called his name again. No answer.

Flanagan advanced toward him, Lennon moving to the other side, ready to flank him if he moved.

She lifted the pistol, held it in both hands, aimed at the man's back. Ignored the gasps around her, the rising murmur of frightened people.

"Howard Monaghan," she called once more, loud enough to grate in her throat.

Now the man reacted. He turned toward her voice, slow as a cobra studying its prey, and saw the pistol.

"Fuck me!"

He threw his hands up.

"Jesus, don't shoot, don't shoot, don't . . ."

Above his pleading, Flanagan heard Lennon say, "It's not him."

She did not take her gaze from the man, kept her sight aligned with his forehead. "Are you sure?"

"I'm sure," Lennon said.

She lowered the pistol. "Bollocks," she said.

The man kept his shaking hands up. He looked from Flanagan to Lennon and back again. "What's going—"

The shot cracked and boomed through the atrium, a shower of echoes from above.

A hush as the reverberations faded, then screams. A torrent of people at the top of the escalator above, charging down, pushing, shoving, the larger and faster of them throwing aside the others.

"My God," Flanagan said. "What's happening? Calvin, can you hear me? What's happening?"

"Level one," Calvin said, his voice strained. "He's there, I see him, he's got a gun. I'm trying to get down there, but the people, the people, I can't—"

Flanagan ran for the spiral stairway, Lennon limping behind her. They forced their way against the tide of terrified men, women and children, fighting for each step. She held her identification up with one hand, clasped her pistol with the other, but it made little difference.

She heard Lennon cry out as he was swept down by the flow of human bodies, heard him swear and curse as he regained his footing. Finally she pushed through onto the first level and saw him.

Howard Monaghan, the Sparkle, a semi-automatic pistol in his hand, scanning the fleeing crowds, seeking his next target.

A young man lay dead or dying before him, his blood spreading out like the expulsion of his soul.

And there, on the other side of the platform, Calvin, suddenly free of the river of people, in clear air.

He didn't stand a chance.

57

The Sparkle's nerve endings jangled beneath his skin, from head to toe, a rush of power and pleasure like he hadn't felt in decades. The screams. The floods of frightened people.

All for him.

All flocking to his luminescence.

No one had paid attention when he first took the pistol from his bag. These sheep were all too busy gawping at their mobile phones, more absorbed in their shiny little screens than in the world around them.

He had picked out the child first. A small boy, not much more than a toddler, walking with his parents. A runt. Like the Sparkle had been. He had aimed at the center of the boy's chest, squeezed the trigger, and . . . nothing.

The safety catch. He had thumbed the lever, but by then the small boy and his family had been swallowed by the crowds. There, a young man in a tracksuit, all elbows and knees and spots, the kind of boy who drove too fast in a pathetic souped-up little car, horrible music throbbing from within.

Of course, the Sparkle could never know such things about people, but it amused him to imagine the life he was about to end.

It was like simply reaching out and knocking the young man down. He felt the shot in his ears, and in his wrist, as the pistol jerked. And then the boy lay flat on the floor. And the people went very quiet, as if these hundreds of human beings were trapped in a vacuum. Then they screamed. And then they ran.

Wonderful.

The Sparkle shivered with pleasure. He had told that cop Lennon that killing was never the point. But perhaps he was wrong. Perhaps it had been the point all along.

One way to find out.

He scanned the swarming crowds, seeking another. But they were rushing away from him, showing only their backs, so he couldn't decide. Maybe a woman or a little girl. But there were so many. So many. If only he could touch them all.

The Sparkle felt heat in his eyes, a thickening in his throat. He wanted to weep with the joy of it. The simple beauty of the act. Choose someone, he thought. Anyone.

Then through the tears, he saw a man fighting against the tide of people. A smart, neat young man in a suit and a tie. The man shouted something, but the Sparkle could not hear. The man broke free of the people, arms wheeling as he staggered forward, his shoes skidding on the polished floor.

The Sparkle took aim.

The young man stopped. His eyes wide.

A surge of peace and happiness, a calmness that radiated from the Sparkle's core to his furthest extremities.

The young man had something in his hand. He raised it up, a dark thing.

The Sparkle heard a shot, felt something sear the air by his head. He squeezed the trigger, flinched as the empty cartridge bounced off his cheek. A piece of the young man's shoulder came away in a constellation of red. The young man fell down, whatever had been in his hand clattering away. His legs twitched.

Then the Sparkle saw clearly what had fallen from the young man's hand. A pistol much like the one he himself held, smoke ribboning from its muzzle.

Why did this young man have a gun? Was he a policeman?

"Howard Monaghan."

The Sparkle blinked. His own name seemed strange to him at the best of times. Why had someone called it here? Had he really heard it? Or was it one of the spectres that haunted his skull?

"Howard Monaghan, put the gun down."

A woman's voice. He turned his head toward it.

The female cop he'd seen on television. She held a pistol in both hands, aimed at him. The police had been waiting for him. But why? How?

He raised his hands above his head, the gun still held in his right, pointed toward the floors above, his finger outside the trigger guard.

She advanced toward him. "Howard, put the gun down, or I will shoot."

The other cop behind her. The Sparkle smiled, felt a warm tear roll down his cheek.

"Hello, Jack," he said.

Lennon held no weapon. He kept his hands out, away from his sides, ready.

Another man broke free of the crowds, a pistol raised. The Sparkle noticed the wire hanging from his ear, snaking into his clothing.

The woman cop spoke again. Told him to put the gun down. Or else. What was her name? Yes, Flanagan, that was it.

"Yes, I'll put it down," the Sparkle said. "But I want to tell you something first."

"I will shoot you," Flanagan said again.

"No you won't," the Sparkle said. "You can't. This isn't America. I'm not pointing it at anyone. I'm not touching the trigger."

"Put it down now."

"I will. But I want to tell you a secret first. About Graham Carlisle."

"Graham Carlisle is dead," Flanagan said. Ten feet away now. "What?"

"He was killed last night by his wife."

The Sparkle turned his attention to Lennon. "Is that true, Jack? Is he dead?"

"It's true," Lennon said. "How do you think we knew you'd be here?"

"Did he tell you what a bad boy he'd been?"

"We know all about him," Lennon said. "Now don't be stupid. Put the gun down."

A needling anger in the Sparkle's gut. Like a child who'd missed out on blowing out the candles on their own birthday cake.

The Sparkle shrugged. "Well, that's that. It's over, Jack, isn't it?"

Lennon walked to the side, along the railing, past the elevator bank. Getting closer. "That's right," he said. "It's over. Now put the gun down so no one else gets hurt."

"I should've killed more," the Sparkle said. "Now it's over, and it's not enough. I wanted more."

Lennon at the top of the stairs, two arms' lengths away. Flanagan at the other side, the pistol in her steady hands.

"You've done plenty," Lennon said. "Now let's stop it here."

"All right," the Sparkle said. "But just one more."

Time to let the lightning out. Time to level the world, scour its surface clean. Time to burn.

He pressed the muzzle to his temple.

58

"No!" Lennon shouted, throwing himself forward before he was conscious of his own movement.

His shoulder connected with the Sparkle's flank. He heard the pistol's boom, felt the burn of the muzzle flare on his cheek. The Sparkle's body slammed against the railing, crushed by Lennon's weight and momentum. Lennon might have heard a wheeze of expelled air from the smaller man but for the high whine the gunshot had left in his ear.

The pistol bounced end-over-end across the floor. Hands grappled for Lennon's throat. He tucked his chin down tight to his chest, wrapped his arms around the Sparkle's torso, and squeezed. Like wrestling a frightened dog, snapping and clawing as he tried to bring it under control.

"Get away from him, Jack!"

Flanagan's voice from miles away, barely audible through the whine and the teeth snapping at Lennon's ears. No strength, no balance, all he had was his weight. He used it to keep the Sparkle pinned against the railing. But it wasn't enough.

The Sparkle got his feet under him and pushed back. Lennon resisted, but he didn't have the power. He staggered back toward the stairway, the Sparkle's feet tangled in his. His fingers dug into the other man's clothing as the floor disappeared from beneath him. The world turned around them both, nothing but air rushing past, then the punishing edges of the steps against Lennon's back. He tensed his neck and shoulders, but he couldn't save himself from the blow to the back of his skull.

All went black for a moment, then he was aware of his descent, the stairs hammering against his shoulders, his knees, his neck, the Sparkle coming with him, both tumbling down the glass-walled spiral.

They came to rest between the two levels, Lennon on his back, head down, feet kicking at air, black stars in his vision. The Sparkle lay across his chest, gasping. He rolled onto his stomach, keeping Lennon pinned, brought his mouth close enough to feel his breath.

Lennon tried to lift his head. He felt a warm trickle on his scalp. He saw the Sparkle's teeth, felt the fists grabbing bunches of his hair. His neck jerked through no will of his own, up, then down, an explosion in his skull. Then another. The world skewed, snapped in and out of focus. He brought his hands up, reached for the Sparkle's face, forced his thumbs into the other man's eyes.

The Sparkle shook his head, dislodged Lennon's grasp. Then slammed his head down, his forehead connecting with Lennon's cheekbone. Blood consumed Lennon's sight in that eye. Through the other he saw the Sparkle's teeth once more, this time snapping at his flesh. He felt pressure then pain in his other cheek, something pulling and tearing.

Lennon's consciousness blinked in and out like a faltering radio signal. As the Sparkle's hands closed on his throat, as the blood blinded him, Lennon barely registered Flanagan's presence over the other man's shoulder.

She called out something, but Lennon only saw her lips move.

If the Sparkle heard, it didn't show. The muscles in his jaws bulged as he squeezed harder.

Thunder joined the whine in Lennon's ears. He saw Flanagan's lips move again. He saw Beattie push past her, an extended telescopic baton in his hand. He saw the Sparkle's head rock with the force of the blow, and again, his eyelids fluttering and Lennon felt the Sparkle's fingers slip away from his throat.

Then they were face to face, the Sparkle's cheek against his, the weight of his slender body on Lennon's chest, the killer's eyes and mouth open, and a childish giggle that Lennon felt resonate against him.

59

Flanagan found Lennon in a curtained bay off the A&E ward, stretched out on a bed. One eye was swollen shut, a gauze pad taped beneath it, his face a patchwork of bruises and cuts.

"How many stitches?" she asked.

"Five on my cheek," Lennon said, the words squeezed through tensed lips. "Another two on the back of my head. I've had worse."

"Did they give you anything for the pain?"

A confused look on his face. He raised a finger to his ear.

She repeated the question, louder.

"I'll manage without," Lennon said.

"When will they let you go?"

"The X-rays say my skull's in one piece, but they'll keep me overnight in case of concussion."

She pulled the curtain closed, sealing them off from the bustle and chatter of the ward. He followed her with his eyes, keeping his head still, as she came closer.

"And what then?" she asked.

"I don't know," he said. "So long as I get my daughter back, that's all that matters. What about Calvin?"

"He's out of surgery. He'll be fine." Flanagan took a breath. "Listen, I want to apologize."

"No need," Lennon said.

"Yes there is. I wanted an easy answer, a quick resolution. I should have paid attention to what you told me."

Lennon shook his head, the smallest of movements. "You acted on the information you had in front of you. I would have done the same."

Flanagan stood by the bed.

"I'm going to help you," she said, "as far as I can. You deserve that pension you've been chasing. I can't promise anything, but I've arranged a meeting with the ACC for tomorrow afternoon. I'll go in front of the Ombudsman and the Policing Board if I have to."

"Thank you," he said.

"It's a pity, really. I could always use a good officer on my team."

A hint of a smile on Lennon's battered face. "You'd have kicked me off within a month."

"Maybe," she said. "I guess we'll never know."

She went to the curtain, her hand on the slick material, ready to pull it back.

"Dan Hewitt," Lennon said.

Flanagan turned back.

"What about him?"

"He knows you've seen my file on him."

"That's right."

"Then watch your back," Lennon said. "He's dangerous."

"Funny," Flanagan said. "He told me the same about you."

"I'm not sorry for what I did," Ida Carlisle said.

The cell smelled of bleach and urine. The wall chilled Flanagan's shoulders as she leaned against it. Ida sat on the thin vinyl-covered pad that served for a bed, her hands folded in her lap, a gauze pad taped to the wrist she'd tried to cut. She wore pyjamas made of paper.

"You should be sorry," Flanagan said. "At least, that's what I'm supposed to tell you. But I can't."

"What time is it?" Ida looked up to the impenetrable window, the blackness beyond.

"Close to midnight," Flanagan said. "You should try to get some sleep. You'll be up in front of the judge at nine."

"What will they do with me?" Ida asked.

"Hard to say. We'll recommend leniency, but you'll do time. There's no avoiding that. But it'll probably be low security."

"Will I be allowed to go to Rea's funeral?"

"Of course," Flanagan said. "I'll escort you myself."

Ida smiled. "Thank you. You're a good person."

Flanagan returned the smile. "So are you. You were just in a bad situation."

Ida dropped her gaze. "I'm not a good person. I thought I was, but I'm not. A good person would've stood up for her daughter."

Flanagan went to her side and sat down. She took Ida's hand in hers. "Like I said, a bad situation."

"What about him?"

"Monaghan? He'll recover, and he'll be charged with Rea's murder. It'll take some time to figure out what we do with the book, whether there's enough in that to prosecute him, but he'll answer for what he did to your daughter. I can promise you that."

Ida touched a finger beneath Flanagan's chin. "And how are you?"

"I'm okay. Tired. But I'll live."

"Have you told your husband?"

"No," Flanagan said. "Tonight. I'll tell him tonight."

"I bet he's a nice man," Ida said.

"He is."

"Then he'll want to know. He deserves to know. And I expect he'll be everything you need him to be. He'll hold your hand through it all. That's what good men do."

Flanagan pulled her close, wrapped her arms around her.

The drive home took less than thirty minutes. She had texted Alistair as she got into her car to say she was on her way. She opened the Volkswagen's windows, used the chill of rushing night air to blow the fatigue from her mind.

Flanagan knew she should have spent the journey going over the conversation she was about to have with her husband, but her thoughts lingered with Ida Carlisle, and her poor daughter. She wondered who Rea Carlisle was in life. In most murder cases she had got to know the victims, as if they were old friends that had slipped away from her orbit and suddenly returned. But not Rea. Flanagan had been too fixated on Lennon, too eager to see it done.

She resolved to get to know Rea. She owed her and her mother that much.

When she got home, Alistair was waiting for her at the kitchen table, pouring a glass of his favourite beer, an American pale ale that cost too much. He had fixed her a gin and tonic. A slice of cucumber trapped between the ice, bubbles clinging to its surface.

He got to his feet, brought the glass to her. She took it from him and set it on the table. His back stiffened with surprise when she kissed him, then his body softened as they embraced.

When they parted, he asked, "What was that for?"

"Just because," she said. "How're the kids?"

"They're okay. They've been asking for you, but I said you'd see them in the morning. Bit of trouble convincing Eli to go to sleep, but fine other than that. I didn't let them see the news."

"Good," Flanagan said. She lifted her drink and sat down. Alistair did the same.

He watched her from across the table.

"How bad was it today?"

"Bad enough," she said.

"Could you have been hurt?" he asked. He tried to hide the tremor in his voice, and she loved him for it.

"It's always a possibility," she said. "You know that. But I wasn't, and that's what matters."

His expression hardened, but his voice remained kind. "What matters is the children. I live with this constant fear that one of these mornings I'm going to have to wake them up and tell them you're not coming home."

Flanagan saw the shake in his hands, the brimming of his eyes.

She said, "Darling, I've got something to tell you."

60

Lennon lingered at the rear of the crowd. Far enough back that he didn't have to hear the sobs of Roscoe Patterson's widow and children at the graveside. Grey clouds billowed over the cemetery, bringing with them a light drizzle.

He knew many of the faces. He'd arrested most of them at one time or another. And some recognized him through the stitches and the bruising. He ignored the hateful glares.

As the mourners dispersed, he sought out Dixie Stoops. He found him shaking the hands and slapping the backs of Rodney Crozier and Dandy Andy Rankin, a pair of men Lennon had witnessed trying to kill each other two and a half years before.

Rankin turned as he approached, looked him up and down. "Jesus, a funeral brings the shit to the surface, doesn't it?"

"How's the ticker, Dandy?" Lennon asked.

"Shove it up your arse," Rankin said as he nudged Crozier's elbow, and they both walked away, leaving Lennon alone with Dixie.

"Sad day," Dixie said.

Lennon nodded. "I'm sorry it happened. And I wanted to thank you for your help. Howard Monaghan would've got away if you hadn't identified him."

"Aye," Dixie said, "and Roscoe wouldn't have got killed if I hadn't named him. I've got to live with that now."

"I imagine you live with worse already."

Dixie looked to the city skyline. "That's true. You'll never know the half of it."

Lennon allowed Dixie to face his memories for a few seconds before he asked, "Were you able to do that favour for me?"

Dixie nodded and trudged along the path, away from the crowds, toward the lonelier parts of the cemetery. Lennon followed.

When all around was quiet, and unkempt graves surrounded them, Dixie stopped walking. "Have you got your end?" he asked.

Lennon nodded.

Dixie beckoned with his finger. "Let's see it."

Lennon took the envelope from his pocket, fat and heavy. "It's all I have left," he said.

Dixie reached into his own jacket. "Then you shouldn't have wasted it on this."

He presented a packet around the size of a paperback book. Lennon handed the money over, and took the packet.

"You didn't get that from me," Dixie said.

Lennon nodded. "Of course not."

He walked away, followed the pathways out of the cemetery, and back to his car.

Bernie McKenna answered her door after one knock.

"What do you want?" she asked.

"You know what I want," Lennon said.

She shouted across the street. "Margaret? Margaret!"

Lennon heard a door open behind him. He looked over his shoulder and saw the teenage girl.

"What?"

"Get your daddy."

The girl disappeared.

Lennon turned back to Bernie. "Where is she?"

"Never you mind where she is. She's none of your concern. Not any more. Now, go on, get out of here before Kevin comes over and gives you another dig in the mouth."

"I'm not going anywhere without my daughter," Lennon said.

"I told you the last time, talk to my solicitor. You get proof you're that child's father, and then we can see about access."

"Bring her out here now," Lennon said. "That's your last warning."

A movement in the hall behind Bernie, then, "Daddy!"

Ellen ran toward the front door, arms outstretched, but Bernie intercepted her, scooped her away. A cousin, Lennon couldn't remember which, appeared from nowhere and took the child from Bernie's arms.

"Are you back for more?" Kevin McKenna's voice called from behind. He stopped when he saw Lennon's face. "Fuck me, somebody else got to you first."

"Walk away," Lennon said.

"Fuck off," McKenna said, jerking his thumb in the direction of Lennon's car, idling in the middle of the street.

When McKenna was ten feet away, Lennon drew the small revolver from his waistband, the pistol Dixie Stoops had sourced for him, and aimed it square at the big man's forehead.

McKenna froze.

"Go back inside your house," Lennon said. "Close the door behind you. I won't tell you again."

McKenna gave an uncertain laugh. "Oh, so we're waving guns around now, are we? Don't show me that unless you mean—"

Lennon cocked the hammer.

"All right," McKenna said. "But you better keep one eye over your shoulder, boy. I'll catch up with you before too long, don't you worry."

He backed away, across the street, into his house, slammed the door shut.

Lennon turned his aim on Bernie.

"You're insane," she said.

Lennon ignored her. "Ellen, come with me, love."

Ellen writhed in her cousin's grip. "Let me go," she hissed.

Bernie sneered. "Oh, the big tough man with the gun. Taking a child from her family."

"I'm her family," Lennon said. "Let her go right now."

"She's not going—"

The cousin squealed as Ellen's teeth closed on her hand. Ellen ran toward Lennon, slapped Bernie's clutching hands away as she passed. She hugged Lennon around his waist.

"Let's go," she said.

Lennon kept his aim on Bernie as he backed toward his car. "Never contact me again," he said. "And stay away from my daughter."

Curtains twitched all around, faces at windows. Lennon had no fear of a call being made to the police. Not on this street.

He didn't hear Bernie's response as he bundled Ellen into the back of the car and strained his way into the driver's seat. He saw Bernie and the cousin in the rear-view mirror, running along the street behind him as he accelerated away.

"You shouldn't bite people," he said. "Put your seatbelt on."

"You shouldn't point guns at people," Ellen said. "And put your seatbelt on. Are we going home to Susan and Lucy?"

"No," Lennon said.

"Then where are we going?"

For want of a lie, Lennon said, "I don't know."

Acknowledgements

As ever, I must thank those who helped me through the writing and publication of this book.

First and foremost is my agent, Nat Sobel, whose support and advice helped me through a very difficult time while trying to write this novel. And also Judith Weber and all at Sobel Weber Associates, and Caspian Dennis at Abner Stein Ltd.

My editors Geoff Mulligan and Juliet Grames; it is a great privilege to work with such talented people, and they make editing the most pleasurable stage of the process for me.

All the great people at Vintage Books and Soho Press, including Alison Hennessey, Bronwen Hruska and Paul Oliver. I'm very fortunate to have these partners in my career, and I can't imagine doing it without them.

Special thanks to three people who helped me with some research points: Dr. Denise Shirley for the medical insights; Caroline Kerr for explaining the legal stuff in simple enough terms for a dimwit like me to understand; Colonel Ant for the nuts and bolts of policing. And also Billy Scott for showing me all the parts of Belfast I never knew before.

All the writers, publishing pros, booksellers, reviewers, and my closer circle of friends, who are far too numerous to name. As ever, I'll single out David Torrans and his fabulous bookstore, No Alibis, for his unwavering support. And Fiona Murphy for the 'Where are my eyes?" story.

My family for sticking with me: Issy, Ezra, and even Sweeney. Finally, my most heartfelt thanks to my wife Jo who put up with a very, very grumpy husband when the words weren't coming. I really, really couldn't have done it without you, my love.